The Unmasking

By

Adriana Kraft

The Unmasking
By
Adriana Kraft

ISBN: 978-0-9894693-7-1

Contains material previously published in 2008 as The Unmasking, under the authors' former pen name, Amanda Burns

B&B Publishing
1970 N. Leslie St. #560
Pahrump, NV 89060

Cover by
Dawné Dominique
DusktilDawn Designs

Dedication

*This book is dedicated to our son's faithful and courageous Rottweiler, Malaki.
We love you and miss you.*

Prologue

Who will be the next goddess?

Images flickered across the large screen TV. The dark-haired woman had her back to him. She'd shut off the shower and was toweling herself vigorously.

"Very nice," the man muttered, tugging the brown robe tighter about his torso.

She turned.

"Full breasts." He licked his lips.

She tossed the towel over her shoulder, exposing her lower body to the hidden camera.

"Imposter!" he shouted, punching the fast forward button. His heart pumped. Her blond curls gave her away for what she was. A pretend goddess – one of those Nordics. Not worthy of being an honored Celtic goddess. Not worthy of his gift.

Another co-ed graced the screen. His pulse slowed. This one stood naked running a brush through long dark wavy hair. A sleeping shirt lay on the bed behind her. She smiled and lightly brushed the dark curls forming the triangle above her treasure.

"Ah." He groaned. "You'll do."

He checked her name. "Mary. A serene name. Mary, I name you Goddess of the Autumn Equinox. You will be blessed with my seed. Many will envy you."

Chapter One

Who will be the next victim?

Nancy Appleby scanned the co-eds in the small lecture hall. Each could be his next prey. Each looked much younger than she remembered being as a full-time student. Each woman hung on Professor Bayfield's well crafted words.

Was it the topic, *Celtic Myths and Rituals*, or was it the aloofness of the tall, dark-haired lecturer with the strong protruding chin that mesmerized? He did command attention. Although his tone was mild, Bayfield played with his audience like a polished actor. Clearly he was in control. Though he gestured but rarely, he moved like an athlete, comfortable in his body.

Nancy jotted notes on a yellow pad pretending to be no different than anyone else in the room. She glanced up at Bayfield, whose eyes had settled on her; they were piercing and inquisitive. Then he shifted his gaze, but he'd noticed her, was thinking about her. Why? She'd done everything she could to blend in. He hadn't seemed particularly troubled by her presence, just curious.

Nancy redirected her attention to the individuals sitting in front of her. She'd arrived early to claim an aisle seat in the back row. The raised auditorium layout provided an advantageous observation post. About sixty women and twenty men were in attendance, no doubt a decent turnout. Blackthorn College had a student body of less than two thousand.

Nancy scribbled more notes and then focused on the men in the room.

Was *he* in the lecture hall? Would he strike again, tonight? Or would the rapist stay in his hole, biding his time?

Professor Bayfield concluded his lecture. Nancy leaned back in her chair, flexed her cramped fingers and welcomed the assurance of the small service revolver pressing against her lower back.

Sergeant Nancy Appleby of the Stevens Point, Wisconsin police force had been on the Blackthorn campus for two weeks and had made no progress in identifying the rapist. She'd enrolled in two classes and moved into a small off campus walk-up, attracting little attention.

Only two persons in Trillium, Minnesota knew her true identity, and why she was there: the president of the college, Joan Williams, who also happened to be Nancy's favorite aunt; and Lucy Washington, an officer with the college police department. The president had sought outside help to solve a string of rapes because she believed that not only was the security of campus women at stake, so was the future of the college. On leave from her own department, Nancy registered for classes as Nancy Crane, assuming her grandmother's maiden name.

She watched Professor Bayfield talk briefly with several co-eds gathered around the podium. What were they seeking from the handsome professor?

4

What did he see in them? He dismissed them quickly and began gathering his things.

Was it coincidence that two of the rapes had taken place only hours after his lectures on Celtic culture? The rapist might have attended one or more of the lectures. The question remained: Had the rapist *given* the lectures?

- o -

So who was the mystery woman? Matt Bayfield reassembled his notes and glanced toward the newcomer standing in the rear of the lecture hall. He'd been offering this lecture series for nearly a year, roughly every six weeks. This fall, only three freshmen had inquired about last year's handouts. The dark-haired female in the back wasn't one of them.

Odd that she'd sit in the last row, because most women, especially those as comely as the co-ed with full lips and watchful eyes, wanted to sit up front to impress him – as if he were looking. He didn't expect to be hanging around Trillium, Minnesota long enough to develop any romantic interests. And he had an ironclad rule against such liaisons with students.

Nonetheless, the woman in the bulky gray sweater and black slacks didn't fit. Matt prided himself on having honed some keen observation skills in his fieldwork as a sociologist. The other students chattered with one another. The interloper remained silent and observant, almost aloof.

Bayfield recoiled. Aloof – that was what Carol Macy accused him of being. He'd found it quite ironic that it was his lesbian colleague who seemed most concerned about his lack of romantic relationships. Her periodic nagging was an irritant he chose to put up with because he counted Carol as his best friend at Blackthorn – one of few.

He shrugged into a tweed sports jacket. Snapping his briefcase closed, he looked up into two of the most calculating gray eyes he'd ever encountered. They belonged to the woman from the back row.

"Can I help you?" he asked, stuffing his hands in his coat pockets. "I can't take long, but I've time for a question or two."

The hint of a smile played across the woman's full lips. The lips seemed large, yet they were right for her. Just then they parted into a pleasant smile showing straight white teeth.

"Sorry if it's a bad time." The co-ed extended her hand; he shook it. It was a cold hand, matching her eyes rather than her smile.

"It's been a harried two weeks," the woman said. "I've just transferred here, and I apologize for not having come to your office to ask about this lecture series. I was told it would be okay to just show up."

Who had misinformed her?

"I really enjoyed your lecture. I'd like to come to your office and pick up any handouts you have from last year and ask you some questions about topics you've already covered."

He didn't have time to waste on someone who hadn't bothered to stop by before tonight. The woman's outward expression was one of exasperation, yet he sensed she was very much in control of herself and the situation. What game was she playing?

"You see, it's quite important to me that I understand Celtic philosophy and practice."

"Why is that so, Ms...?" Matt absently ran fingers through his hair. "I'm sorry, I don't know your name."

"Crane. Nancy Crane. Well, I've been told my grandparents came to this country from Wales. So, I guess I want to learn more about myself."

"I see." Matt scowled and glanced at his watch. "I'm not a genealogist, Ms. Crane."

"I understand that, but..."

He held up a hand, stopping short her plea. "Okay, but not now. I have to go. Can you come by my office tomorrow – at two o'clock? I'll have some materials for you. You can ask your questions then, though I doubt that I'll be very helpful."

Matt walked toward the side door still feeling Ms. Crane's appraising eyes. Did she size up all her professors so thoroughly? Genealogy! He doubted she had very much interest in the subject. What was she really after?

He took long strides down the corridor toward the outside exit; an image of broad lips forming a sexy pout teased him. He groaned. *Get hold of yourself, Bayfield. This is only the beginning of the new academic year. Don't make it any longer than necessary by fantasizing about some inexplicable female. You don't have time for fantasies.*

This year he had to produce at least two solid articles in order to move up to the next academic tier. He didn't mind the students at Blackthorn; some surprised him with their insights and abilities. Still, he wanted to have more impact on the field of sociology than he could ever have based at a small liberal arts college. His sights were set on a research university with doctoral students, but no such offer had materialized when he completed his graduate work. Instead, he'd ended up taking the only position available.

It wasn't a matter of fame or money; neither was particularly attainable in his chosen field. He wanted more engagement with colleagues about the issues he considered important, and that was hard to do in a department consisting of three professors.

He was eager to move on. Besides, the weather was abominable – Trillium was practically in Canada.

Myths and fantasies were objects of his academic study; in reality, he prided himself on being a hard-nosed pragmatist, not subject to the allure of outrageously kissable lips.

– o –

Nancy left the building convinced the circumspect Professor Matt Bayfield could be more helpful than he thought. He'd seemed preoccupied when she approached him after the lecture. Was he frosty with all students, or did he have some quirky sense of who she was? When she'd asked to meet with him at his office, he acted like she wanted to trespass on his private sanctuary.

Her own reaction to the professor surprised her. She was good at quickly sizing up people. That skill had gotten her out of more scrapes than she could count. She'd bet a month's pay that Bayfield was not the rapist; that would be too easy.

He proved he could captivate an audience. Up close, there was a hint of more to the man than academics.

What was he hiding behind that veil of academic objectivity? His dark eyes flickered passion – out of fear, because of her?

His passion for Celtic culture was evident. That was a passion fueled by intellectual curiosity. What she'd just seen in his probing assessment of her was more basic, more elemental. She'd sparked his interest. Why?

She'd never imagined finding a professor intriguing. If she wasn't working a case, she might enjoy cracking the professor's stiff exterior.

Still, she had to strike Bayfield from her suspect list. That he was a chameleon, of sorts, did not make him a rapist – but it didn't mean he wasn't.

She'd know soon enough.

Nancy stayed in the shadows waiting for Bayfield to exit. Only moments went by before he emerged from the building. He strode quickly down a walkway leading away from campus. Apparently, he was going home rather than back to his office. Or was he preparing to lie in wait for some unsuspecting co-ed? Careful to remain within the protection of darkness, Nancy followed.

No more than ten minutes elapsed before Bayfield turned up a sidewalk toward a modest house, stopped on its porch and retrieved some mail, unlocked the front door, and stepped inside.

Nancy made her way up a small hill to a clump of aspen in the park across the street. From there, she had an unobstructed view of the professor's house. She nestled into a wind blown pile of leaves and breathed the night air deeply. The setting made the stakeout almost enjoyable.

Within an hour, the downstairs lights in Bayfield's house went out. An upstairs light came on. Nancy rolled her eyes. Didn't the man know he was putting on a show for anyone sitting in the park watching his house – not that there was a crowd. Damn, she should've brought a pair of binoculars. Then, the bedroom went dark. "Show's over," Nancy muttered, stretching cramped muscles.

She stared into the darkness, waiting, doubting that many perps got undressed and climbed into bed before setting out to rape. Still, she waited.

She checked her watch. Each of the attacks had taken place between the hours of eleven at night and two in the morning.

At two-thirty, Nancy stood, stretched, brushed off her bottom, and headed back toward the parking lot to retrieve her car. It had been a long stakeout. At least, Bayfield hadn't raped anyone that night.

A cold wet nose nuzzled Nancy Appleby's bare ankle below the hem of her blue fuzzy bathrobe. She remained hunched over her early morning work, transfixed by words on the computer screen. Automatically, she reached under the kitchen table to scratch the Rottweiller's ears. The dog lapped at her ankle with increased urgency.

"Okay, okay, Mal. I'll get you some breakfast." She left the laptop on and rose to pour some kibble into a large metal bowl. She waited while the animal gobbled his meal. "What would I do without you, Malaki?"

She knelt and hugged the dog who in turn licked her face. "You're a lifesaver. Don't know hardly a soul in Trillium. With you along, it doesn't really matter."

The detective refilled her coffee mug and returned to the kitchen table. She reviewed her computerized notes. She needed a live lead. The rapist wouldn't stop until she caught him.

Very little was actually known about him. Estimates of height ranged from five foot seven to six feet. Weight descriptions varied from one hundred and fifty pounds to two hundred. The perp wore dark clothing and a dark ski mask.

After overpowering his prey, the man would bind and blindfold the woman and take her off campus, driving what seemed like two to three miles, before raping her. Two women reported that the attacks had occurred outdoors while the other two said they had been taken to some type of shelter or shed, but not to a house. The air was described as dank and musty.

Nancy sipped lukewarm coffee from a chipped mug. She continued scrolling. The perp had threatened to beat or kill the woman. No weapon had been reported.

Next, Nancy considered what was known about the victims. They were all co-eds. The four women shared one significant anomaly: each attended Prof. Bayfield's Celtic culture lecture series. Two were raped hours after attending a lecture. One was raped a few days after a lecture. The fourth victim, however, didn't seem to fit into the pattern. She was raped two months after the last lecture of the previous academic year. The victims had also frequented the same bar before being attacked.

The rapes occurred about six weeks apart: February fifth, March twenty first, May first and August first. Nancy frowned at her notes. Why no rape in June or July? And the August rape made no sense. Although the college had a summer session, Bayfield's lectures only took place during the traditional academic year.

Bayfield? Nancy suppressed a smile remembering his reluctance to meet with her. Although he wasn't a hot lead, he did fit the rough descriptions of the rapist – but so did seventy-five percent of the males residing in and around Trillium. He must be about six feet since she was five-five, and he loomed a good six inches or so taller. She had yet to determine where he'd been when the rapes had occurred. Certainly, he was in town for the two that happened the night of his lectures. His whereabouts at the time of the August rape could be the key to striking him from her suspect list.

She'd find out if he taught during the summer session or whether he spent his summers elsewhere. It was not difficult to imagine him sailing. Somehow he had obtained a very nice summer tan giving him a rugged, weathered look. Maybe he spent his summers canoeing and fishing the nearby Boundary Waters. Now *that* would be a great way to spend the summer.

She saved her files and shut down the laptop. There hadn't been enough time for fishing this past summer. Nor enough time for men.

Nancy pushed the chair back from the table and Malaki sprang to attention. "Okay, big boy. I'll get dressed and then we'll go for our run. Then a quick shower. A class on botany. Lunch and then a date with the good Dr. Bayfield. What do you suppose we'll learn about him, today?"

Nancy sat across from Professor Bayfield in his cramped office. Book shelves overflowed with volume after volume. The metal desk was functional. A computer and printer sat on a table beneath a window with a view onto the quadrangle. Very little of the floor was visible because of stacks of papers and more books. He wasn't a slob; the stacks were neat and seemed well organized. Did he ever finish a project, or did he just need more space? He'd moved a pile of papers from the corner of the desk to give her a surface upon which to write.

She uncrossed her legs and tugged at the russet skirt that had climbed to mid-thigh, mildly irritated at the short skirts so in fashion with co-eds. She'd do what it took to blend into the campus scene, but she wasn't accustomed to showing off that much of her thirty-one year old body in this kind of setting – though she was proud of her well toned legs. Running and yoga definitely had their benefits.

Bayfield seemed antsy trying to find any place to look – above her right shoulder, above her left shoulder, at the floor, out the window – to avoid being caught looking at her legs. Maybe his discomfort gave her an edge.

She stopped fumbling with the hem of the skirt and studied the movement of his mouth. He was one of those annoying people who could talk while hardly moving his lips.

He smoothed out his dark green turtleneck and continued responding to her question. She stifled a yawn. What had she asked? Oh, yeah. Whether there was any truth to the notion that in ancient Celtic culture women were on a more equal status with men than in other cultures of the time.

"So, you see..." Bayfield said, interlacing his fingers, keeping his eyes focused on her nose. She'd never considered her nose one of her more endearing assets. "Based on Classical authors, archaeology, and vernacular myths, it seems quite plausible that at least some women held positions of considerable power. They appear in stories as warriors, as priestesses, as politicians, and there is considerable evidence that a number of women were buried with much ornamentation, a sure sign of power and prestige."

"What about the common woman – the woman at home?"

Bayfield shook his head. "That's much more difficult to determine. If I had to guess, I'd say the man ruled as in most cultures and in most historical periods. But history does very little to preserve the stories of the common woman, or man, for that matter."

"Fascinating." Nancy leaned forward slightly, feeling the movement of her breasts against her thin blouse. She noticed Bayfield bite his lower lip and squirm slightly in his chair.

She was struck by the absence of anything personal in his office. Nothing except book titles spoke to the character of the man – no artwork, mementoes, or college banners. The lack of pictures of a wife or sweetheart pricked her curiosity.

"So, do you get all of this knowledge from books? Do you go through dusty libraries? Do you dig in dirt?" While she maintained a poker-face, she doubted Professor Bayfield let dirt get under his fingernails.

Bayfield gave her a patronizing smile before answering. Had she pierced his armor?

"Actually, all of the above. I know you must find it boring to think about, but it is quite challenging. It's sort of like doing a maze, or a labyrinth, or a crossword puzzle." He tilted back in his chair. "I'm just now finishing writing up notes from this summer's fieldwork."

"Really," Nancy said without having to feign interest. "What was that about?" She scrunched forward; Matt Bayfield was about to tell her something she really wanted to hear.

His eyes softened, reflecting a gentler side. He was focused on a distant memory.

"I just spent the most satisfying summer working on a dig in Ireland. It was very rewarding. I should get at least two, maybe three articles out of that work. Maybe even the beginnings of a book. Then, maybe I can get out of..." He drew himself up short. "Anyway, to answer your question, yes, I do both dusty libraries and digs – that sort of goes with the territory."

Nancy sighed, surprised at the wave of relief she felt. She couldn't entirely explain the appeal she found in the man. He was arrogant and aloof.

But then there was that gentleness. He was a paradox. Too bad she didn't have more time.

"Three months is a long time to be away from home, professor."

Bayfield flinched. "I imagine that depends on your home. There's not much tying me down, and I like it that way. I'd love to spend a year teaching abroad. Maybe, someday."

Oops. His exterior had cracked just a bit. Nancy checked her notepad to give the professor a moment to recover. With him off her list of suspects, could Professor Bayfield become a useful ally? She swallowed. She shifted in her chair; her skirt inched a little higher. She didn't pull it back down.

- o -

Matt pushed his chair further away from the woman and crossed his legs. Why had he made such a revealing remark? At least, Nancy Crane was more relaxed than when she'd first arrived. She'd been ten minutes late, and seemed as scattered as most of his students. Yet, she was different. She didn't speak to him with the deference that students used. He ran fingers along the crease of his pants. It was difficult looking at her and seeing a student.

Ms. Crane was older. Probably not much younger than he was, if that. What brought an older woman back to school, particularly a private liberal arts college? Divorce, boredom, ambition?

She didn't wear a wedding ring. He'd predict divorce.

Sculpted legs and thighs; signs of an athlete. He welcomed the return of short skirts, but it was damn difficult sitting there carrying on a polite academic conversation while ignoring a woman whose entire persona screamed sex. Maybe Carol Macy was right; maybe he had been too long without a woman.

Was Ms. Crane aware of the vibrations she emitted, or of his discomfort? Last night she'd been camouflaged under a bulky sweater. Today, she sat in front of him revealing a smoldering sensuality. Her shoulder length ebony hair was as dark as his. Ample breasts shifted beneath the thin blouse whenever she gestured, which was often.

The woman's lips mesmerized. They were thick – probably too large by most people's standards – yet, they fit Ms. Crane's smile perfectly. Actually, they were too inviting.

Bayfield fiddled with a button on his sport coat. He looked up at his visitor's eyes and then glanced quickly out the window toward the quad. What would it take for her smile to reach those steel gray eyes?

"You said you transferred. Where did you come from, Ms. Crane? And why Blackthorn, of all places?"

"In fact, I've been away from school for some time." She hesitated, peeking at her notepad. "I wanted to get a fresh start. Blackthorn has a decent reputation, and I love the northland."

"Oh...I guess it does appeal to some folk. So, you're from the area?"

"No, I grew up in Milwaukee."

"Really! You're a city person. I'm from the Bay Area. San Francisco. And you still enjoy the northland?"

"You seem to find that preposterous, Professor Bayfield." The woman's eyes burned bright and then softened; somehow he'd gotten behind her cool composure. "I grew tired of the cut-throat existence of the city," she said. "I love the solitude this part of the country offers, and all the fishing, hunting, hiking, canoeing, and cross-country skiing. If you like the outdoors, then just about everything's at your fingertips."

"You hunt!" Matt knew his shock, if not disgust, was transparent. What did it matter if she hunted grizzly bear stark naked? He flushed at the image. Was she some female Celtic warrior come back to taunt him?

"Don't be squeamish, professor." She actually giggled. Was she trying to goad him? "I didn't mean to offend. But abhorrence at a female hunting seems in sharp contrast to what we were just talking about in ancient Celtic culture – sounds like some of those women hunted."

Don't rise to her bait. Just let the discussion drop. It's not important. She's not important. "Has nothing to do with you in particular, or women hunting. I just find hunting to be an archaic pastime that's outlived its usefulness."

"Oh, well then." Her features darkened. She

19

tugged at her skirt. "I guess – no, it doesn't matter." She abruptly dropped her pencil into her purse and closed her note pad. "This has been most instructive, Professor Bayfield. Now, if I can get copies of last year's handouts, I'll be on my way. I'm sure you are a very busy man."

"Of course." Matt opened a desk drawer and gave her the handouts. "I hope these will be helpful. I'm sure it's difficult jumping in midstream, but the college wanted this lecture series to span across two years in order to keep up student interest."

The Crane woman stood to leave. Matt rose. He wasn't sure he was ready for her to go, but he couldn't think of anything else to say. He'd already said too much.

"Oh, that reminds me," she said, slipping on a light jacket, "are the lectures open only to students?"

He crossed his arms, ignoring the impulse to help her with her jacket. Why was she concerned about who attended his lectures? "The series is open to the entire college community, even to the town of Trillium. Mainly students come, but occasionally a few others show up."

"But you don't know who they are?"

"Of course not. We don't take roll. Why do you ask?"

"Just curious, I guess." Nancy Crane gave him a wide, warm smile. "Thanks, professor." She reached for his hand and shook it. "I'm eager to read these materials. If I have more questions, I hope I can come back and pursue them with you."

"That would be fine." Bayfield nodded. He'd been pleasantly surprised by the woman's keen mind and genuine interest in the Celts. "That's why I'm here. Just don't expect too much. It is a general lecture series."

Before the woman could reply, a shrill buzzing emanated from her purse. "Excuse me," she said, reaching for her cell phone. She punched a button and held it to her ear. "Yes."

A shadow crossed Ms. Crane's face and her body shuddered briefly. Matt's pulse quickened.

"Okay," she said, to the caller. "I'll be right there." She hurriedly stuffed the phone back into the black purse that appeared to double as a carry-all bag.

"A problem?" Matt inquired. Instantly, he wanted to take back his words; her problems weren't his.

"Yes, you could say that," she said. "One of the students was raped early this morning."

Matt gasped and took a step backward. "Raped! That can't be!"

"I'm afraid it can and it did. I've got to run – I volunteer at the Woman's Center. Thanks for your time, Professor Bayfield."

"Of course." He raised his hand to wave. "Any time. It's always nice to find a student interested in Celtic culture."

Had she heard him? She was in such a rush. Raped! Here at Blackthorn? That was something that happened in Frisco or L.A., not Trillium,

21

Minnesota.

He pondered the closed door. Nancy Crane certainly was a go-getter. It hadn't taken her long to get involved at the Women's Center, and she wasn't intimidated by him in the least bit. Was she ever intimidated?

She was enigmatic, exuding sensuality while remaining distant, feigning subordination while staying in charge. Much about her didn't add up. Undergraduates seldom shook hands with him.

He pivoted and stared at the chair she'd just vacated. He couldn't recall ever meeting a co-ed who carried a gun in her purse.

So who the hell was she?

Chapter Two

Pale yellow curtains hung over the observation room windows in the old frame building that housed the campus Women's Center. Nancy figured their color didn't matter much to Mary Lathrop, sitting rigidly on a cushioned chair. Her vacant eyes matched her pallid complexion. Even the woman's dark hair lacked luster.

Beside the co-ed knelt Ginger Maki, a member of the Center's staff, speaking soft words and occasionally massaging Mary's hand. Officer Lucy Washington stood off to the side with her police notepad at the ready. It appeared to be of little use at the moment; Mary Lathrop stared straight ahead acknowledging nobody's presence.

Nancy cocked her head at Officer Washington. Together, they stepped out into the hallway. "What do we know?"

"Not much," Lucy Washington said, flipping open her pad and checking her notes. "She's only been lucid a couple times. She'd been at a bar and was walking back alone toward campus when someone grabbed her from behind. He stuffed her in the trunk of a car and drove off."

"Did she recognize him?"

"Nope. Ski mask. Dark clothes – like the others. He drove for a while, blindfolded her, and then raped her. That's about all she's saying. So far, there's no emotion. She just recites her story like she's sharing a recipe for chocolate chip cookies."

Nancy nodded. "Sounds familiar. Anything else?"

"One odd thing."

"What's that?"

"The victim can't get over the fact that the man wanted to make sure she wasn't too cold."

"Huh?"

"Yeah. Guess he commented as much while he was raping her, and then later, when he dropped her off a mile out of town. He hoped she wouldn't catch a cold getting back to her dorm. Can you believe it?"

"Afraid so." Nancy sighed. "These guys aren't well screwed together, or they wouldn't be doing what they do. Maybe I've seen too much, but nothing surprises me anymore."

"Guess I'm still pretty new at all of this." Officer Washington fidgeted with her notepad before putting it away.

Briefly, Nancy considered the blushing redheaded officer. She likely wasn't more than a year or two out of college. Nancy winced. It was hard to remember ever being that innocent. She'd been that way once; she wished she could remember when.

"It's okay," she said, lightly. "If you stay in this work for long, you'll see more than you ever thought possible."

Nancy walked back to the observation room and peeked in. Mary Lathrop still had that far away look. Turning back to Officer Washington,

Nancy said, "She's in capable hands here. Think I'll head over to the bar this evening and see what I can pick up. Let me know if you get any more from Mary. I assume you'll be interviewing the bartender?"

"Yeah, me – and probably another officer."

"Does anyone, besides you, take these attacks seriously?"

Officer Washington shrugged, averting her eyes. "Don't know, really. I hear a lot of *it's just those college kids strung out on booze and drugs.*"

"Shit! Can't they tell the difference between effects of drugs and booze and this?" Nancy gestured toward the black haired co-ed whose cheeks had yet to witness a tear. They would, Nancy was certain of that. "Let me know if you turn up anything. I want to get the bastard before he strikes again." She retraced her steps toward the Center's entrance.

Later that evening, Nancy sat at a small table in the far corner of the Northland Bar and Grill. She tapped the table surface with an index finger. It wasn't a very original name. But then, it was probably difficult to be creative when there were twenty-three other bars in a community of ten thousand people.

This area of northern Minnesota was noted for its iron mines, and, before that, for its great white pines. The white pines were long gone, though loggers still worked the vast network of second and third growth across the region's marshes and bogs. The mines were closing, one by one. Trillium was home to hard working folks; apparently, many of them drank hard, too.

Business was slow. Four middle-aged men and a woman sat on stools at the bar. Several college students crowded around a couple tables. Most tables were empty. There was no live music. A local country western band had played the previous night. From the advertising flyers posted in the entryway, it was evident the owner had no particular musical preference. In addition to country western bands, jazz, folk, and even Celtic bands were highlighted as forthcoming attractions.

Would Professor Bayfield come out to hear the Celtic ensemble? She doubted he often rubbed shoulders socially with the locals, likely never with students.

Nancy lifted her beer to her lips and swallowed slowly. Damn, what she'd give for a Point beer. Couldn't hardly find the stuff outside Stevens Point, but it was recognized far and wide as one of the better brewed beers in the world. Next time she went to Milwaukee to see her mom, she'd have to fill her trunk with a case or two of Point beer.

Hardly anything of interest had happened since she arrived at the bar, and now the bartender was washing glasses preparing for closing. She'd had plenty of time to admire the sixteen point buck mounted on the wall behind the bar as well as the large mouth bass and northern pike hanging on the near wall.

Nancy ran her fingers along the grooves of several engraved hearts filled with initials and words of love roughly gouged into the wood table where she sat. Who carved their hopes and dreams in oak? How many of those immortalized relationships had actually worked? Were any of the artists now embarrassed by seeing their names linked with a former lover?

There was a time when her heart had been filled with such innocent love and expectations. Those expectations had been shredded, bit by bit.

The notion of finding love in this bar seemed starkly out of place given her reason for being there. She shuddered, remembering the women who had been raped after leaving the bar. What had they come to this place for? Had they sought a good time, to be loved, lasting relationships?

Dwelling on those co-eds now wasn't going to help her do her job. She squeezed her eyes shut. So, why hadn't she attracted anyone?

Maybe she hadn't dressed sexy enough. She'd thought the v-neck sweater and Victoria's Secret Miracle Bra gave her enough up top to interest somebody. And the miniskirt and calf-high boots should attract more than one appraising eye. Maybe it was the auburn wig.

She'd picked it thinking it complemented the light green sweater and white skirt quite nicely. And the black boots should have been pure knockouts; at least, that was what she'd been told by two girlfriends back in Point when they helped her plan wardrobes for these stakeouts.

Smoke tickled her raw throat. Nancy coughed. Apparently, enforcement of non-smoking sections wasn't high on the bartender's list of duties. She wrapped her fingers around the cool beer stein and suddenly looked up into a set of leering eyes.

"Hellooo, little woman," said a wobbling, sandy-haired man who must have been in his mid-forties. He looked local, not college. And he was short, way too short to be her man. "You look awfully lonely tucked over here in the corner all by your lonesome, missy. I'll bet you'd like some male company."

As he reached for a chair, Nancy rose to her feet. "Sorry to disappoint, but I've got to scoot. Early class in the morning. Too bad you didn't come over sooner."

"But..."

Nancy smiled from ear to ear. "Stuff it, mister. You do look like you could use a shoulder to cry on. But you're too late, and you're really not my type. Drive safely."

Without looking back, she heard the man slump heavily onto a chair at the table she'd just vacated. He'd get over it.

She stepped out into the chilly night air. Her senses went on alert. Her eyes, her ears, even her nose canvassed the parking lot – from light to dark, from noise to silence, from smoke to dankness.

Nothing moved. Nothing seemed out of place. She strolled toward her car. A train whistle sounded from the north end of town. She unlocked her car, climbed in and started the engine. She let out a breath, shifting the vehicle into reverse.

She'd come up empty again. This case was taking longer than she'd hoped. How many more women had to be raped before the man made a mistake – a mistake that led to his capture, or a mistake that led to the killing of a co-ed?

Nancy glanced back toward the bar before pulling out of the parking lot. There in the dark shadows of the building glowed a tiny red light. It looked more like a red dot. She flinched. Probably nothing to be concerned about, but someone had definitely watched her leave; someone who smoked cigarettes or cigars.

- o -

He watched the red Jeep Cherokee pull out and turn north toward campus. He ran his tongue across his lips. She'd been a stunning beauty, dressed to attract. More mature than most of the co-eds that frequented the bar. He preferred black hair, but auburn would do. She had the curves to be a worthy goddess. As with the others, he'd collect more evidence to be certain she qualified, but he had little doubt that she would.

The woman in the black boots would have to wait her turn. Samhein. If only she had black hair. Samhein – a time of masks and visits from other worlds. She'd have to wait until Samhein.

His lips curled. He wondered if the goddess was good

29

at waiting. He was; his gift, like a good wine, could not be rushed. Everything had a purpose and a time. His was to give to the goddess. Hers was to receive his gift.

He grunted. The time for this goddess would be Samhein.

- o -

"Sorry to bother you so early in the morning, but you weren't home last evening. I wondered if you could tell me how the student who was attacked is doing?"

"Oh, it's you, Professor Bayfield," said Nancy, slightly flustered, immediately recognizing his deep voice over the phone. She reached for the robe lying on the bed. There was no reason to inform her caller she'd just gotten out of the shower.

"Yes, I apologize for not identifying myself. I think this whole situation has me out of sorts. I didn't know who else to ask. I got your number from the registrar."

Nancy cussed under her breath. It was that easy to get her number? "That's okay. I'm sure the young woman would be pleased to know someone cared enough to ask. Yesterday, she was still pretty much in shock. That's quite typical."

"Was she beaten? This isn't the kind of thing you'd expect to happen here at Blackthorn, or Trillium, for that matter."

"Well, it did." Nancy put a clamp on her rising ire. The man sure was naïve, but then his view

30

was likely the prevailing sentiment in any small college or small community. "No. She wasn't beaten – not on the outside. But she was raped, physically and emotionally. At this point, who's to say how she is? She probably doesn't even know the answer to that question herself."

"I'm sure you're right." Was that a catch in the professor's otherwise calm voice? "Guess I shouldn't have bothered you, Ms. Crane. I hope the young woman comes out of this okay."

"You didn't bother me, professor." Nancy kept her voice distant, not inviting further questions. How much had she said when she'd taken that call in his office? She strained to remember. Damn, she shouldn't have said anything.

"Fine. Okay. Well, good-bye. If you have more questions about the Celts, you know where to find me."

The connection went dead before Nancy had a chance to respond. The caring in the professor's voice was genuine; she didn't question that. Yet, he seemed nervous about calling her. Was it guilt, or something else? Or was he uncomfortable sharing his emotions?

From what she'd seen and heard in his office, Bayfield wasn't overly fond of the college or of Trillium. He seemed skilled at maintaining distance from his students, but learning about the rape had apparently put a dent in the man's aloofness.

Yes, she could find Professor Bayfield when she wanted him. She shook out her wet hair. Even though she'd swear with every bone in her body that Bayfield was no rapist, she'd also swear he fit into the whole puzzle somehow. She knew she'd have more questions for the man with the provocative chin and deep calming voice.

Over the next few weeks, Nancy's life fell into a routine: attending classes, volunteering at the Women's Center, staking out bars three nights a week. She knew what a rat must feel like chasing haphazardly about trying to find its way out of a maze. She'd had background checks done on janitors, professors, probably half the men residing in Trillium. Nothing came back suspicious.

By now, it was late October. She'd lost count of how many times she'd been hit on at the bar – almost always by short men. Was she that short? Maybe she'd have to start wearing platform shoes. Ugh! No one had followed her home. And, other than the first night, she hadn't seen anyone watching her leave the premises.

There was hardly enough time to keep up with her classes; she hadn't even gone back through all the lectures Professor Bayfield had supplied her. She hadn't talked to him since his early morning phone call. His story had checked out; he'd been out of the country from June fifteenth to the end of August the previous summer.

"Enough of that," she muttered. "This is going to be a different kind of day. It's Sunday." Nancy set the comics in her lap and glanced around the apartment with satisfaction – it had become hers. A Green Bay Packer stein sat at the center of the table in the small eating area off the kitchen. A bronzed moose sculpture and a crystal eagle rested on the fireplace mantel. These were prize possessions that traveled wherever she went. She hadn't brought much artwork: a piece celebrating a federal stamp of the loon hung on a wall. On another, she'd displayed a canoe paddle. She'd hoped to find time to go up to the Boundary Waters, but with an early fall, ice would be setting in soon. Hopefully, she'd have time to get to her family's cabin in northern Wisconsin to do some ice fishing, but, if she had to, she'd buy a Minnesota license and check out a local lake or two. She loved eating fresh fish fried in beer batter.

And, of course, there was Malaki, stretched to his full length without an apparent care before the fireplace in which burned one of those cute fake logs. She much preferred the real thing – real logs, that really snapped and crackled. But this would do. She grinned. It was a peaceful day; a day for resting. That was what she planned to do.

The phone rang. Was it louder than normal? Nancy hesitated, allowing the answering machine to take a message. Why hadn't she left the apartment for the day? She should have made a picnic lunch and taken Malaki to the park.

"Hi, dear, I need to talk with you about something very important. No, it can't wait until

you get back to Point or Milwaukee. Nancy Ellen –
are you hiding behind that infernal machine?"

"Hello, Mother," Nancy said sweetly into the
phone. "Do you have eyes of Super Woman?"

Nancy's mother laughed. "Maybe I do. So how
are you doing? Are you working yourself to the
bone as usual? How is it being back in school?"

"Mother," Nancy interrupted. "When you talk
this fast, you're nervous about telling me
something. Now, what is it?"

"No," her mother cooed. "I asked you first.
How are you?"

"I'm fine. I could rest and relax more, if people
would leave me alone. Not you, of course. Being
back in school is not fun. I haven't read this much
in years."

"I'm sure it's good for you. Now...are you
sitting down?"

"Yes...." Nancy leaped to her feet, immediately
began pacing and nearly tripped over the phone
cord.

"Nancy, I never thought it would happen to me
again. Not twice in one lifetime."

"What are you talking about?"

"You know I loved your father very much."

A chill niggled at the base of Nancy's spine. "Of
course you did; we all did."

"I've found another man to share my life with. I
know you'll like him a lot. He won't replace your
father. We both know that, but he's good for me
and I think I'm good for him."

Thick silence hung somewhere between

34

Milwaukee, Wisconsin and Trillium, Minnesota.

"So what do you think, dear?" Nancy's mother prompted, at last.

Nancy shriveled. Think? How the hell could she think? *Don't screw this up Appleby; your mother deserves to be happy.* God, how long had it been, nearly ten years? "I'm happy for you, Mom…if you're certain," she squeaked. "Do I know this lucky guy?"

"No, I don't think so. His name is Jack Farley. We met a couple years ago, but we didn't start dating until early this summer. I didn't want to say anything at the time, but now I do."

"That's pretty quick, isn't it?"

"Nancy, at this age perhaps you better be quick."

"Maybe so. Mom, I trust your judgment. So is this marriage?"

"Well, of course it is. What did you think I was talking about? We're thinking maybe July fourth. We thought that might be special."

Nancy gagged. "Yes, I'm sure it would be. So when do I get to meet this fabulous man?"

"Whenever you can get away, I suppose. Thanksgiving? Christmas?"

"Don't know if I'll get there before Christmas. Things are taking longer here than I'd planned, but we'll have a Christmas break. Is the family still gathering at the cabin for Christmas?"

"Of course we are. Jack will be with me. He can hardly wait to meet you."

"I bet. I'll look forward to it."

"And what about you?"

"What?"

"Is there a nice young man in your life? I hoped, with you being in a new community, you might find romance."

Nancy chuckled. "Not hardly. Not here. Probably not in this lifetime. I've got to run, Mom. I am pleased for you. You take care."

"Oh, I will, dear. Apparently, better than you. Bye."

Nancy laid the phone in its cradle and slid down the wall, crumpling on the floor. Malaki stood and stretched before nudging his way onto her lap.

"Wow, Mal! We're hardly gone two months and the entire world changes. My mother's getting married." Nancy gulped in air. Why did it bother her so? Her dad had been killed, in the line of duty, almost a decade ago. Her mother was still vibrant and had always taken good care of herself. She was well enough off financially, but certainly not prime game for a fortune hunter.

She'd have Jack Farley checked out upside down and sideways. Was Farley spelled with an e, or without?"

"Ouch! Behave yourself!" Nancy pushed the dog's head away. "How many times do I have to tell you not to poke my boobs?" She buried her face in Malaki's thick, furry neck. "Can you believe it? My mother's getting married, and I can't even get a man to follow me home."

Nancy walked into the campus bookstore and made her way directly toward the tall, dark-haired man seriously searching book titles in the sports section. She'd unobtrusively followed Bayfield to the store, but hadn't expected him to stop in that particular section. He hadn't struck her as a sports enthusiast.

She sidestepped down the aisle to within a few feet of him and pulled a book on canoeing off the shelf. Bayfield never looked her way. Nancy leaned over to see what had captured his attention. The title came into focus: *Guns for Upland Game and Big Game*. Her eyes flew wide and she quickly swallowed her nearly audible gasp.

"You plan on hunting birds or big game, Professor Bayfield?" The man lurched backwards, giving her a look of horror. He fumbled with the book, pushing it back onto the shelf as if it were afire. Nancy stifled a giggle. Would he be any more embarrassed if she'd found him perusing the *Kama Sutra*?

"I have no plans to take up hunting," Bayfield said, shoving his hands in his coat pockets. "I merely wanted to know the derivation of shotguns versus rifles. It could be that their varied purposes can be traced back to primitive cultures, like the use of spears versus blow guns."

Nancy closed her mouth and blew air into her cheeks. This guy is good, very good. She'd bet that wasn't his real reason for picking up the book, but then, no alternative explanation came to mind.

He didn't strike her as a hunter, past, present, or future. "If you want to know about guns, maybe I can help. I've always hunted – birds and big game – and, my dad had a collection of antique guns I've maintained in recent years. Afraid I don't know much about blow guns, though."

His face darkened. He cleared his throat to speak, but hesitated. At last, he said, "Why are you here, Ms. Crane? I didn't ask for your assistance. You keep...popping up. Is there something I can help you with?"

"Actually, now that you mention it," Nancy said, shelving the canoe book, "if you've got a few minutes, I'd like to pick your brain some more about the Celtic lectures. I've been meaning to stop by, but haven't found the time. How about letting me buy you a cup of coffee in the Union?"

Bayfield took another step backward, creating more space between them. She saw him scan the nearly empty store. Probably he wouldn't want to be seen fraternizing with a student, but as planned she'd caught his interest by wanting to probe his passion: Celtic culture. Did the man allow himself any other passions? What might it take to get him angry, or sad, or overjoyed? What might it take to make him lose some of that self-control he seemed so adept at maintaining?

His poker face intrigued her; challenged her, really. She pushed her hair over the collar of her coat, waiting for him to respond to her invitation. Good God, he was so damn self-possessed he could be a cop.

"Why not?" he muttered at last.

That was it? *Why not?* Such enthusiasm. Would he have shown any more emotion if she'd invited him to her bed? She cocked her head to the side and quickly led the way out of the bookstore, giving him no chance to change his mind.

- o -

Matt Bayfield checked out the Union cafeteria before ordering coffee and finding a table. They were indeed alone. Three o'clock on a Friday afternoon had always been a safe time to browse books and even stop for a latte. Until, that is, he'd been accosted by the female sitting across from him, who seemed unable to stop grinning.

Did she chew on her lips to make them so pronounced? She looked like she'd just been kissed thoroughly, if not roughly.

He moved his head back and forth loosening neck tension and cleansing his mind of that image. "So, what can I do for you, Ms. Crane?"

She scowled in response. Now what had he said wrong? Nothing. It was *her* idea that they talk over coffee. The woman was too damn mercurial.

"First," she said, running a finger around the rim of her coffee cup, "I owe you an apology, and need to ask something very important of you.

Matt sat up straight, his curiosity piqued. "Go ahead. I know of nothing for which you have to apologize."

"When I was in your office and the call came from the Women's Center, I shouldn't have revealed anything about the rape." Her lips tightened. "I guess I was in a rush, or something; it just slipped out. And I knew better than that."

"You never said who was raped."

"No, of course not. But even the fact there was a rape shouldn't have been shared. Have you told anyone?"

He shook his head, surprised to see her so vulnerable.

"You must promise never to tell anyone."

"Or you could get into trouble?"

"Perhaps." She warmed both her hands by wrapping them around the coffee mug. "But more importantly we don't want to create a climate of fear at the college or in the community."

Matt nodded. "I understand. You don't have to worry about me; I won't say anything." He arched an eyebrow. "So, we share a secret, Ms. Crane. I'm quite good at keeping secrets."

"I'll just bet you are."

"So what else is on your mind?" He watched her give him a quizzical look. He wasn't at all certain he wanted to know her inner thoughts.

As if reading his mind, she pursed her lips and then smiled broadly. He felt his temperature rising. Was it the latte? Had the Union staff turned up the heat? Or was the heat emanating from the dark haired female sitting across from him?

She was evidently of Celtic extraction. Her hair, her lips, her cheekbones all spoke of a heritage that could be traced back to Druid priestesses and Celtic warriors. The snug maroon cardigan sweater and large gold loop earrings gave her a vivacious flair.

Slow down, Bayfield. She's just a damn student. She's no Celtic warrior/goddess come to joust with you, verbally or otherwise. The woman merely wanted some answers to academic questions; she wasn't seeking him as a male consort. *Ms. Crane is a student – bright, perky, sexy – but, first and foremost, a student.*

"Relax, professor," she said, tucking stray hairs behind an ear, "I'm not going to bite you. And, if I did, I promise it wouldn't hurt at all."

Damn, she *was* flirting – or was she? He'd never been very good with that kind of repartee and innuendo. The fast track he'd been on through college and grad school hadn't left him a lot of time to pursue relationships, and the few he'd had seldom lasted long. That was okay by him, and he hadn't been involved with a woman since moving to Trillium.

He narrowed his eyes, trying to decipher the beaming Ms. Crane. She looked liked she'd burst out laughing at any moment. Why wasn't he laughing? Because he'd made a pact with himself: never get involved with a student.

"Shapeshifting."

"What?" Matt sputtered, trying to keep up with the woman's train of thought, if there was one.

"In your second lecture, you talked a little bit about shapeshifting – that Celtic shamans would

41

change form in order to travel to another dimension to get information, or to make a conquest."

"Yes, of course." He relaxed some. The woman no longer was a feminine provocateur preparing to pounce on her next quarry; she was a student seeking information. She'd actually done her homework; she'd read his lectures. There was never enough time to go into enough depth on any topic in the lectures. The dean of Arts and Sciences had wanted the series to be very basic so it might appeal to a broader audience. Matt had never been pleased with the idea of being some kind of campus entertainer.

"So, tell me more. Why would a shaman change shape into an animal?"

"Could be several reasons." Matt got up to remove his sport coat. Sitting back down, he continued, "A shaman might take on an animal disguise in order to borrow the strengths of that particular animal – for example, becoming a hawk would enhance eyesight. Or, it might be a way of hiding the human form, making oneself invisible, if you will, permitting one to travel in this dimension or another without being identified."

Ms. Crane gave him a low laugh. "So, if I took on the appearance of a skunk, I might be able to scare off certain enemies?"

"Yes, quite a few," Matt said, trying not to imagine Ms. Crane as a seductive skunk. "Similarly, a shaman might shapeshift in order to stalk, with maximum stealth, an enemy or lover."

"Really!" Ms. Crane's eyes shot wide.

A surge of unexpected pleasure coursed through him at her apparent interest. "Myths and stories abound of shamans, gods, and goddesses changing form to track down a lover who had otherwise eluded or jilted them."

"Come on." The co-ed's eyes sparkled. "You're putting me on."

She was teasing him, but he couldn't help but prove her wrong. "There was, for example," he said, "Aengus mac Og, the god of youth and love, who dreams of a beautiful maiden and falls in love with her. After stalking her for quite a while, he learns that she spends her time in the shape of a swan. He is told that if he turns into a swan himself, he may find her. But he has to select her from a hundred and fifty swans."

Matt sipped his coffee and took in the view of his eager listener leaning over the table.

"So, damn it, what happened? Did he find her? Did they live happily ever after?"

Matt chuckled. "Don't you have any patience?"

"Sometimes," she said, raising her chin.

"Well, he does find her. They swim around the lake together, getting to know each other, I guess. They fly together. Eventually, he wins her over. But he does so by taking on her form."

"Intriguing. And there are lots of stories like this – of shamans, gods, and goddesses?"

"Yes."

Apparently lost in thought, Ms. Crane crossed her arms below her breasts and absently pushed upwards. Matt wet his lips. Damn, he'd like to be doing that. He caught himself: no way. She was a student; a student who carried a gun in her purse.

Ms. Crane hugged herself as if warding off a chill. He, on the other hand, was sweating, resisting tempting thoughts.

"So, what do you think, professor – can people really shapeshift?"

His laugh resonated from deep within. He hadn't known what to expect her to say, but certainly not that. "I don't know, Ms. Crane. I've never had the experience." He paused. "Shapeshifting was an esteemed practice in many ancient cultures, and is currently adhered to, yet today, by many persons who practice nature-based religions." He nodded at her amazement. "That's right, there are many shamans around the world, including in this country, who at least believe they shapeshift and travel to other dimensions."

"No shit." Nancy covered her mouth quickly. "Sorry."

"I've heard the word before," he interjected.

"So..."

Now, why did she look so perplexed? They were only talking about a shared academic interest.

"So, when people shapeshift, do you think they are aware of what they are doing? Are they responsible for what takes place around them?"

"I don't know, Ms. Crane. Like I said, I've never had the experience, and it's not been the focus of my research. I simply know many people believe it happens. Why does this phenomenon trouble you so?"

Immediately, her face went blank. She was a woman of many faces. He wasn't sure he liked this face much – she was hiding something.

Chapter Three

"So who's the babe?"

Matt recognized the familiar taunting feminine voice. Groaning his annoyance, he fumbled with his office key. He didn't have to look down the hallway to know Carol Macy stood there with an "I've got a secret" grin spread across her face. From the moment he'd arrived at Blackthorn, she'd befriended him. She'd been on the faculty for five years and had shown him where many of the skeletons of past deans lay. Actually, she'd been a good friend, except she thought he needed to be in an intimate relationship. Carol had made clear from the beginning that she wasn't available given her own relationship with a woman who taught in the English department.

He heard her footsteps coming down the hallway. Trapped. She meant well, but she should butt out of his personal life. Five minutes ago would have been just fine.

Matt tossed his keys on the desk, removed his coat and peeked over his shoulder. Sure enough, the tall blonde with a single braid reaching to the small of her back leaned against the doorjamb.

"Well, come on Bayfield, spill your guts. I just happened to be walking back from the bookstore a bit ago and checked out the Union to see if there was anyone I could join." She peered at him over the rims of her glasses. "It didn't look like you, or the shapely young woman at your table, would welcome the intrusion. So, I came back here to lie in wait. Who is she? How long have you known her? Where have you been hiding her?"

Matt flopped into his chair. He dug at his temples with both thumbs. Two women in one day was at least one too many. "It's nothing, Carol. She's just a student. Crane. Ms. Crane. I think Nancy is her first name. She saw me in the bookstore and had some questions."

He didn't like the lazy smile creeping across Carol Macy's face. "And then one thing led to the other. Right, professor?"

"She's a student, for god's sake. I don't get involved with students, you know that."

"You're right," said his colleague, stepping further into his space. "That makes this all the more intriguing. I've never seen or heard of you entertaining a student at the Union."

"I wasn't entertaining her!" Matt lowered his voice. "She offered to buy me a cup of coffee because she had some questions about my Celtic lectures."

"So...you're telling me," Carol said, resting a hip against the corner of his desk, "that this attractive co-ed just happened to bump into you at the bookstore on a late Friday afternoon, and just happened to have some questions for you?" She furrowed her brow. "Come on, Bayfield, you're brighter than that."

"What do you mean?" He didn't like the fact that his voice sounded strained.

"She's either after your body or something else. It's Friday afternoon, remember. The campus is deader than Lazarus. And how many times have female students offered to buy you coffee, Bayfield? You have the reputation of a piranha. Oh, you do fine with small groups of students. But female students don't flock to you. A few women may try to attract you from a distance, but they give up quickly in the face of Stonehenge."

"Stonehenge. Me?" Matt scowled at his colleague's probing gaze.

"Yep. Stonehenge. That's your code name among the deprived females of Blackthorn College: brainy, but remote; passionate, but not about women."

"Depraved, more likely," Matt muttered. "And how would you know anyway?"

"Women talk, my friend. Even women who are not particularly interested in men. Did you think locker room talk was limited to men only?"

"I don't know anything about locker room talk."

Carol Macy shook her head side to side. "No, I imagine you don't. So, who is this Crane woman? I haven't seen her around. She's not fresh out of high school, that's for sure."

"No, you're right about that. I don't know much about her. She just seems…seems to be around." He lifted one shoulder. "I gather she's a transfer student but has been away from college for a while." He leaned back in his swivel chair. "Actually, I don't even know her major. She showed up at my first lecture in September, has come by once to ask some questions, and then I saw her this afternoon."

Matt frowned, remembering another contact, but there was no need to tell Carol Macy he'd tracked down Nancy Crane's phone number and called her. Or that she intrigued him in ways he couldn't quite grasp.

No, there was much about Nancy that he wasn't about to share with the curious faculty member staring at him, searching for any tidbit of information. He pulled on his nose. Now, why had he thought of her as Nancy? He'd always refused to be that informal with female students, even in his thoughts.

"I do find her interest in Celtic culture refreshing," he said finally. "She seems quite eager. She's already volunteering at the Women's Center."

"I have a friend on the Center's board; maybe I could check her out for you."

Matt closed his eyes and shook his head. "Don't go meddling trying to make something out of nothing."

"Don't worry, professor, you know I'd never do anything like that."

"Like trying to set me up with that biology instructor over at Conner's Hall?"

"That wasn't one of my better moves, I admit. But this is different. This Crane woman bears watching, Matt. Whether you like it or not, you two looked very cozy – very entranced. At least she's not one of *your* students. That could get messy."

"Nothing's going to get messy," Matt snapped, rising from his chair. "I value our friendship, Carol, but I can take care of myself. Don't meddle. Now, it's long past time for both of us to be headed home.

"Yes, I suppose so," Carol said, pushing away from the desk. "But, you have to admit Nancy Crane looks quite cute, and you must be a little curious about her or you'd never let her buy you coffee.

"The man I saw this afternoon was not the offish Matt Bayfield whom I have come to adore and champion during this past year." Carol Macy walked toward the doorway and threw him a last teasing smile. "Maybe she'll get you to drop your guard some. Don't look so dismayed, Professor Bayfield. It might do you some good to let someone get close to you. You might even learn to enjoy it."

- o -

"Are you okay, Mary?" Cautiously, Nancy appraised Mary Lathrop, who huddled on a soft cushioned chair in the corner of the rec room. A Center staff member had called saying the woman had remembered something that might be helpful. Nancy glanced at Washington waiting with her notepad handy.

"No." The response came slowly. The young

51

woman took a deep breath. "But I will be," Mary added. "Everyone here has been so kind. Don't know what I would've done without you all."

"We want to do whatever we can." Nancy hesitated, not wanting to rush the woman with further questions. She had to be given all the choices she could at this point; the assault had undermined her fundamental sense of self-control.

Mary hugged herself and smiled weakly. "Thanks for coming by. I hope I didn't put you to too much trouble. You're not skipping a class or anything important, are you?"

Pleased to see a sharpness return to Mary's eyes and a pinkish tone to her cheeks, Nancy said, "Not at all. Sounded like you had something to tell us you thought might be significant."

"I don't know how significant, but you did say to call if I remembered anything else."

"That's right," Nancy said, drawing up a chair across from Mary. "Do you want to share what you remembered now?"

"Yes, of course." With trembling fingers, Mary brushed dark hair back from her forehead. "There was something burning."

"What?" Nancy scrunched forward. "Burning?"

"Yes, burning. Not right away. But at the place where..." Mary focused on the Picasso print of colorful figures dancing in a circle hanging on the far wall. "Where he hurt me. No – where he raped me. That's where I smelled it. It was foul."

Only the radiator made any noise.

"Can you tell us what it smelled like?" Nancy

52

asked.

Mary paused, thinking, remembering. "Maybe a combination of damp leaves smoldering and rotten eggs."

"Yuck." Officer Washington's response was involuntary. She reached to cover her mouth. Nancy grinned up at her.

"Mary, how do you know the smell was from something burning? You were blindfolded."

Mary's brow creased. "I didn't see anything burning, but I did smell it. It was like smoke in my nostrils."

"Okay, I'm not questioning what you experienced. I'm just trying to understand."

"I know. Anyway, that's what I remember. It's probably not going to help, but I thought you might want to know."

"Absolutely. Thanks for telling us." Nancy rose to her feet and reached over to squeeze Mary's hand. "At this point, we don't know what will be the key that'll nail this guy. Any little thing might do it. If you think of anything else, don't hesitate to call us. Okay?"

"Okay, I will. It's been five weeks. When do I stop remembering?" Mary blinked back tears. "Again, I appreciate what you're trying to do."

Nancy Crane Appleby inhaled the candle-scented air deeply. Her head rested on the rim of the footed bathtub. With eyes closed, she relished the steaming water and bubbles ebbing across her skin. She reached for the soap bar and slid it across her chest and over her flat belly. Her skin hummed to the touch. She could drown in this kind of luxury.

With some reluctance, Nancy pulled herself back to the primary reason she'd filled the tub. She often did her best thinking while soaking.

So what did she have? Not much. A rapist who struck about every two months or so, assuming that each attack was reported. Some of those attacks came at or about the time of Bayfield's campus wide lectures – coincidence or not? Victims were transported off campus. Wrists were loosely bound – some behind the back, some at the waist. Each victim had been blindfolded. And Mary Lathrop had smelled a foul odor she believed was from something burning. Maybe. Each victim had been walking back to campus from the same bar; a couple had remembered something foul and musty smelling wherever they'd been taken.

She'd staked out that bar so many times she thought she knew every nail and crossbeam in the place. Nothing. Well, nothing but the usual hits from guys who thought she would be a willing next sexual conquest.

Which brought her back to Bayfield. A lazy smile crept across her lips. Professor Matt Bayfield. So reserved, yet the man had passion. She'd seen it when his eyes lit up while he told her about shapeshifters. More than once she'd caught him looking at her with bedroom eyes. Was he undressing her in his mind? Nancy chuckled, running fingers across curls that led to pleasure. She'd undressed *him* a couple times herself. Could reality ever match fantasy?

Nancy arched her back and pulled on her tightening nipples. She wet her lips. Damn, it had been too long. She settled back into the water, letting it rise to her neck. "Focus, Appleby," Nancy muttered, "focus."

Bayfield stood squarely in the middle of the puzzle. She was sure of it. While he was no longer a suspect, what he did at the college fed into the mystery. Nancy kept coming back to his lectures. Did they trigger the attacker?

But then there was the August rape, and Bayfield had been thousands of miles away getting dirt under his fingernails. Damn, she wished she'd seen that. She'd give most anything to knock that smug look off the professor's face.

She needed to confirm the lecture dates with Bayfield. Apart from the August rape, one other didn't quite jibe, but there might be an explanation. The water was cooling down. Nancy wrapped her toes around the hot water faucet and turned it until she had the temperature right.

Monday night might provide the break. Bayfield would be presenting the second lecture of the semester. She hoped the fact it was Halloween wouldn't diminish the attendance. She'd go to his lecture and then stake out the Northland Bar. It seemed fitting that a Celtic group would provide live music.

She wiggled her toes. Once again, she'd be the

bait. Why didn't the creep come out of his hole? He had to know she was around. The place was too small to go unnoticed. So why wasn't she able to find him?

Nancy opened her eyes. Shadows cast from the flickering candles danced across the ceiling, each one distinct and then blurring, each one shifting from one form to another.

So what kind of animal strength should she draw upon as she changed form come Monday night? She'd always been a master of disguise; she'd just never known she was a shapeshifter, until she met Matt Bayfield.

Nancy glanced over at two large sorrowful eyes begging for attention. "Okay Mal," she said, reaching out a hand to scratch the dog behind his ears. "I've probably daydreamed long enough. Now, if you get your big head off the tub, I could get out."

She stood to dry herself off and Malaki backed away, giving her plenty of room. "With a bit of luck, Mal, we might be headed home soon." The dog responded with a deep growl. "So you don't agree, huh?" She wrapped the towel around her midsection. "So what do you know that I don't?"

Mal settled at her feet, his head resting on his paws. "After we crack this case there won't be anything keeping us here." She folded her arms, cradling her breasts. Her body warmed.

Bayfield's smug smile filled her mind. She'd never expected to be fascinated by a professor – but there wasn't time for shenanigans with any professor. Not that he would ever get off his podium long enough to test out her fantasies.

"Oh hell, Mal," she said, looking down at her confidant and protector. "He's probably a dishrag in bed anyway. I've got enough dishrags."

From the rear of the lecture hall, Nancy had an adequate view of the lecture attendees. She'd watched each person enter. Like the last time, about eighty people sat in the small hall. Not bad for a night before many papers were due.

Only a handful of men fit the height qualifications. Three of them were stocky, likely jocks, certainly powerful enough to subdue a woman. The others were more interesting. Her hunch was that the attacker was not a student, at least not the traditional student who attended college right out of high school. Victim accounts gave her the feeling they were dealing with an older man. At times, the man seemed almost fatherly.

Two men in the hall were older. One sat three rows from the front. He was balding with a hawk-like nose; his pen hardly stopped moving. This guy was serious about Celtic culture. Could he be her rapist?

Nancy directed her attention to the man sitting in the second row from the back. He slouched in his seat. A moustache flowed over his upper lip. He wore faded green bib overalls. Was he janitorial staff simply waiting for the room to clear out? She'd have to check back and see if the attacker had attempted to kiss any of the women. A moustache should have been noticed, unless he'd grown it recently. Nancy's brow creased. How long did it take to grow a bushy moustache?

Nancy focused on Bayfield's words. He sounded as confident as ever. That typical hitch of condescension in his voice rang clear, as if he doubted anyone within hearing fully understood what he was saying. His eyes settled on her. They were like a vortex. Nancy braced herself. His eyes drank her in. Were they laughing, taunting, or seducing?

Although she could hardly breathe, Nancy listened carefully.

"This should be of particular interest to the women present this evening," Bayfield said, grinning subtly as if he was about to share a secret. "Women played a major role in numerous Celtic legends. In many such cases their male consorts are secondary, almost superfluous. In the ancient Celtic religion, goddesses were seen as more powerful than gods. Medbh, for example, sheds her lovers frequently because as Queen she is the pure example of Sovereignty. The king is tied to the land; kings will come and go, but the land will remain. The goddesses remain constant, reflecting an earlier matriarchal period of Celtic culture."

Nancy's chin lowered to her chest; her eyelids narrowed. She jerked herself awake. Bayfield was much more interested in the supremacy of Celtic women than she was.

"Furthermore," Bayfield said, "female goddesses in this tradition melded two dynamic powers: fertility and war."

Nancy grinned. Now, you've got my attention, professor. She picked up her pen and scribbled some notes.

"Goddesses embodied life and death, fertility and war, sexuality and destruction," he said. "To understand Celtic culture you must grasp how their cosmology balanced polar opposites. Their belief system, their experience focused on balance and harmony. Examples abounded in the natural world in which the Celts were spiritually and emotionally immersed. Each animal, each tree, each rock, each blade of grass played a role in the ultimate balance of the world and the underworld."

A mousy co-ed near the front raised her hand tentatively. That took guts. Bayfield didn't welcome interruptions. He tried ignoring the woman, but the student was persistent.

"Yes, Ms. Lamppi?" Bayfield pulled a pen from his pocket and wrote something on his lecture notes. Was he taking down the student's name, making sure he didn't miss his place, or reminding himself to do something important?

"Professor Bayfield, excuse me, but I can't help but wonder," the student asked. "Before the Christians converted the Celts, did they worship trees? Some of the loggers in the area today claim environmentalists are nothing more than folks who worship trees."

59

Nancy smothered a grin. Bayfield was turning red; he was not a happy man. Professors were bombarded by questions from left and right fields; she understood why some might not like to leave much time for questions.

"I'm not an expert on contemporary environmentalism, Ms. Lamppi," Bayfield said, resting his hands on the podium. "I suppose one could make a case that the Celts were environmentalists of the first order in their own time. All living matter was sacred. For many, the oak tree was most sacred. Druids would seek out oak groves for their places of worship and ritual practices. It was their belief that the oak groves brought them closer to that which was supremely sacred and the object of their worship. Did they worship the oak tree? I think not."

That familiar smugness tugged at the corner of Bayfield's mouth. He'd found his pace and was once again in his element.

"Perhaps the relationship between the Celt and the oak tree is somewhat analogous to a Christian and the cross." Bayfield paused for effect. "To the Christian, isn't the cross an important symbol directing attention to the holy, to God? And to worship the cross, itself, would be a form of idolatry. I expect some Christians *do* practice that idolatry, and I imagine some Celts did worship the oak tree, but in both cases the symbol was taken too literally and may have in fact precluded the believer from making that next step toward the holy.

"Anything else, Ms. Lamppi?"

The flustered co-ed clutched the gold cross hanging from a chain around her neck while shaking her head. Surely, the woman wasn't put off by Bayfield's analogy. Nancy thought Bayfield had been quite perceptive and eloquent.

Another hand rose. Nancy inched forward in her seat; the older man with the hawkish nose waited to be acknowledged.

"Yes?" Bayfield said, brow furrowed. He didn't seem to recognize the man.

The questioner cleared his throat. "What about Samhein? Isn't it tonight? And is it true the Celts used the night to do crazy, wild things? Including orgies. And isn't that what Halloween is really supposed to be about, instead of begging and threatening?"

"That's certainly more than one question," Bayfield replied, smiling thinly. "Yes, tonight is the celebration of Samhein. It marks the halfway point between the equinox and the solstice. The Celts believed that on this night, the veil between this dimension and others was at its thinnest, and if individuals were properly disguised they could pass from one world to the other. Many Samhein celebrants dressed in animal skins. And yes, Halloween is apparently modeled somewhat after Samhein.

"From what I gather, there were some wild goings on. As to orgies, I don't know. They may have happened or they may have been the fantasies of those who came along generations later eager to record a debauched history of primitive peoples, perhaps giving themselves license to follow suit."

Nancy nodded. Bayfield paused and scanned his audience. He was a maestro at this, and she respected that. Actually, she was more than a little envious.

"Your question feeds directly into one of the major points of this evening: polarity. Celtic thinking does not allow us to look at only one thing, be it animal, emotion, or rite.

"The search for balance leads us to polar opposites. Samhein's polarity is Beltane, which occurs on May first. They are six months apart on the calendar. While Samhein celebrates the magic of decay and death and the open passage between two worlds, Beltane lifts up the magic of earth, blossoming, and freshness of new life.

"One cannot exist without the other. There is a natural balance and harmony between the two seasons. And I would suggest, sir, that yes, it is quite clear Beltane was a time for sexual excess, even ritual orgies. So, hopefully, this response to your question does get us back to where we belong.

"Often, then, occurrences in Celtic culture and spirituality were not as they first appeared to an outsider, whether contemporary or centuries removed," Bayfield continued with his prepared lecture, "because the outsider did not share this fundamental understanding of harmony and balance. Thus when the Romans came to Ireland, to Scotland, to Wales, they could not fathom why the Celts regarded trees and water as sacred.

"Outsiders thought the Celts worshipped trees, pigs, stags, rivers and so on. While instead, the Celts regarded all of life as part of the same unity, of the same harmony, of the sacred oneness. Perhaps one of the lessons to learn from all of this is not to quickly presume we understand another's culture. Things may not be as they appear."

Bayfield glanced at his watch. "That's enough for tonight. We'll get back together just before the Christmas break, on the twentieth of December."

Nancy sighed, leaning back in her seat. She watched the attendees exit the hall. There was no certainty the man she was looking for was in the room, or that he'd attack tonight. The hairs standing on the back of neck told her otherwise. He was here; she could smell his stench.

She looked down at Bayfield collecting his notes while answering the questions of a voluptuous blonde. Recalling Bayfield's closing comments, Nancy's body went rigid. *Things may not be as they appear.*

"Holy shit," she mumbled, looking frantically about her. Too late. Only a few individuals remained. Was it possible? Could the man have been sitting within thirty feet of her disguised as a woman?

- o -

"Good job, Doc."

Matt looked up from the drinking fountain and spied the janitor. "Oh, hi, Clyde, noticed you joined us tonight. Nice turn out."

"Yeah, Doc. You bring 'em in, all right. Were more townies tonight than usual. Probably thought you'd say more about Halloween than you did."

Matt smiled at the older man in bib overalls. This was backstage at the college level. Janitors often seemed to develop a familiarity with professors that surpassed his expectations. Yet, the man holding the handle of the large broom seemed as interested in Celtic culture as any of the regular students. He often stopped Matt after lectures to either say "good job" or ask a question.

"Thought that mouse Lamppi wasn't gonna give up on asking stupid questions tonight."

Ignoring the janitor's comment, Matt started to walk away. "I've got to run, Clyde. Good to see you again."

"Yep, you too, Doc. Don't let them co-eds get to you," the janitor cackled.

"You can count on that," Matt said over his shoulder. He wasn't about to get in a discussion with a janitor about any of his students, including Ms. Lamppi.

Once outside, Matt pulled his overcoat tighter about his neck to ward off a nippy wind coming out of the northwest. Winter was fast approaching; not his favorite season of the year. So why was he stuck in a section of the country where winter could last six months? Good question, but one he'd gone over countless times in the past. He was doing everything he could to get back on track, into a quality university and to a warmer climate. But the question that really nagged at him this evening was why the hell the woman had disappeared without saying a word.

Their paths hadn't crossed for a while. He'd actually been looking forward to sparring with Ms. Crane. He hadn't decided what to do if she suggested going for a cup of coffee. Matt shoved his hands deeper into his coat pockets.

What had she thought of his reference to the goddesses combining polarities? Bayfield slowed and watched the shadows of the campus lights play across the walkway. Light and dark. Polarity. That was an apt image of Nancy Crane. One moment she was exuberant, apparently without a care in the world. The next she was deadly serious.

His breathing quickened. Why did it matter that she hadn't stopped by after the lecture to ask a question or poke fun at his demeanor? She was a student, making her *verboten*. So why did he become half aroused whenever he saw her? Was it her lush lips? Or those large gray eyes that seemed to probe his soul? Or her quick wit? Or her easy laugh?

"Pull yourself together, Bayfield," he mumbled. "She's a student, for god's sake. End of story. End of attraction."

Two hours later, Nancy Crane sat on a barstool next to the open space where patrons came to place their orders. Her purse lay on the stool beside her so there would be plenty of room for her perp to sit down if he ever arrived. She'd wait another half hour and then make her exit. She was nearly certain the man was somewhere in the smoky bar.

Slowly adding another layer of lipstick, Nancy studied her image in the mirror that stretched the full length of the row of liquor bottles behind the bartender. She hardly recognized herself. Her own dark hair was tucked under an auburn wig. Fake contacts made her eyes appear dark brown instead of gray. The sweater she wore dipped low, revealing much more of her breasts than she preferred, but then she was trying to fulfill every man's dream. She hoped her red leather mini-skirt screamed availability. Once again, she had on the calf length black boots. They provided her with some sense of being covered up as well as warmth. Now all she needed was a man – the right man.

She took a sip of Coors and watched a new patron enter the room still huddled over from fighting the cold wind. He straightened and stepped into the light.

Nancy raised a hand to cover her largely exposed breasts. It couldn't be, she screamed to no one. It couldn't be. She looked away and then peeked back at the man approaching the bar. Holy shit! It was.

Be calm. He won't recognize you. You're in disguise. And what in the hell was Matt Bayfield doing here? This wasn't his kind of scene. She closed her eyes taking in the lilting Celtic music. Of course it was tonight. She should have remembered that. She shivered and then warmed to her task. It might be fun observing the man when he didn't realize she was even nearby.

Nancy concentrated on her beer and nearly snickered when Bayfield came to the bar to order a drink. His fingers drummed against the bar surface no more than two feet from her arm. The bartender was busy at the other end of the bar and Bayfield's impatience was evident.

At last, the bartender nodded at Bayfield. "What can I get for you?"

"A glass of chardonnay," Bayfield said, distinctly as if the man might be hard of hearing.

The man wiped his hands on his once white apron. "Drinking heavy tonight, huh?"

Nancy gave Bayfield credit for not rising to the bartender's bait.

Out of the corner of her eye, she watched Bayfield accept his drink and change. His gaze swept above her trying to locate a seat in the crowded tavern. His eyes lowered meeting hers. She tried to control her racing pulse. He shook his head. And then his eyes bugged.

"Ms. Cr – "

Before he could mutter another syllable, Nancy

leaped to her feet, wrapped her arms around his neck, and planted the biggest, wettest kiss she could muster on his mouth, swallowing the rest of her name and his breath. He stumbled backward. She refused to let him go, imprinting her lips on his.

She started to release him, but then one of his hands pressed against her back and the other curved over her buttocks. Her eyes widened. Professor Bayfield was kissing her! Not about to pass up this opportunity, Nancy closed her eyes and enjoyed the moment.

His tongue pushed into her open mouth; she greeted it with her own. He brought a hand between them and squeezed a breast. Her eyes flew open. Would she burn up right there in the damn bar? As if he sensed her changing mood, Bayfield's eyes sprang as wide open as hers. He started to pull away.

Applause and hoots broke out from bar patrons. Steins were raised in salute.

Nancy and Matt looked sheepishly at the other patrons. "Don't say a word, Bayfield," Nancy said, still holding him close. "I can explain everything, but we've got to get out of here, now." He started to open his mouth. Brushing her lips across his, she whispered, "Please, don't say my name. It could be a matter of life and death."

With approval, she watched his jaw clamp shut. "Come on, lover," she said, loud enough for those nearby to hear. "These folks aren't going to pay us to put on a show."

She shot him what she hoped was her most provocative smile. "They'll call the cops on us for lewd behavior if we hang around here any longer."

She led the professor toward the exit to more applause and catcalls. At last, she could breathe again. She had a lot of explaining to do; Bayfield wouldn't be put off easily this time.

While Bayfield hadn't blown her cover, he'd just about blown her mind. She never dreamed he'd set her body ablaze with a single kiss.

Chapter Four

Matt slammed a shoulder against the exit door and flew down the stairs leading to the parking lot, dragging Nancy Crane behind him.

He spoke not a word, giving no credence to Ms. Crane's protestations.

What the hell had just happened? After the lecture, he needed to relax. He'd gone to the bar to listen to live Celtic music and have a glass of wine.

And then out the corner of his eye he'd spied those lips, those tantalizing lips that so often cluttered his mind of late. It had to be her. No one else in the entire world had lips as full and moist as hers. But she wore a wig and was all dressed up like a…like a tramp.

He'd only begun to express his shock when she was all over him. Those lips tasted even better than he'd imagined. They'd entrapped him, engorged him. He remembered not being able to breathe and then succumbing to her wiles.

He opened the passenger side of the Triumph and shoved Ms. Crane in, trying not to recall how much he enjoyed that kiss.

For a moment there, he'd actually lost control. Good God! He could still feel the warmth of her breasts against his chest and the firmness of her butt gathered in his palm. All the hooting and hollering of the tavern crowd galled him. He hoped Carol Macy hadn't been hidden somewhere in the deep shadows of the bar. He'd never hear the end of it, if she was.

He scurried around to the driver's side. But who was she? Polarities? The woman must be made up of multiple polarities. Why was it so important for him not to say her name? He slid into the driver's seat with hands trembling slightly. And what about "life or death?"

She owed him an explanation, and now. He turned on the overhead light. She wasn't going to hide in darkness, not anymore.

Bayfield looked across the narrow space at Ms. Crane. She sat there quietly defiant with her eyes firmly fixed on his. Somehow they were dark brown, not the dusty gray he'd admired. Her hands, balled into fists, sat in her lap. He didn't know whether he or the ubiquitous woman was more furious. The air surrounding them throbbed.

Bayfield tried to calm himself by swallowing deeply. "So what do you have to say for yourself, Ms. Crane? That was quite an act you put on inside. Was that some weird Halloween stunt?"

Nancy twisted in her seat to face him. She tried unsuccessfully to cover her bare legs with her coat, but it was too short. He watched her eyes narrow to pinpoints. Was she still working on her story?

"You've always seemed quite talkative before, Ms. Crane," he goaded. "I do think I deserve an explanation. It's not every day than I'm accosted by a pretty woman, even one in such a disgusting disguise as that.

"Are you going to just sit there, Ms. Crane?

What's the next step? You talk? Me talk? We have sex? I don't welcome overtures by students." His voice cracked. "It's unprofessional."

Inexplicably, Nancy began to laugh. It was a throaty laugh. She placed a hand over her offending mouth. Her eyebrows arched. He leaned away from her. What had he said that was so damned hilarious? *She* was the ludicrous one here, not him.

"Unprofessional. You!" She giggled. "I doubt that very much. The world would stop spinning." She jerked the wig off her head and tossed it on the dashboard. "I guess I do owe you an explanation," she said, fluffing up her hair. "I must say, though, you were the last person I expected to see in that bar tonight. You caught me completely by surprise."

"Apparently," Matt replied, absently brushing his fingers across his lips.

Nancy smiled demurely. "Not a bad kiss? I agree. Maybe we'll get back to that. But first there are some things you need to know about me."

Matt tried to marshal his senses to concentrate on what Ms. Crane was saying, not on how she looked. Although that was becoming increasingly difficult since her coat had parted displaying those delightful breasts that had so recently pressed against his chest. And that mini-skirt didn't even fully cover black panties. He quickly shut and opened his eyes trying to regain focus.

"First, you can call me Nancy. I'm not really a student. Well, I am, but I'm not."

"If you don't know what you are, Ms. Crane, how am I supposed to know?"

She tilted her head to the side, ignoring his snide comment. "You remember the rape that happened in September."

"Certainly. That was awful."

"Right. In fact, the woman was the fifth rape victim since last February."

"Here at Blackthorn!"

"Exactly."

"So what do you have to do with them?" Remembering the gun stowed in her purse, he felt a tingle of realization work its way up his spine.

Nancy Crane inhaled deeply and slowly exhaled. "I've got to trust you. Are you trustworthy, Professor Bayfield? You already know too much, and you're a bright man. It won't take you long to figure it out anyway. I'm an undercover cop working on the rape cases."

Matt nodded his head slowly. He bit his lower lip before responding. "Yes, that makes sense; it fits. And I almost blew your cover tonight."

She nodded in agreement.

A cop! He blew air through pursed lips. An undercover cop. She wasn't a student. That was good. But a cop!

The corners of Ms. Crane's mouth turned up. "Have you ever kissed a cop before, Professor Bayfield?"

He shrugged. "Can't say I have, Ms. Crane. Have you ever kissed a professor before?"

"Nope, you're the first." She glanced down at

her lap and then back over at him. "So can I trust you not to put me at risk?"

"Of course. What would make you think otherwise?" He hoped she wouldn't doubt his word. For some reason he wasn't prepared to fathom, it was important to him that she trust him.

"All right then, you might as well take me home," said Nancy, reaching for the seat belt. "I can't go back in there tonight. Everyone knows I left with you."

"You didn't drive a car here."

"No, the point was either to be picked up in there or, more likely, to be accosted walking home."

Matt reached across and grazed her shoulder. "You mean you were setting yourself up to be attacked? Does anybody else know what you're doing?"

"Two others do. But I can protect myself."

"I suppose you mean the gun in your purse. Maybe there wouldn't be time to get it out."

Nancy turned her head sharply. "How do you know about the gun?"

"I saw it the day you were in my office and got the emergency call on your cell phone – the call from the Women's Center."

"Damn. I'm slipping. Sometimes it's in the purse; sometimes other places." She frowned. "So are you going to take me home, or do I have to walk?"

"No. I'll take you. It's not safe to walk alone by yourself at night." Matt turned the key in the ignition and the engine started immediately. He slipped the Triumph into drive and muttered, "But why am I telling you that?"

- o -

Perspiration beaded his brow. His breath quickened. He nearly choked on the bile rising in his throat. She was his. She'd been sitting there at the bar preparing herself to receive his gift. He glared out the tavern window and watched the Triumph pull out of the parking lot.

Why? Her time was tonight. Samhein. Why did that idiot Professor Bayfield have to show up? And why had she rushed into the professor's arms? She'd betrayed him. She was supposed to receive his gift tonight.

He lurched to his feet. He was empty. She'd forced him to find a substitute. He didn't like giving to strangers. It was always so much easier to give to a goddess he knew.

- o -

Neither driver nor passenger spoke other than to give and receive directions during the short drive to Nancy's apartment. After Matt guided the Triumph into the parking spot Nancy had indicated, she said, matter-of-factly, "You might as well come up. I'm sure you must have more questions by now. I can't have you spilling what you know because you're bursting with curiosity. Besides," she sent him a coy smile, "I owe you a glass of wine."

"What the...?"

"Down, Mal!" Nancy knelt to grab the Rottie by the collar before he had any more opportunity to slobber over Bayfield. "He's a guest, Mal. Don't mind Malaki," she said, glancing back up at the open-mouthed professor, "he's just fine as long as he knows you're a friend. Why don't you bend down and scratch him behind the ears like this?"

Bayfield hesitantly stretched out his hand. Malaki raised his head up meet the professor's fingers. She decided he'd have to learn a lot more about animals before he'd develop a comfort level with them.

Within a minute, Mal lost interest and retreated to his blanket before the fireplace. "So, let me take your coat, Bayfield." Nancy hung both of their coats in the entryway closet. She glanced at Bayfield who was taking in every detail of her tiny apartment.

"You're quite the observer, aren't you? Will white Zinfandel do?"

Bayfield followed her toward the kitchen. "Yes, to both questions." He chuckled. "If I were attending a lecture, I'd be sitting in the back row. It's where observers sit. I thought it was just sociologists, but now I have to add room for cops."

"That you do," Nancy said, pouring wine into a juice glass. She grabbed a Point beer from the refrigerator. "Sorry for the quality of the crystal, but I hadn't planned on staying in Trillium long."

"Neither had I."

Nancy took a seat in a leather chair opposite the couch and gestured for Matt to sit across from her. "Damn these contacts. Excuse me one minute." She retraced her steps to the kitchen and removed the contacts. Upon her return to her chair, she said, "There, that's better. They do disguise the eyes fairly well, but after a while I feel like I can't see so well. My imagination, I suppose.

"So you must have a question or two." She watched his eyes travel from her lips, to her half exposed breasts, to her skirt climbing nearly to her crotch. He'd just have to gawk because she didn't quite trust herself to change with him sitting out here in her living room. That had been one hell of a kiss.

"Where are you from? How did you get here of all places? And you're really not a student?"

Nancy chuckled. She recognized the signs of both desire and fear in his compressed lips and widened nostrils. In the past hour, Matt Bayfield had become much more male and much less professor. The little game they'd been playing off and on during the past several weeks now had few limits. She knew that, and she expected *he* knew it, too.

"Like I told you, I grew up in Milwaukee. I come from a family of cops. My dad was one before being killed. Each of my two brothers is on the Milwaukee police force – as was my husband."

"Husband?"

"Ex-husband." Was that a sigh of relief escaping Bayfield's lips? "Short story. He thought I grieved too much and too long after my dad's funeral. So I finally told him he could find a different bed to sleep in. Our friends, mostly cops, stuck by him, so I moved to Stevens Point in north central Wisconsin, where I'm a sergeant on the college police force and a detective with the Stevens Point Police Department."

Bayfield let out a low whistle. "And I thought you were an overly eager co-ed."

"I'm glad. That's what I was trying to be. As far as your second question goes..." Nancy leaned over to pet Malaki. She grimaced. Too late, her sweater had already fallen away to show Bayfield even more skin. She really wasn't used to wearing such revealing stuff. But oh, hell! She felt like she was riding one of those mechanical bulls at a country western bar and someone had turned up the speed by two notches.

She settled back and took a swallow of beer. What did Matt Bayfield really make of her? "I'm here because the president of Blackthorn happens to be my favorite aunt. She wanted someone from the outside to look into what was happening here. The local campus police seemed less than vigilant. Women were getting high and getting laid and then regretting it the next morning – that about sums up the local viewpoint."

Bayfield shook his head. "And that's supposed to surprise anyone?"

His eyes went blank. He stood and turned his

back on her. "So where do I fit in?" He turned back to face her. "I assume your bumping into me at the bookstore wasn't an accident."

She'd dreaded the question, knowing that it would come, had to come. She glanced down at her lap and smoothed out what she could of her skirt. "Not entirely." She looked up at him. "There are some facts in this case that you aren't aware of."

"I don't doubt that at all. Can you enlighten me so I might understand why I've been so central to your investigation?"

"Don't get bent out of shape, Bayfield." She tried to soothe his hurt feelings with her voice. "I'll try to explain. It'd be easier though if you'd sit down. Your towering over me doesn't make be very comfortable. And this is already uncomfortable enough."

"Oh, sorry." Bayfield sat back down on the couch and crossed his long legs at the ankles. "So why me, Detective Crane? Was I a suspect?" He gasped. "*Am* I a suspect?"

"No, not any longer." Nancy's voice box strained. Why did this hurt so much? "Four of the five women raped had just attended one of your lectures."

"Holy hell." Bayfield scrunched forward. "Why?"

"I don't know. That's one of the things I'm trying to figure out."

"But one woman was raped and there was no lecture?"

"Right, this past August."

She watched him mull over this new bit of information as if he was arranging all the pieces of her story. She'd forgotten he liked to work puzzles, mazes, and labyrinths.

"So that's why I'm not a suspect – any longer. You checked out my story about working abroad this past summer."

"Uh, huh. Does that bother you?"

He shook his head. "No, you had to check it out. It was your job. So, you thought if you stuck by me maybe you'd gain some insight into what had been happening or why?"

"In part. I also enjoyed listening to you carry on about your work." He blushed a little before slouching back into the couch. She grinned at his apparent embarrassment. "You are a bright man, Professor Bayfield, and charming in a strange sort of way. Plus, you weren't trying to get into my pants. We were safe because of your personal code of conduct regarding students."

"But you're not a student?" His eyes held a challenge.

"Not really." She hurried on. "Somehow I expected I might be able to pick up clues in all the information you provided from your lectures and our discussions. I'm convinced this creep is somehow keying off your lectures."

"But there was no lecture in August."

"I know. I know." Nancy tucked a bare foot under her torso. "It doesn't fit, yet it has the same M.O. otherwise. Now that you know what I'm doing maybe I can ask you more direct questions about some of this Celtic stuff. I'm sure there's some kind of link."

"So you still want to hang around me?"

Nancy's arms tingled. What was he really asking? "So professor, would you like me to hang around more?"

Bayfield narrowed his eyes. "I asked you first."

Nancy rose to her feet. Malaki got up also and stretched as if saluting the sun and then took a protective stance by his mistress's side. "I'm willing. I hardly know a soul here in Trillium. You don't seem any more tied here than I am. I don't know when I'll leave, but I will."

"And so will I."

"So I've gathered. I find you fascinating and stimulating. Even your arrogance is a challenge. So what do you think?"

"Sounds like we're talking about more than a professor discussing a case with a detective."

"It does, doesn't it?" She felt her voice grow husky. "That was one hell of a kiss, professor. I must confess I've wondered if there are any more of those left."

"Me too," he said, rising to face her. "Since apparently confession is the thing to do tonight, I will admit I've wondered how those lips would taste." He traced her puckered lips with the tip of a finger and she drew it into her mouth. She suckled it until he groaned, then reluctantly let it go.

"You were supposed to be safe," he whispered.

"But I'm not," she sighed, moving into his arms.

"No, you're not. Not at all. Carrying nitro to a dig would be safer than getting close to you. But, thank God, you're not really a student."

She liked the way he smelled her hair and rubbed his chin across her forehead. She stood on her toes and wet her lips inviting him to kiss her again.

The phone rang.

"Damn it!" Nancy glanced at the clock on the mantel. How had it gotten so late? One thirty in the morning. Her police training kicked into overdrive. "I've got to get that," she said, dashing toward the kitchen and the phone.

"Hello."

"It's me, Washington. I'm at the hospital. He struck again."

"Son of a bitch. When?"

"About an hour or so ago. Odd, this time the guy gave her a ride to the hospital. Dumped her off blindfolded and wrapped in a robe. Her clothes were in a bag."

"There ought to be prints somewhere."

"Doubt it. He wore thin gloves."

"Damn."

"Yeah. He seems to know what he's doing."

"I'll be right down."

"No. No need. They've already given her an IV sedative. She won't be out from under that until mid-morning. I just wanted you to know."

"I appreciate that, Lucy. Get some sleep. I'll

plan on getting to the hospital before noon. See you then."

Nancy hung up the phone and walked heavily back into the living room. She looked up at Bayfield and scrunched her mouth trying to recall why he was there.

"It should have been me," she yelled. "I blew it!"

"If you did," Matt said, staring at his hands, "I blew it for you. Do you even know if the woman was at the bar?"

Nancy jerked her head up and then shook it. "No, I forgot to ask. I'll get all the details in the morning. I just bet he was there in that bar. Why wouldn't he come after me? I've given him so many opportunities."

"Maybe you don't fit what he needs or wants."

"You may be right. We'll go over everything again and again. Clearly, we're missing something."

"So, can I call you?" Bayfield asked, his voice thick with desire.

"You better call me, or I'll come after you."

Matt held up his hands. "And you have the gun."

"Right. A lot of good that will do for me with you. Come on, professor, time for you to head on home. Just don't dream about co-eds when you hit the pillow."

"How about cops?"

"That would be fine, if it's about a certain female cop we both know." She grabbed him by the hand and led him to the door. "But you've got to kiss me before you go. I can't wait much longer for that. I'm not big on self-sacrifice, you see."

"Oh, I didn't know."

She smiled boldly and slanted her lips across his. At first they just brushed lips. Then he traced hers with his tongue and she reciprocated. At last, he settled into a lingering, deep kiss – *yes!* The man had passion!

She worked her tongue into his mouth. She swung a leg around his legs and held him tight. His hands roamed freely over her breasts. One hand slipped inside her sweater and rubbed a nipple through soft fabric while the other hand followed the contour of her leg until it settled on her butt.

There was no mistaking his arousal pressing against her belly button. He hunched over and she scrunched upward on the toes of her foot. They found a better fit. And she arched against him. His breathing quickened as did hers. When he broke the kiss and pulled away, she felt abandoned. She bent over and gulped in air. His broad hands gently kneaded her tight shoulder muscles.

"I've got to go." His voice cracked. "Now! We've both been through too much tonight. When we climb into bed together, I don't want to wonder later if it was because of shock." He gave her a hint of a smile. "And frankly, I'd like to be less exhausted than I am right now."

"Well put, professor," Nancy said. "I'm sure I'll agree with you in the morning."

Bayfield walked out into the night and Nancy closed the door behind him, placed her back against it and promptly slid to the floor. Her body vibrated with unfulfilled passion. What the hell had she gotten herself into this time? She licked her lips. That was powerful. Maybe too powerful. But damn if she'd shy away from that man.

"So what do we do now?" Joan Williams, President of Blackthorn College, cast a long face at her niece.

Nancy had never seen her aunt this agitated. They sat in the parlor of the President's House. Its décor was old English, Nancy supposed. The wood and the furnishings were dark and heavy, not her way at all. Too stuffy. Bayfield would probably adore it. She blotted him from her mind, not welcoming that distraction. "Not a lot we can do but continue sifting through the stories, trying to find new clues. Beef up the effort to inform women about protecting themselves without causing a panic." She shrugged. "Hopefully, the next time we can redirect him to me."

"That's another thing," the white haired, tall, elegantly dressed woman said, pacing back in forth in front of where her niece sat. "I don't like you running around out there in skimpy dress trying to lure the crazed man like casting a Royal Coachman to a wary trout."

Nancy's eyes twinkled. One of the things she liked most about her aunt was the way she could be so polished one moment, and the next she could regale you with stories of fly fishing or paddling the Boundary Waters. The woman was no porcelain doll, that was for sure. "Don't worry about me. I can take care of myself. Besides, Officer Washington knows when I'm on a stakeout."

Her aunt came to a halt, apparently bracing to counter Nancy's argument, and then her shoulders slumped. She sat down in a winged chair. Shaking her head, President Williams said, "I have to worry about you, Nancy." She pinched the bridge of her nose. "Your mother will never forgive me if anything bad happens to you here."

"The entire family are cops. She's learned to live with the danger."

"Maybe," Joan Williams said, thoughtfully. "I wonder if one ever really gets accustomed to danger, or even if it's wise to try to do that. Couldn't that lead to carelessness?"

Nancy nodded. "Complacency is always a risk, but accepting danger doesn't mean you forget it's there."

"No, I'm sure you're right. And your mother never can forget. I still miss your father. He was a good man."

"He was terrific, and he was a good cop. And he still got shot."

Her aunt nodded her agreement and then a faraway look spread across her face. Was she remembering earlier times? Weddings, births, baptisms, funerals, rites of passage and times that could bind families together, or tear them apart.

The grandfather clock in the corner struck twice. President Williams looked at the clock. "I should be getting ready for a finance meeting with the board." She cracked a smile. "But I much prefer playing detective with my niece. Are we quite certain that it's only one man behind all of this?"

"Fairly. Having this many rapes in less than a year at such a small college is very unusual in the first place. Unless there's something bad in the water turning nice guys into rapists, I'd be quite confident we're looking for one twisted creep. And the attacks share a lot in common."

"Yes, most have occurred after Professor Bayfield's lectures. I wonder if we should put a stop to his lectures." President Williams paused. "I'd hate to do that. Students have given the series rave reviews, but if he's inciting..."

"No," Nancy interrupted, "I don't know what the connection is, but the lectures may yet lead us to the attacker."

"And what is this you said about the last victim? The man put a wig on her head?"

"That's right. The other victims were dark haired – black or brunettes. This woman was a blonde. Apparently, the rapist put something on her head before raping her. She was blindfolded, but said it felt like a wig, at least some kind of covering. So, it seems like he prefers dark-haired women."

"Or at least not blondes."

"Exactly."

"So we have a man who stalks women in the dark, kidnaps them, binds their hands and blindfolds them, puts them in his trunk, and transports them out of town, and rapes them. And is apparently concerned for their welfare afterwards."

"Odd, isn't it. He threatens them, rapes them, and then wonders if they're too cold or drops them off at the hospital."

"Maybe he's a split personality."

"If not, he's damn good at compartmentalizing."

"So your mother is remarrying. What do you think about that?"

Where had that come from? Nancy shrank back into her chair. Aunt Joan was famous for shooting zingers after disarming her audience, but this was too much. "I've not had much time to think about it."

"Uh, huh. Why don't I believe that? I imagine Henry and Nathan have checked him out thoroughly."

"No history of scams." Nancy tugged at the sleeve of her sweater. "Apparently, they think the guy is okay. He seems to make mom happy. So we all should be pleased."

"So why aren't we all pleased?" President Williams' mouth turned up slightly, apparently enjoying her niece's discomfort.

"I'm not sure," Nancy sighed. "It'll be better after I meet him. Guess I never expected her to remarry. But she did sound so happy."

"Well, good," Joan Williams said, rising to her feet. "I'm sure we'll all adjust. This family has always been good at adjusting."

"Yes, I suppose so," Nancy said, following her aunt's lead and preparing to leave.

"Keep me informed, Nancy. I do hope we're doing enough to protect our students." She scowled. "I've given some thought to going public with this. But I'm not at all certain Blackthorn could survive the scandal. And as you've said, publicity may simply encourage more rapes."

The two women stopped in the grand entryway. "Now give your aunt a hug. And be careful, Nancy. Be very careful."

"I'm doing my best. I just wish we had better results."

"Yes. Unfortunately, the guy must be quite clever."

"He'll trip up. It's a matter of time."

President William's hand flew to her mouth; her eyes sparkled like those of a child on the verge of a discovery. "I nearly forgot."

That look brought back memories of a favorite aunt teasing a little girl in pigtails. Nancy held herself in check.

"What do you think of our Professor Bayfield?"

"What?" Nancy chirped.

"Professor Bayfield. Don't be coy with me. I'm your aunt. It has come to my attention that you might be interested in him and he in you – beyond the case, that is."

"How? Who?" Nancy sputtered.

"Nothing is private long at a small college. If you have a conversation with a man more than twice, then rumors start."

Nancy peered at her aunt for any clue to what she was feeling. "Does that bother you?"

"Not in the least. You're both adults. Old enough to make your own mistakes."

"He has a code about not getting involved with students."

"You're no more a student here than I am. Maybe I should be more concerned about that, but you're hardly fresh out of high school and you don't have him for a teacher." President Williams folded her arms. "Someone needs to loosen Professor Bayfield up some." She grinned slowly. "And I expect my niece might be just the person to untie some of his laces. He is handsome isn't he?"

With effort, Nancy avoided touching her rapidly coloring cheeks. "He's not hard to look at, though he can be pompous, arrogant and a know-it-all."

"Yes, well, I can see you've had time to get to know our Professor Bayfield. So, does he interest you?" Her aunt cocked her ear eager for more gossip.

"Aunt Joan!" Nancy rolled her eyes. "I haven't heard from him for two weeks. So, nothing's happened. The Blackthorn rumor mill will have to find some other tidbits for its grist."

A throaty chuckle emitted from the president. "Sounds like a little cat and mouse game to me." She placed a finger to her chin, obviously enjoying herself. "I wonder which one of you is the cat and which is the mouse. Maybe you change roles from time to time. That always makes for delightful play."

"And how do you know about that?"

"Don't underestimate your aunt. I don't just read books. And I expect Matt Bayfield will come to his senses. He just can't figure out how to measure up to his own standards. You'll make him bend. And he'll likely enjoy joining the real world, once he's had a taste of it." Joan Williams winked at her niece and waved goodbye before turning to stroll toward the hallway leading to her office.

Nancy closed her mouth, put on her coat and stepped out into the crisp afternoon air that pleasantly stung her lungs. Low slate gray clouds loomed overhead. The wind had picked up since she'd entered the President's House. Winter was coming. It was time. Mid-November in the northland should mark the beginning of snow and cold temperatures. Her cross-country skis were ready.

God, how she loved winter!

Chapter Five

"Damn, I hate winter!" Matt Bayfield growled into the stiff headwind, holding the hood of his sweat suit with one hand while tugging the zipper with the other.

Seven inches of snow covered the ground. Park crews had worked the entire morning and much of the afternoon to plow the roads and jogging paths. It was Saturday; he ran on Saturdays, Tuesdays and Thursdays. Unless the weather was too damn miserable. Today was cutting it close.

Matt turned and jogged along the southern edge of the park. At least the wind wouldn't be in his face. Kids on a nearby hill used sleds, plastic sheets and shovels to slide down the snowy incline. Their screams spoke of a pure joy he'd seldom experienced, certainly not as a child.

A mile out, the wind died down and he turned north by the soccer fields. The snow sparkled like a blanket of diamonds. The only evidence of civilization was a ski trail cutting diagonally across the blanket. Grudgingly, he admitted it was a pretty afternoon. Thankfully, he'd remembered his sunglasses or the bright reflection off the snow would have given him a headache.

His head already pounded, but not from the glare, nor from exertion. Why hadn't he called her? Why hadn't she called him? He'd said he'd call, but that didn't mean she couldn't, if she really wanted him.

That was part of the problem. Was she feeling guilty for suspecting him to be the rapist? He didn't want any thank-you fuck. "Oh sorry, I thought you were somebody else. Did I hurt you? Let me stroke your ego and your cock and everything will be okay." He didn't need that kind of charity.

A green SUV turned the corner sharply. Slush splattered Matt waist high. The driver pulled away without a backward glance. "Son of a bitch," Matt shouted. Had the bastard done that on purpose?

Another half mile and Matt swore his lungs were frozen and his breathing grew labored. He eased his pace. This was when what was healthy for you nearly killed you.

What the hell was he going to do with Ms. Crane? He knew what he'd *like* to do: throttle her for disrupting the serenity of his life. *Right.* He pushed the hood off his head. There were a few other things he'd thought of doing to her, and she seemed more than willing.

Against his better judgment, Matt slowed to a walk to let his heart stop pounding. Was it pounding from the workout or from his erotic thoughts? Even if she was willing, truly willing and interested in a sexual romp with him – not out of some sense of owing him something – she was still a student. Well, she was a cop posing as a student. While he knew that, to rest of the campus she was a student, and if he let himself get involved with her he'd be judged as a professor screwing a student. Though at some point, once she apprehended the rapist, the truth would come out.

Why did that bother him so much? She'd never take a class from him. And she was a cop, for god's sake. She certainly could take care of herself.

So how many more days or weeks was he going to allow this internal debate to rage on? The debate was not going to resolve itself. What would her aunt say if she knew of his designs on her niece? Nancy Crane was everywhere: the niece of the president of the college and a cop. That had to be double trouble. Of course then he hadn't planned on a long stay at Blackthorn anyhow. But an affair with the president's niece was hardly the way to obtain a glowing recommendation.

Matt allowed himself to smile. Well, maybe from the niece, but not the aunt. So which was more important? He ran in place briefly and then resumed his jogging pace.

- o -

"Miss, may I pet your dog?"

Nancy smiled at the bent over, gray haired lady, tucked in a scarf and drab overcoat.

"I've seen you and your dog in the park many times. He's such a beautiful animal. What's his name?"

"Of course," Nancy said. "Malaki is his name. Mal, sit. He'll be fine."

95

With a smile, the woman leaned over and ran a gloved hand over Mal's head. "You're so handsome, young man. My name is Mrs. Lindenhammer." She glanced at Nancy. "He sure has muscles. He reminds me of my Zeno. He was a Rottie, too, but that was a long time ago. Thank you for letting me pet him. Next time, Malaki," she said to Mal, "I'll have a treat for you."

"Be careful. It's quite icy out here today."

"I will be." She lifted her cane and pointed at its sharp cleats. "It's such a gorgeous day, I didn't want to miss it. The doctor wants me to walk everyday unless it's raining or blowing snow.

Nancy watched the older woman hobble down the sidewalk. She hoped she was that determined when she got to that age. Turning back to Mal, she said, "You old lover, you. You've made a friend and I have none. Don't worry, I won't dwell on that." She stepped into her skis, put her hands through the ski pole loops and pushed off. Could there be a more beautiful day?

"Let's get going, boy. Time's a wasting."

- o -

Shielding his eyes from the sun, Matt made out two dark figures approaching. One was on skis; the other raced ahead of the skier. "Oh, damn," he moaned, recognizing Malaki, who had come to a halt in the jogging path blocking Matt's way. There was no question about the identity of the skier in the glistening red pants and jacket.

96

To his surprise, Nancy Crane broke into a smile when she saw him scratching her dog. At least she wasn't going to throw ice-balls at him. There was still a chance he might get out of this entanglement alive.

"Well, if it isn't the forgetful Professor Matthew Bayfield," Nancy said, sliding to a spiffy halt before him.

Matt ignored the snow that splattered his legs. The cold weather, if anything, made the woman even more chipper. Her cheeks were rosy; her ebony hair hung in a ponytail, making her look even younger. She hardly puffed from the workout. Her lips didn't look cold at all. He knew they could warm him better than any expensive brandy.

"I see you've adapted to winter quite nicely, Ms. Crane."

"Why shouldn't I – I love winter!" Nancy beamed a broad smile at Bayfield. "You look a little ragged and done in, Bayfield. Don't you know this is a season for skiing, not jogging?"

"Don't know how to ski. Not that it matters." Matt crossed his arms. Why was it important that she understand? "I've never thought about trying," he blurted out. "I seldom see a lone skier."

"I'm alone," Nancy said, pouting slightly. "Well, I do have Mal." She cocked her head to the side. "Though I did think maybe I wouldn't be alone. There was some man who was going to get back to me. He was one hot kisser, but I guess that must have been all he had in him. All promise, but no delivery."

Matt shelved his immediate response. "Okay, I guess I deserved that." He knelt down on his haunches and gave Malaki a firm scratching. "You're a real puzzle for me, Ms. Crane."

"I thought you liked playing with puzzles."

Was her pout genuine or was she teasing? "Come on, Ms. Crane, demure is not becoming on you. I don't know what to do with you, about you, or whatever."

A giggle bubbled from Nancy Crane's throat. "My, I must be a problem, if you can't even say what's bothering you. You don't usually have a problem with words, professor."

"Well – you're a cop."

Nancy Crane crossed her arms and stretched as tall as she could. "I knew that, Bayfield." She jabbed a finger at him. "I knew that'd stick in your craw. For your information, Mr. Professor, cops take their clothes off and screw like everyone else."

Matt stepped back from her assault trying valiantly to ignore that image. Ms. Crane's lips curled into a smile as if she knew exactly what he was imagining.

"So, what else is bothering you, professor?"

"That's just it, I am a professor," he said, seizing on her words. "You may not really be a student, but you appear to be one. And if I allow myself to be overcome by your charms, everyone from the janitor to the president is going to believe I'm having an affair with a student."

"And you think that matters?"

"Yes."

"But you know. And I know. It would be our little secret."

"Not so little."

"And after we catch the bad guy, everyone will know you weren't screwing around with a student after all."

"That's true." Any remnant of resolve was crumbling rapidly. His manhood stood to salute the woman's words. She should be a trial lawyer.

Nancy took off her gloves and pulled the ski pole loops off her wrists. "And then I'll go back to Point and you'll stay here or go wherever, and no one's hurt or bothered. Isn't that what we both really want? A little fun, a little sex. Nothing too messy or emotional."

"Right," he mumbled. "A little fun, a little sex. Nothing too messy or..." Her lips blotted out the last word. Matt sighed deeply into her open mouth. To hell with the janitor and the president, this was good.

Even in the cold afternoon, her body warmed his. They had every right to enjoy themselves. He decided to do just that.

"I don't live too far from here," he said, breaking their kiss. "You want to come and have a glass of wine or something warm to drink?"

She laughed. There for the first time, he saw her smile reach to her eyes, and she wasn't laughing at him, but with him. That warmed him immensely.

"I'd love to share a glass of wine with you,

professor, if you don't think that will bring the wrath of President Williams down on you."

He reached over and lifted her chin and brushed his lips across hers. "I'm ready to take that chance, detective. What about you?"

"Oh, I'm more than ready," she said, sliding her skis back and forth. "I expect the president will be the least of our problems. Why don't you lead the way?"

- o -

The threesome made their way across the park toward Matt's neighborhood. Nancy tried to keep a rein on her senses. The winter scene before them was like a Christmas postcard. The houses along the way were quaint, built in an era of frugality and far-north efficiency but with taste. And – she sucked in cold air – she was about to go to bed with Matt Bayfield.

They'd danced around that question long enough. It was time. Her body said past time. Was he the kind of lover those kisses promised? Would he measure up? She gulped. Would she measure up? She'd know soon.

They turned up Matt's driveway. Nancy left her skis on the porch and followed Matt inside. Malaki bounded past her and skidded across the waxed wood entryway coming to a halt in the living room. "Good grief! Mal, come here boy." She looked up into Matt Bayfield's frown. "I'm sorry. He can be exuberant."

"Not unlike his mistress." Bayfield's eyes sparkled.

Nancy warmed under his gaze.

"Is he going to be okay? I can run him home and come back."

"No way!" Matt tugged on her ski jacket zipper. "We've come this far. I wouldn't want to risk either one of us getting cold feet."

She pulled on his sweatshirt zipper. "I don't know about you, but I'm pretty hot, actually. Mal will be fine if it's okay for him to be on the rug in front of the fireplace."

"That'll work," Matt said, shrugging out of his sweatshirt. "If you don't mind, I should take a quick shower."

"Me too. After you. That'll give me some time to get Malaki adjusted. He'll have to explore some before settling down."

"There's not a lot to explore. The place is big enough for me, and rents reasonable. Make yourself to home. I won't be long." Matt climbed the stairs two at a time.

After removing her ski pants, Nancy toured the downstairs helping Malaki settle in. Actually, she was quite curious about what the place might tell her about her soon-to-be lover. The house was clean and neat. It almost looked like it wasn't lived in, and he hadn't even been expecting company. No dishes cluttered the counter. Magazines were neatly stacked. She smelled furniture polish. Goodness, did he think her place was a pig sty?

She worried about Malaki's welcome. Matt

Bayfield didn't look like the pet owner type. No dog. No cat. She hadn't even seen a birdfeeder outside. The furniture was practical and tasteful, but not overdone. His stereo system was top of the line, but the primary decoration had to be books.

There were books everywhere, even in the kitchen. And they ranged from fiction, to classics, to history, to music, to cookbooks. The man had a variety of interests. Nancy laughed when she spied a copy of the Kama Sutra. What might he have learned from that?

Ten minutes later, she heard Bayfield coming down the stairs. She stood in the kitchen doorway and smiled at the dark-haired man wrapped in a burgundy robe. His hair was damp and slicked back. His eyes darted from her to Malaki standing by her side.

"So is he going to be okay?" he asked.

"Yes, I hope he doesn't bother you." Nancy scratched Malaki's ears. "I could still run him back to the apartment. It wouldn't take that long."

Matt hesitated before shaking his head. "No, he'll be all right. He is housebroken?"

"Of course."

"I guess I should put some water in a bowl or something."

"That would be nice."

"Does he want anything to eat?"

"Not yet, maybe later." Nancy scrunched her lips and flashed an eyebrow. "I better go take that shower."

"I laid a towel and washcloth out for you, and I

hung up a robe you might want to use. It's way too big, but it'll keep you from getting chilled. The bathroom is the second door on the right."

Nancy brushed her lips against his and ducked quickly to avoid being caught in his arms. "I won't take long."

"I don't have any beer. You do drink wine, right? You don't just keep it on hand for guests?"

"Sure. Though I much prefer beer. If this becomes a habit, I'll have to supply you with some Point beer." She grinned at his look of incredulity and then dashed for the stairs.

She walked down the hallway toward the bathroom. The house had a Gambrel roof, giving each room a slanted alcove look. Charming. Matt's office was in the first room. More books, a desk, computer and printer, and an easy chair. How many books did the guy own?

Without hesitation, Nancy walked further down the hall and peeked through the open doorway on the left. "Wow," she gasped. "Not bad." The centerpiece to his bedroom was a queen-sized bed with a handmade orange and blue quilt. Its design showed a sun casting its rays three hundred and sixty degrees. The room, actually two rooms, contained two easy chairs, a dresser, a couple mirrors, and more books. Floor to ceiling windows overlooked the park. What amazed her most, though, was the number of candles. There seemed to be candles everywhere. Did they merely stem from Bayfield's Celtic interests? Perhaps Matt Bayfield was a romantic after all.

Within minutes she stood under a hot stream of water pelting her skin. Fantastic! There were some muscles that she hadn't heard from for some time complaining about the cross-country ski workout. She used the huge bar of soap liberally. It was a man's bar of soap. Nancy closed her eyes and smiled. This was nice. Most men she'd known would have jumped her as soon as they crossed the entryway. Hell, she would've jumped most men in the same circumstance. There was something to be said for a self-controlled man, a considerate man.

She dried off and stuck her arms through the soft brown robe he'd left for her. She bunched the sleeves at the elbow in order to poke her hands out, wrapped the material around tight and tied the sash, and bent down to carry the hem of the robe in her hand. Nancy giggled. She must look a sight, but then she didn't plan on keeping the robe on for long.

Matt met her at the bathroom door with a glass of wine in each hand. "You look like a butterfly peeking out of its cocoon."

The fire in his eyes warmed Nancy from her crown to her toes. He might be considerate, but there was no question that he wanted her. Even his formidable patience was beginning to wane.

"Why don't we go to the bedroom?" he said. "We'll take our time and enjoy our wine, but the ambiance will help set the mood."

"I'm not doing badly on mood as it is," Nancy

said, aware that her voice sounded huskier than usual. "But a little wine won't hurt."

She followed his lead. Matt set their glasses down and lit several candles; soon the room was filled with a soft glow and flickering shadows. Together, they pulled back the sunbeam comforter, propped up some pillows, leaned back against them, and sipped their wine. "This is a beautiful room, Matt. Did you decorate it yourself?"

"Sure. You'd didn't think I'd like beautiful things?"

"I didn't know."

"I was attracted to you, and you're beautiful."

"My, you are a romantic," Nancy whispered, ducking her head to sip more wine.

Matt laughed aloud. "I believe you are the first person to accuse me of that. A little unusual. A neat-freak. An egotist. A history buff. But nope, never a romantic."

"Maybe you're an unusual, egotistical, neat-freak romantic. So how did you wind up in Trillium, Minnesota? It doesn't sound like your choice of locations."

"It's not. I'm a California boy – born and raised in San Francisco. I did college and graduate school at Berkeley where my father is a history professor. When I finished my dissertation there was a glut of sociologists on the market. It was here or Podunk State."

He folded his arms across his chest. His neck muscles bulged. "I'll be out of here in a year or two. There are two or three decent articles in the pipeline that will allow me to move up."

"You sound like guys I've talked to in prison – counting the days until they could hit the street."

Matt swiveled his head and gave her a wicked grin. "They probably spend their time thinking about women and money."

"And you don't?"

"Nope. I don't need a lot of money, and I have a vivacious woman sitting on my bed right now." Matt reached over and tugged playfully at the sash on Nancy's robe. "So, how are you coming with that wine? Or are you playing detective again by getting me to tell you my life story?"

"Just curious." She laid a hand on his arm. "I might prefer playing doctor. Of course, I could play detective and try to find out what you're hiding under that robe."

They both looked down at Matt's lap where the robe had sprung to life forming a tent. "Closing this case might not take long at all," Nancy snickered, setting her wine glass down on a nightstand and then turning back to Matt. Slowly, she ran her tongue around her lips. "Am I going to have to do this alone?"

"I think I can be talked into helping," he said, putting his drink aside. Matt wrapped her in his arms and Nancy slid hers around him. She smiled into his shoulder basking in the warmth of his hug and the kisses he was planting on her head. She leaned back against his arms and studied his eyes. He bent to kiss her forehead and then her nose.

Her blood was coming to a rapid boil; he did have a thing for her nose. At last, his lips slanted across hers, and she opened to him.

If he had a thing for her nose, he was fixated on her lips. Her lips thrummed under his caress. She'd always been a little self-conscious about them being too large, but Matt Bayfield certainly seemed to think they were just right.

He broke the kiss and reached again for her robe sash. This time he undid it, exposing all she had to offer him. She didn't dare move. He drank her in through his eyes. She shivered with anticipation and delighted at the color rising in Matt's cheeks.

"You're gorgeous," he said, lifting a breast with each palm. Would he look any happier on Christmas morning? The awe in his voice brought tears to Nancy's eyes. She closed her eyes; she wasn't the weepy type. So what the hell was happening to her? She'd been admired before, yet Bayfield's broad grin already had her on the edge of a cliff.

Was he mesmerized? She ached. "Touch me," she whispered. "I won't break. I promise."

"I know. I just want to savor the moment. There will never be another first time for us."

Nancy bit down hard on her lip, and found the patience to match his.

At last, he brushed a nipple with a finger. She sighed in relief encouraging him to reach for the other one. And he did. "Oh, my God," she said. "How did you know my nipples are so sensitive?"

107

"A good guess," he said, leaning closer to study her response. Her nipples pebbled even more under his close scrutiny.

Nancy could hardly hold herself together. His tongue snaked out and lightly tapped first one nipple and then the other. And then he caught one between his teeth and bit down gently while tugging on the other.

"I'm gone," Nancy moaned, grinding her teeth. She grabbed Matt's shoulders, bracing against him. She sat precariously at the apex of a giant waterslide. She teetered. She tried to hold back. She dared herself to let go. Then there was no choice. She slid and screamed until she hit bottom. And then she curled up in a ball waiting for air to fill her lungs once again.

Moments later, Matt said, with hunger still burning in his eyes, "I enjoy a woman with sensitive breasts."

Nancy managed to smile. "Thanks. That was quite a ride." She lay back again and breathed deeply, pleased he knew enough not to return immediately to her breasts. They'd had enough to last a while. Well, not too long. His tongue traced the outline of her belly button. "What are you doing?" she asked, as if she had no clue.

She felt his smile press against her belly. "The wine left me hungry," he said. "And you appear to be a feast fit for any king."

"Oh." Clever. A line he used with all his women? Nancy scowled at that thought. Maybe he was transporting himself back to the time of the

Celts. In any case, who was she to deny a hungry man? She spread her thighs wide. His smile moved lower until his breath intermingled with her moist heat. She wanted to wipe her brow, but instead clasped his head between both her hands, encouraging further exploration.

He didn't need much encouragement. His tongue lapped at her mound as if he were a cat cleaning its mate. He traced the perimeter of her heat. She flexed her buttocks, demanding more. She heard a smothered chuckle. "Come on, professor, don't dilly-dally," she nearly screamed. "Tongue, finger, whatever, I need more!" She moaned, low and then higher, matching his lapping motion. She was so ready.

At last his tongue entered her sex and then two fingers followed, probing, discovering a good fit. Her eyes sprang wide open. "Yes," she sighed. She raised her legs upright giving him more access. All of those years of yoga were paying off. She did a split and relished Matt's labored breathing.

"You're delicious," he mumbled, skimming her bud with the tip of his tongue while driving his fingers deeper.

Nancy opened her mouth to taunt him with something clever, but no words came – only tiny mewing sounds. Her entire body pooled in her center and then released slowly at first and then more rapidly. She came in wave after wave. Her legs collapsed to the mattress. Bayfield continued lapping her flow.

At last, he leaned back and licked his lips – the

perfect picture of male satisfaction. She grinned back, more than satisfied herself.

"You look like you could use a brief break," Matt said. "I'll go refill our glasses."

"But don't you want..." Nancy said, trying with difficulty to lift herself to a sitting position.

"We've got plenty of time. Refuel. I'll bring up some cheese and crackers."

"I wasn't enough to satisfy your hunger?" she said, giving him her most wicked smile.

"That was one hell of an appetizer, Ms. Crane," Matt said, giving her a mock bow, "but I believe the main course is still ahead of us."

"Oh God," she gulped. "But that appetizer course was better than most."

He brushed the back of his hand against her inner thigh. Again, her pulse quickened. "Now, let me go so we can continue this multi-course gourmet extravaganza."

Nancy watched Bayfield disappear through the bedroom doorway and head down the stairs. He certainly wasn't the slam, bang, thank you ma'am kind of guy. She'd had enough of those types. Her eyes fluttered shut and a tiny smile played at her lips. Did he have any idea how unusual he really was?

- o -

In the kitchen, Matt refilled the wine glasses and then spread specialty crackers in a circle on a clear plate. In the center of the circle he placed two kinds of cheese. After putting the food and drinks on a tray he seldom used, he wiped the counter and turned to retrace his steps upstairs to the bedroom.

Standing in the doorway, blocking his path, was a very large dog with pleading eyes. Matt winced. What did dogs eat? Cheese? Maybe. Bones, but he didn't have any bones. Milk? That was cats, but maybe dogs too.

Matt opened the refrigerator and stared at its contents. He glanced down. At his hip, Malaki stood making his own assessments of available food.

"Okay, Mr. Malaki, I haven't the foggiest idea what you like, but its imperative that you remain satisfied – well, at least occupied. How about a couple hot dogs? They're pre-cooked. Why not some milk? Ah! How about a leftover pork chop or two? I'll just find a mixing bowl and put it all together, then you can choose what you want."

The only sound the dog made was a single "ruff." Malaki stuck his nose into the bowl. The food disappeared like it had been dropped into a black hole. He'd swear Malaki turned and grinned at him.

"You stay here," Matt said. "It's time for a long winter's nap."

Matt headed for the stairs and for the woman waiting in his bed. His step was light. Nancy Crane had turned out to be much more than he'd expected. She was a passionate and expressive woman out of bed, so it shouldn't surprise him that she was equally passionate and expressive in bed. He enjoyed making love to a woman who could let him know what she liked rather than just lie there waiting to see if he could pass some kind of unspoken test.

She was turning out to be quite the woman. Nancy not only had delectable round breasts, they were exquisitely sensitive to tactile stimulation. He adored the way she hummed and purred – she was a complete sensory turn on, visual, sound, touch, smell and – wow – taste. Matt shuddered and hoped he hadn't been as hasty as Malaki had just been with his treat. But she'd tasted like some unfamiliar juicy dessert prepared in another time dimension. Would he ever get his fill of her?

Matt stepped through bedroom doorway and was greeted by a live erotic fresco. He grinned from ear to ear; his erection stood instantly. There on his bed sitting straight up on her haunches was the object of his erotic revelry, with fingers of one hand splayed from nipple to nipple and the other hovering over that dark triangle whose tangy taste still covered his lips. With her dark hair cascading around her shoulders and her thick lips spread in an enticing smile, she was his ideal picture of a Druidic priestess – beckoning, offering, and very much to be adored.

"Ah," he said, "you seem to have revived quite nicely."

"It looks like you have too." Her gaze was fixed on his arousal. She wet her lips. Fingers of her lower hand teased herself and him. "I think the food you brought up will have to wait. I've got another hunger that still needs feeding. Top priority. A.S.A.P."

Matt didn't need an engraved invitation. He set the tray on the floor and pulled a drawer out from the nightstand. He fumbled around until he found some condoms and left them on the nightstand. Then he knelt on the bed. "What did you have in mind?"

"This," she said, leaning over to encircle his shaft with her fingers.

He breathed in sharply. Her fingers slid rapidly up and down his length. He tensed, not wanting it to end so quickly. Her hand stopped moving. A sigh escaped his lips.

He didn't dare open his eyes. Her breath was warm. Her mouth was warmer still. That warmth teased and then traveled his full length. He was trapped in warm velvet. He never wanted to be set free.

She arched back slowly, letting cool air whip at him. Quickly, her dark hair bobbed up and down two times, three times, four times. And then she pulled away. His eyes sprang open. He tried not to cry out.

"Sorry," she apologized, "accept that as a promise, but I'm not as patient as you. I have to have you inside me, now, or I'm not going to be responsible for my own behavior."

"Oh." Matt was gratified that he could fill the woman with such obvious lust. "Of course."

"Of course?" Nancy shook her head and

laughed. "Why don't you lie back down and let me take the lead?"

Matt followed her advice and waited. She leaned over to reach a condom. After tearing it open, she put it on him. There were no more preliminaries. She straddled him. She closed her eyes and bit her lower lip and then easily slipped him inside her body.

Matt blinked. If her mouth was hot, this was scalding – almost uncomfortable, but not quite. He adjusted to her heat and peeked at the point of their joining. He half expected to see steam rising from between them.

Nancy encased him, her body rigid as if at attention. Where was she? Had she gone outside her body? Had she left him?

Suddenly, Nancy jerked and then became a blur – moving straight up and down, corkscrewing to the left and then the right. Every muscle in his body strained trying to hold back the inevitable. She never let up – she seemed determined to have her way with him. That familiar gathering in his loins began. His head buzzed. "Oh shit," he groaned: he'd gone past any point of control.

At last his body took over, leaping, meeting hers thrust for thrust. "Yes," Nancy shouted, riding him with the skill of a bull rider. There was no loser. His fluids rose to join hers.

She collapsed, crushing her breasts against his chest. Her ragged breaths warmed his neck. "My God," Nancy said haltingly, "I never thought a professor would be this good."

Laughter rolled out of his mouth. He couldn't stop laughing.

"So, what's so damn funny, Bayfield? We just screwed our brains out and all you can do is laugh?"

"You're something else, Ms. Crane." He laughed some more. "And I never imagined a detective could be so good."

Her giggle filled his ear and then her tongue. "I guess we're both open to surprises. That's a good sign. Don't you think?"

"Absolute necessity, I expect – for a researcher or a cop."

Nancy yawned and snuggled. He kissed the top of her head and pulled a sheet up over them. The steady rise and fall of her sleeping body was oddly comforting. He closed his eyelids to join her. Wasn't it *men* who were usually accused of falling asleep right after sex?

He smiled a lazy grin. *Not bad – not bad at all*. This promised to be a better winter than the last one. Good sex. Good repartee. A stimulating mind. What else could one ask for? And on top of that, there were no strings, no expectations.

After she caught the bastard rapist, she'd go back to Devon Point, or wherever she'd said she was from. And he'd keep his vita floating out there in the meat market of the academic world.

He sighed, sank further into the bed and ran a finger down Nancy Crane's backbone. *Not bad at all*, he reconfirmed. This would do just fine, for now.

Chapter Six

Wetness pressed against Matt's right arm.

He tried lifting an eyelid. How many times had they made love during night? And now she wanted more! The woman was incredibly insatiable. Did he have another round left in him?

Wait a minute! She'd fallen asleep on his left side, and he was on the edge of the bed. There was no mistake about it. A tongue licked his bare arm. His eyes sprang open. Slowly, he turned his head to the right. Large, baleful brown eyes greeted his.

He pinched the bridge of his nose. Crap. The only problem with his current situation loomed next to him in the form of a large black and brown dog. It was her dog. She should get up and take care of whatever the animal wanted. He placed a hand on Nancy's bottom and squeezed. Her regular deep breathing never wavered. He shook her harder. His reward was a muffled snore.

Throwing the covers roughly over Nancy, Matt struggled to sit up. Malaki sat politely waiting. Why had the dog adopted him as his savior? Because you fed him, you idiot! Matt groaned. Wasn't that the nature of beasts – you feed them and they want more, expect more, demand more.

He threw on a robe and lumbered down the stairs to the kitchen. Yawning, Matt opened the refrigerator door and then glanced back over his shoulder. No Mal. "Now where the hell are you,

you dumb dog?"

Matt followed the low growl coming from the living room and discovered its source. "Double damn," he swore. Malaki danced back and forth in the entryway.

Even Matt knew what that meant. "This can't be happening," he muttered, poking his arms through his winter coat and thrusting his bare feet into winter boots. "Where'd she put your leash? Oh, there it is," he said, spying it hanging from Nancy's jacket pocket. He snapped the leash on the dog's collar. "You better be quick about this."

The dog was as strong as he looked. Matt stumbled and ran following Mal to the closest tree, fearing his arm was going to be pulled right out of its socket. He huddled in his coat and glanced up and down the street to see if any of his neighbors were watching in the pale pre-dawn gray. No one seemed to notice.

At least, Nancy's dog was serious about his business. Matt looked down and scowled. He was no expert on dog excrement, but he hadn't expected white and runny. He groaned, making a face. "Let's get back inside. How the hell do women run around all winter in skirts and dresses?" He yanked his robe tighter around his legs and dashed back to the warmth of the house. Obediently, Malaki followed.

Later, much later, after preparing scrambled eggs, English muffins, orange juice and coffee, Matt made his way back up to the bedroom. He was greeted with a sneeze.

Nancy sat propped up against pillows; a Kleenex box lay on her lap. At least half of its contents were strewn across the bed and floor. She didn't look like the same woman who had greeted him the last time he'd entered the room. Her eyes and mouth drooped. Her chin rested on her collarbone.

"How are you?" he asked in his best morning after voice.

"Miserable!" Behind a hint of a smile she said, "Don't look so pained. You were great. We were great. But I must've caught a cold yesterday."

"I'm sorry." Matt put the tray down and sat on the edge of the bed. "Can I get you some tea? I've got green tea, Chinese, herbals and just about any other kind you can imagine."

Nancy grimaced. "I suppose you do. Sure, why not? It can't hurt." She sniffled and blew her nose noisily. "I'm not a very good patient, Bayfield. As soon as I can, I'll get dressed and get out of your hair."

She looked blank and then closed one eye and peered at him with the other. "Where's Mal? I completely forgot him. Where is he? Is he okay?"

Shrugging, Matt offered, "I think so. His stomach is gurgling some, but I imagine that's his way of digesting food. He seems quite friendly actually."

"Gurgling." Nancy cast him a concerned look. "What did you feed him?"

"Well, I don't have dog food."

119

"I know. He handles most table foods. So what did you feed him?"

"Last night, he had hotdogs, pork chops, and two-percent milk. Today, scrambled eggs, an English muffin, and I substituted water for milk."

Nancy pursed her lips. "You had to take him outside didn't you?"

Matt nodded.

"It wasn't pleasant was it?"

He shook his head.

"Sorry about that. Mal has a milk allergy; he doesn't digest it well at all."

"I noticed."

"You're a real trouper, Bayfield. I would never have guessed. Why don't you get that tea, and I'll try to stand up long enough to take a shower." She narrowed her eyes at him. "I hope you weren't expecting more...more sex. I feel like I've gorged six back-to-back holiday meals."

Matt chuckled, "I'm not disappointed. And I'm more than full, for the time being."

"Oh, don't worry," Nancy sniffled, reaching for another Kleenex. "I'll be hungry again. I expect over and over again."

- o -

Standing at the entry of her two-flat, Nancy waved at the receding Triumph and flashed Matt the biggest smile she could muster. He'd given her a ride because he didn't want her cold to worsen; most men wouldn't have noticed. They never did manage to get her skis in the Triumph. It'd been difficult enough squeezing Mal in. Leaving him behind wasn't an option; Mal had likely worn out the professor's welcome. She'd told Matt he might want to consider getting a more practical vehicle for the northland. He'd grumbled something nearly incoherent about not planning on being there long enough for that.

Malaki barked and lumbered toward the porch. When Nancy opened the door the dog took the stairs to her second floor apartment two at a time. She dumped her things on the floor longing for the comfort of her bed. She was exhausted. First, though, she'd make some more of that tea Matt had given her.

Humming, Nancy reached for a pan and basked in the memory of how considerate a lover Matt Bayfield had been. Considerate, yet passionate. Slow, yet also robust. He could be athletic, as athletic as a tumbling waterfall, and then as lazy as a millpond.

While the water heated, she went to her bedroom to change into fresh clothes. The room and the bed looked smaller now. And oddly, she felt more alone in this reduced space than in Bayfield's two room alcove. She slipped out of her panties and bra. As she opened the lingerie drawer, a flash from the street caught her eye. Tiny hairs on the back of her neck stood up; she stepped cautiously to the window and peered out through a tear in the pink lace curtain.

The gray sedan across the street hadn't been

121

there when Matt dropped her off. She was sure of that. Like any cop, it had become second nature for her to observe her surroundings. She'd swear that car had pulled up in the ten minutes or so since she'd been back in her apartment. The driver remained in the vehicle slouched down in the seat as if hiding. If she'd been on the ground floor she'd probably have missed seeing him at all. The car would simply look like someone had parked on the street while visiting one of her neighbors.

The man with the heavy coat and stocking hat wasn't visiting. It looked like a Vikings hat. "Damn," she groaned, "where's my deer rife when I need it." With its scope she would have had a clear image of the man.

Was he waiting for someone? Or was he spying? He turned and faced the house. She was fairly certain he couldn't see her. He was pointing something at the house, at her. She stepped away from the window. There was no crashing glass, no loud reverberation of a gun blast.

With two fingers, Nancy inched aside the curtain. He was still pointing something at the house. It looked like a camera. Now why would any one be taking pictures of the house while hiding in a car? And the guy was definitely trying to hide.

Nancy whirled from the window, pulled on a pair of panties, threw on a robe and dashed down the stairs with Malaki following wildly behind. As soon as her feet hit the porch, the gray sedan spun its tires and sped away. The license plate was caked with mud. "Son of a bitch!" Nancy shouted, with clenched fists. "The bastard." She turned and climbed the stairs again.

A burnt smell assaulted her nostrils. Nancy raced to the stove. "Shit!" she hollered, turning off the burner and holding the badly burned pan in her hand. So much for tea. Who wanted tea anyway!

After putting food down for Mal, Nancy retreated to her bedroom and without removing her robe climbed into the bed. She didn't have the energy to lift her head off the pillow.

But she had to think. Who was the guy in the gray sedan? And what was he doing taking pictures of the house? Think like a cop, damn it. How many times had she heard *he was average in appearance* or the car was *mid-size gray*. Yet this time those descriptions were apt. She'd never had a clear view of the man. Other than the Vikings stocking cap, nothing stood out. And there had to be hundreds of Minnesota Vikings stocking caps in Trillium. The car was likely a Chevy – at least a General Motors product. A fairly late model, but not new. That didn't help a hell of a lot either.

Maybe he was an insurance adjuster and needed pictures of her landlord's house? Then why didn't he get out of the car to take his pictures? It was definitely this house that had held the man's interest. Did he know she'd been watching him? Was he trying to take pictures of her? Good God, she'd been naked at the time! But he couldn't have seen her through curtains, could he? As soon as she could get out of bed, she'd pull the shades.

Did they make cameras that could see through things? Maybe it wasn't a camera. Maybe it was some kind of scope. If he had the right kind of high tech scope, he could have been looking right at her through the frilly curtain.

Nancy hugged her pillow. If so, he might have seen more than he'd expected.

How did the man happen to show up immediately after she'd gotten home? Had he been stalking her? Had he been watching Matt and her through a fancy scope? Nancy shivered. Who the hell was the creep? She wasn't going to relax completely until she found out.

Nancy rolled over onto her stomach and fell into a fitful sleep. Her dreams were filled with smoky bonfires, incantations and stone altars. She wore nothing under a white robe tied with a simple rope. Hands, not hers, framed her waist. Her heartbeat stopped. Fingers danced over and around her full breasts. Lips compressed hers and she relaxed. These were familiar lips; these were loving lips. She could not see him, but vaguely she knew him. Nancy opened herself to her faceless lover and he took her tenderly at first and then more aggressively until she screamed in a language she didn't understand. She pounded his back with her fists his rear with her heels. It was too much. She couldn't get enough of him. She wanted to swallow this mystery lover into her body. And then it was done. He was gone. She was bereft.

She drifted in and out of wakefulness. The smoke from the bonfire, or was it from their lovemaking, still hung thick about her. As the smoke thinned in places, she made out a red dot and a figure of a man in a dark robe watching. His face remained in the shadows of his dark hood. Was that a smile or a sneer? She sat up straining her eyes to see more clearly. The man took a step back into the dark and vanished.

Her dream world switched. She was back in Matt Bayfield's arms in his large bed. Then she slept soundly.

- o -

Settling back in his recliner, he propped up his feet and pulled the black robe across his legs. After taking a swallow from a beer can, he picked up the remote and pressed play. The TV screen turned from fuzz to blue and then images began appearing. It was time to get to know his elusive goddess better. He fast forwarded through the video of her getting into her car at the Northland bar. Those pictures had been purely exploratory. He prided himself on being like the artist who painted the picture of a beautiful woman first naked and then with her clothes on. His chuckle resonated deep in his throat. He worked in reverse – clothed and then naked.

He pushed the play button and glowered at the pictures from Bayfield's house, erasing any that showed the professor. There were some decent shots of the

125

goddess bouncing up and down on the bed. He sighed, appreciating the way her breasts bounced naturally. There was too much silicone out there these days, but none for his goddess. It wasn't difficult to imagine her bouncing on his Robyn.

The pictures on the screen switched to her standing at her apartment window. Her curiosity edged with fear drew him like none of the others had. The others never knew he was there. This one was different. She'd sensed his presence like a deer during the hunt. She wouldn't be easy, but then he was growing tired of easy.

He took another swig of beer and wiped his mouth with the back of his hand. She was a looker. Lush. She was ripe to receive his gift. But now she'd have to wait longer, much longer. He had to play by the rules, and so did she.

She'd been selected to receive his gift on Samhein, but circumstances had prevented that. Now she'd have to wait for Beltane. It was only right to maintain the balance, the harmony of the universe. The wheel could not be allowed to go off kilter or the entire world would be in danger.

He reversed the video and paused it, replaying that moment when he'd had a clear view of her standing naked at the window. He reached between the folds to fondle his Robyn. His breath shortened. Everything worked out for the best. He hadn't realized when he first saw her that she was worthy of being the high goddess of Beltane. He hadn't been able to get more than a glimpse of her naked until now. But she was so perfect: long dark hair, full mature breasts, wide hips. He couldn't have dreamed of a better Beltane goddess. Once again he had to trust the universe. This goddess had been saved to be the goddess of the Maypole. Her gift would be the greatest of all.

He'd been annoyed at first when she'd left the bar with Bayfield. He grunted. The professor didn't know half of what he thought he did. So much for academics. The Samhein substitute had been okay; she'd been appreciative of his gift, but not as much as if she'd known him. He'd been left to give to whoever was available. She'd been a stranger; worse, she was a natural blonde. How he despised the Nordics. That was his penance for nearly defiling the goddess of Beltane before her time. To do so would have been catastrophic for him and for the universe.

He smiled at his good fortune and at the goddess of Beltane peering at him from his TV screen. "The universe provides," he whispered, jerking and spasming. He didn't close his eyes. He wanted the naturally black haired goddess to see the gift he was preparing to sacrifice for her.

- o -

The next morning, Nancy stood in front of the TV with a yoga DVD plugged in. She lunged forward, twisting into Warrior pose. Holding the position, she struggled to clear her mind. Kundalini yoga provided a vigorous workout along with meditative opportunities. Even though she'd practiced yoga two to three times a week for years, this morning she was having difficulty letting go and being present in the moment. Nancy softened and lengthened her neck, closed

127

her eyes and turned inward. Still, the man in the gray car and the red dot from her dream penetrated her mind.

Don't fight it. Nancy took her own advice, slipped to her knees and went into baby pose with her rear resting on her heels, her forehead on the mat and her arms stretched straight out in front. She relaxed into the position, allowing toxins to sweep from her body. She did not resist images or thoughts. Perhaps the universe had something to offer.

Nancy had scoffed at such a notion for years. Her yoga teachers often used such language, embracing a mystery that Nancy respected but never felt. She took yoga because it was good for her body and for stress reduction. She didn't do yoga to be in touch with the spirits of the universe.

She listened quietly and then more intensely. Nothing. No voices. No shining lights. Just darkness. And of course, niggling thoughts about the man in the gray sedan.

Breathing deeply through her nose, she floated. This was a state of relaxation she enjoyed, though there was an edge to it that sometimes frightened. She'd never wanted to climb into a hot air balloon unless the tether remained securely tied to the ground.

She replayed the images of the man in the car pointing something at her window. Her muscles tensed remembering that for a brief moment she was certain he'd been pointing a gun at her. But he hadn't. A camera? A scope? And what about the red dot? At least some camcorders had red dots. Perhaps, a video camera. But why would a man want to make a video of her or her landlord's house? No, the creep had been interested in her; not the house.

There was little doubt that he was middle aged, or at least not a young jock. Nancy rose and ran in place for two minutes to shake out her muscles. She had to have a plan. Matt's next lecture wasn't until around the twentieth of December. She'd get with Washington and go back over all the reports. They were missing some links. What else did the women have in common? The last attack involved a wig. Why? Were there other unusual elements she'd overlooked?

Nancy walked toward the shower discarding her loose fitting yoga clothes as she went. She turned the shower knob to hot and stepped in. Leaning back into the stream of water, she smiled softly remembering what it had been like showering in Matt's bathroom. She grabbed the small bar of soap and ran it across her skin. There was no difficulty at all imagining his fingers taking the place of the soap. She stretched her neck letting the bar slide between her breasts.

Closing her eyes, she shuddered as the slippery soap slithered lower across her navel to the juncture of her thighs. She chewed her bottom lip and lathered the thick black curls guarding her most private place. Holding the bar just so, she maneuvered it upon and down her crevice. With a tantalizing swirling motion, she forced herself to move away and soaped her firm buttocks and then her hips. She bent over to do her legs and feet while hot water cascaded off her back and streamed through the crease of her buttocks. The soap, guided by her fingers, traveled slowly up an inner thigh returning to that tuft of black.

Nancy drew in a deep breath before using the soap bar to separate her engorged nether lips. Widening her stance as much as possible in the confines of the tub, she leaned back and pressed two thirds of the bar and two fingers into her channel. She stood there and waited, challenging herself, tempting herself. How long could she wait? She thought of Matt pulling on her nipples. She imagined his tongue flicking at her bud. The soap bar slipped from her palm and her fingers penetrated deeper.

She bent forward and then back, letting her fingers find the spot, and then she chortled and spun out of control. And in the flash of ecstasy she saw a man pointing something at her; there was a red dot flashing rapidly on and off.

Nancy stumbled out of the shower reaching frantically for a towel. She dried and shivered; any residual erotic fantasies immediately evaporated.

Could the man be recording his potential victims? Did he go through a process of hand-picking his victims in advance? He did seem like a perp who paid close attention to detail. If he selected his victims days or weeks in advance, then there was nothing random about the attacks at all. The rapes seemed to be tied into the timing of Bayfield's lectures.

If the man had videos of his victims, he probably replayed them imagining exactly how he wanted to take each woman. And if he'd watched them over and over again, the man could have developed a twisted kind of empathy for them. He had a relationship, albeit a one-sided relationship, with each woman before ever attacking her.

Nancy tossed on her robe and walked into the kitchen to pour herself a cup of coffee. Was she giving the man more planning credit than he deserved? Maybe. If she was right, she'd certainly crossed his radar screen. That was good. She wanted to be his next target. Then she could nail him and get him off the street. But if she was right, then the man was demonstrating more cleverness and guile than she'd anticipated. All of which made him even more dangerous.

Nancy sat on a bar stool at the kitchen counter sipping her coffee and reviewing her copies of the victim reports. Her eyebrows arched. How many of those co-eds would have been in public arenas where camcorders would have drawn no attention? Gymnastics. Volleyball. Soccer. Maybe even a theater performance. Did the college sell videos of shows and dances students performed? Probably no records were kept unless he'd made a purchase with a credit card. She pursed her lips. Her guy wasn't that stupid.

Hell, the creep could have taken a camera to a park or to a picnic. Almost anything was possible. Yet, he'd come after her in her own apartment –

maybe even in Bayfield's apartment. Probably nothing too revealing. Though if he'd climbed the hill across from Matt's house...maybe. She'd have to check the layout better next time. If the man worked with a long range camera, maybe.

"Too damned many maybes!" Nancy snapped. Glancing over at Malaki scratching at the small braided rug in front of the door, she groaned, "Okay, Mal, you're right, I've been ignoring you. Let me throw some clothes on and we'll go for a walk. Professor Bayfield's tea seems to have worked miracles on my cold." Malaki cocked his head at her as if he knew exactly what she had and hadn't said. She nodded. "You're right again. Professor Bayfield worked a lot of miracles on my body, too." The corners of her mouth turned up. "But then maybe I worked a miracle or two on his body."

The phone rang. Nancy let it ring a second time before picking it up. She immediately recognized the voice. Her reflection in the hallway mirror was that of a happy, satisfied woman.

"I'm fine. The tea took care of the sniffles," she said, not trying to keep the excitement out of her voice. "How are you?"

"I'm good," Matt replied. His voice seemed huskier than usual. "No second thoughts, if that's what you mean. How about you?"

Nancy giggled. "The only second thought I've been having is when we'll be able to get together again." His laughing response caused her to rise to her toes and wrap the phone cord about her midsection.

"I'd invite you to Thanksgiving Dinner." She hesitated. "I can cook, but my aunt has invited me. Would you like to join us?"

She smiled at his groan.

"Not hardly. Thanksgiving with the president of the college is not something I'm up for yet. I've already got an invitation from a colleague."

"I understand about the president…as long as you can get up for her niece."

"I should be able to manage that without too much effort. So what do you want to plan? It'll take me pretty much from now to three o'clock Wednesday to grade papers so my students can take them with over the break. I'll be so exhausted and stressed out that night you won't want to be around me and the next day is Thanksgiving."

"You're slow getting the papers back?"

"I hate grading. But the students owe me another paper shortly after break so they need the feedback."

"I can appreciate that. How about the day after Thanksgiving? Let's make a day of it. We can rent you some skis and go out to one of the forest trails that's well maintained."

She could imagine him shaking his head during the long ensuing silence. "I don't ski. Thought I told you that."

"But I'll teach you." She ignored his cough. "Come on, Bayfield, be a sport. This is the wrong time of the year to be jogging. There's nothing to cross-country skiing. And it's good for you."

"So what do we do after I make an ass of myself?"

Nancy grinned into the phone. "You can play with mine and I'll play with yours."

"Your place, or mine?"

"Why don't we come back here? I'll cook us up something special."

"Sounds great to me. The only problem is the next several days are probably going to drag by. In case you're wondering, I really enjoyed yesterday."

"You sound quite surprised."

"Honestly, I am."

"Oh." Nancy furrowed her brow. "You didn't have high expectations about me?"

She didn't know if his chuckle was reassuring or not. "No, more accurately about myself."

"Oh." Now she was confused.

"Usually, I don't phone a woman the day after I slept with her."

"Once is normally enough?" She winced at the squeaky sound of her own voice.

"Normally."

"But not this time?" Nancy waited, holding her breath.

"Not hardly. You're a real puzzle to explain, Crane. Maybe it's the dog."

"What?"

"That Rottweiler of yours. Maybe he casts some kind of spell on me."

He was teasing, but she played along anyway. "I'll have you know, Professor Bayfield, if there are to be any spells cast on you from this household, it will be me doing the casting."

"Yeah, I don't doubt that. I hate to break up this scintillating conversation, but I must get to my grading. How would you like to grade one hundred and fifty papers before Thanksgiving?"

"I'm thankful I don't have to think about it. You certainly put them off, didn't you? I didn't think you were the procrastinating type."

"Only with papers – and maybe sometimes with women. See you."

"Bye." Nancy replaced the phone. For whatever reason, he'd certainly been a procrastinator with her. She'd have to keep working on the man to try new things, or he might suffocate from his routines.

Chapter Seven

The Trillium police car parked in front of the President's House only exacerbated Nancy's nasty mood and soured her stomach. Her aunt had called her twenty minutes earlier to say they had a problem and to come over immediately. The problem was obvious: her cover had been blown.

"This is Chief Ed Bacardi of the Trillium Police Department," President Williams said, "and the gentleman to his left is Chief Dennis Grimes of Blackthorn campus police."

Both men nodded at Nancy warily. Had she forgotten to put on a bra? Or did she threaten them? While the men were likely quite pissed at her, it was clear from the strained, regal cast of her aunt's face that the president of Blackthorn College remained in charge of this little get-together.

"Please, everyone have a seat," President Williams instructed. She directed her gaze to where Nancy sat on an uncomfortable straight-backed Queen Anne's chair, a replica of some century that escaped Nancy at the moment. "I'm sure you've guessed these men know that you have been working undercover for me on the rape cases."

"The thought had occurred to me." Nancy waited, not wanting to take the lead.

Chief Bacardi cleared his throat and pulled on

the end of his bushy moustache before speaking. He looked like a traditional, hardworking, nose-to-the grindstone cop who never wanted to make waves and would want everything done by the book. Her aunt had definitely thrown the book out the window on this case.

"I think we ought to begin, Detective Appleby," Bacardi said.

Damn, they'd really done their homework. Nancy worked at looking calmer than she felt.

"By first acknowledging our displeasure at your being involved in a case in Trillium and Blackthorn without our knowledge. The president has explained her position and made her prerogatives clear, but that doesn't mean we're happy with her decisions."

"I'd make the same decisions if I had it to do over," President Williams interjected.

Chief Bacardi grunted. "I don't doubt that one bit, President Williams."

Nancy looked sharply at the Chief. Was that a little admiration in his eye?

"I still don't like it," Chief Grimes whined, crossing his arms. The chief of campus police looked so pale Nancy wondered if he ever strayed far from his desk.

Grimes continued, "We don't need any kind of big city whiz kid sneaking in the back door to make something out of nothing. I say she should be sent packing. Immediately."

Nancy directed a glacial stare at Grimes. "You may be the only person to ever have described

Stevens Point, Wisconsin as a big city, Chief. I don't know whether to be flattered or appalled." She held up her hand to prevent the fleshy man from interrupting. "And I beg your pardon, but there is very much happening here at Blackthorn. Young women are being raped."

"Or so they say."

Barely managing to control her temper, Nancy snapped, "Six women have been raped since last February. There may be others that weren't reported. Do you realize those numbers rival the statistics at Big Ten universities? Blackthorn is tiny in comparison."

Grimes shrugged, but remained silent. Chief Bacardi glanced at President Williams and then at Nancy. "No matter what we think, detective, it's clear you're here to stay for a while. Speaking for my department, we'd like to support you in any way we can. Frankly, you know of more rapes than we did. Only two of them were reported to us." He turned to Chief Grimes. "Had you heard of six rapes?"

Chief Grimes reddened. "I'm not sure. Maybe." He threw up his hands. "You can't believe what some of these young girls say. Maybe they got in over their heads. Or want to hit back at some guy who jilted them."

"Maybe," Bacardi replied, pulling on his moustache. "Still, I'd like to know of any complaint."

"Yes, definitely, Chief," President Williams said. "I'm amazed that we don't routinely report such complaints to your department."

"If they're credible." Chief Grime's response sounded lame.

"And who determines credibility?" the president asked, her voice lowering an octave.

Nancy smiled inwardly. The chief ought to be wary of her aunt's piercing glare. The man was on a short rope, and her aunt held both ends.

"We do." Grimes turned red. "I'll see to it myself in the future. But what about her?" he demanded, pointing at Nancy.

"She stays," President Williams declared. "Do you have anyone on either force as well qualified for the job?"

Chief Bacardi chuckled. "We'd love to have you working for us, Detective Appleby. I've gone over your record carefully and had long conversations with your superiors in Stevens Point. I don't know how President Williams came up with you, but for now I'm pleased she did."

"What about you, Chief? Do we have anyone on the Blackthorn force better qualified?"

"Of course not," he sputtered, "but..."

"Good, then both of you will cooperate with her and give Detective Appleby what she needs." President Williams cleared her throat. "This young woman is placing herself in danger to protect our co-eds; I want to make sure you two do everything you can to protect her."

"The first thing you can do," Nancy piped, "is maintain my cover. Does anyone else in your departments know of my presence?"

"Not in mine," Bacardi said.

"Nope, mine either," Grimes agreed.

"Good." Nancy narrowed her eyes. "But someone had to alert you to me in the first place. Who?"

Both men shook their heads and looked at President Williams.

Her aunt's shoulders sagged. "They won't say," her aunt said. "They claim some kind of privilege and wouldn't go along with our plans if they had to divulge their source."

Nancy nodded. She didn't like it one bit, but she knew the importance of protecting sources. She just hoped both men were as determined to protect her. "One more thing," she said, "Do either of you have a man in a gray car tailing me?"

"I wouldn't tail an undercover cop," Chief Bacardi said, sitting up straighter, "unless we were called in for support. What about you, Dennis?" he asked, turning toward the campus police chief.

The response was a laugh and then a sheepish glance at the president. "Can't say I didn't think of it, but we don't have the manpower to have anyone traipsing after her."

Both responses rang true. There was still a man out there, though, with a video camera or a scope, and it didn't seem likely he was a cop.

"So how can we help you, Detective Appleby?" Bacardi asked.

Nancy ran her hands through her hair. She knew she had to give them something or they'd be hounding her every day. She wasn't about to share all her hunches yet – not until she knew she could trust both men. "There may be times when I'll want to have you get some information from your computers." Both men nodded, probably aware she was stalling. "Okay, I stake out the Northland Bar and Grill, usually three nights a week. I vary the nights. I could let one of you know when I'll be there."

"Good, that's my turf. You'll let me know," Bacardi responded. "It's bad enough to have these co-eds raped. I don't want a cop raped. Not on my beat. What else? Do you have any leads we can help develop?"

Nancy shook her head. "Nothing solid. I'm thinking the creep strikes after or shortly after a campus-wide lecture series offered by Professor Bayfield on Celtic Culture and Ritual. From what the women have told me, I'm guessing the man is middle-aged."

"An older student," Grimes said.

"Maybe."

"And what about this professor?" Grimes asked. "Seems like a logical suspect."

"He was out of the country when the August rape occurred."

"So he missed one. How about the ones after that?"

"I followed him home in September. He never left his house." Nancy cocked her head to the side. She might as well level with them, they'd find out anyhow. "And in November, he was with me during the time of the rape."

President Williams coughed and rose to her feet. "Well, I guess that about sums things up, gentleman. I'm sure we'll be able to count on your assistance. Hopefully, together we can get this man before he strikes again."

"You can count on us, President Williams," Chief Bacardi said, extending his hand first to the president and then to Nancy. He smiled at Nancy. "I already have your phone numbers including your cell." He lowered his eyes and smiled faintly. "Maybe you should give me this Professor Bayfield's numbers too. Sounds like the two of you will be spending a fair amount of time together."

"You got a problem with that?" Nancy asked, straightening her spine.

"Nope, not me. If the president doesn't, I don't. But I would appreciate the numbers in case we have to get a hold of you quickly."

"I'll have them to you before the day is out."

"I'll want them, too," Chief Grimes insisted. "Don't seem right to me, but none of this does."

Nancy held her tongue and smiled as sweetly as she could. After both men left the parlor with their hostess, she took in a deep breath.

Her aunt returned shortly sat back down in her chair and howled, "That was great, girl! You sure are cool under fire. I thought you'd go berserk when you found out they wouldn't tell how they found out about you being here."

Nancy shrugged. "Clearly, they protect their

sources, but how do you think they learned about me?"

"I don't know. Maybe I'm madder about that than you are." Her aunt turned pensive. "It had to be some kind of leak around me. Unless, Officer Washington..."

"No way. Nope. She's not the leak," Nancy insisted.

"What do you think of our police chiefs, Nancy?"

"Are you being coy? Bacardi appears to be a straight-up, no-nonsense cop. Grimes seems rather creepy to me and sure doesn't have the foggiest about rapes on college campuses. How did he get the job?

President Williams looked down her nose. "I can assure you I inherited him. If it wasn't for his brother on the Board of Trustees, I'd have a new chief. The man's arrogance infuriates me, but no more than his brother. Town and gown relationships are difficult at best even when you have well intentioned competent people working with you. But what about this guy in a gray car?"

Glancing away from her aunt's steady gaze, Nancy lied, "Don't know. Probably nothing."

"And why don't I believe that? You be careful, girl. You're my favorite niece."

"I'm your only niece, Aunt Joan. Apparently, those two gentlemen who just left don't know about our relationship."

"Apparently not. Wouldn't they be thrilled?"

"Somehow, I doubt that."

"So are you bringing your man to Thanksgiving dinner? We'll have plenty of food."

Nancy stood to leave. This conversation had just taken a wrong turn. "No, he has other obligations." She gave her aunt a broad smile. "I'm not sure he's ready to admit he's involved with the president's niece."

"So you're bopping him already. Good for you! I can hardly wait to see how our stiff Professor Bayfield handles you."

Nancy's eyes rounded. She held her laughter until she reached the driveway, and then she laughed until tears slid down her cheeks. She could have told her aunt the stiff Professor Bayfield handled her quite well, thank you. He was right. The day after Thanksgiving seemed a long way off.

"Malaki, behave yourself!" Nancy gripped the dog's leash short and tight.

"I'm sorry," she said to the stranger. "He's normally so well behaved."

The man walking the small yappy dog nodded. "That dog's going to scare the crap out of my Honey."

"She seems to be holding her own. Maybe we ought to just walk on. I don't think these two are going to be friends."

"The park's big enough – you should be able to find a place for him without encroaching on our space."

Nancy held Mal firmly. "I didn't realize this

was your private place, mister." She made a show looking about. "Nope, I don't see a sign saying it's anyone's."

"The name is Jeffers, young lady, and I've been walking dogs in this area for years."

Malaki sat down at last. Nancy scowled at the man. "Jeffers. This park is called Jeffers Park."

"That's right. Named after my father, who donated the land for it."

"That still doesn't give you the right to claim a particular spot for your dog."

"Maybe not, but most people don't complain. Only outsiders." The man spun on his heel and his dog followed him, yapping at everything and nothing.

"And happy Thanksgiving to you, too," she yelled at the man.

"I'm sure glad you don't make that much noise, Mal." She bent over to scratch the dog. "You didn't like that little prissy dog, did you? Her owner wasn't much fun, either."

Nancy studied the back of the man walking away from her. It would be just like the rapist to make some kind of inane contact with her. He clearly loved to play games. Would he be that bold? Jeffers. She'd have Bacardi check the guy out.

He hadn't raised the hairs on the back of her neck. But something sure had gotten to Malaki. Maybe her radar was slipping.

The Triumph engine turned over once, twice, and then only grinding sounds reached Matt's ears. He slammed his palms against the steering wheel. "Shit! Son of a bitch!"

Temperatures had dropped below zero the night before, but he'd had his car checked only the previous week. Though he wasn't at all sure the local mechanics had a clue about how to maintain a Triumph. But then he didn't either. He'd enjoyed the feel of the car in California. It was, however, almost useless during the northern Minnesota winters.

He turned the key again. Nothing. Was it the battery? Maybe the starter? Maybe the fickle machine had gone into hibernation for the winter.

Matt wedged his tall frame out of the car and slammed the door behind him. He stomped toward his house to call Nancy Crane to pick him up. She would have a good laugh over this one. It was already quite evident she didn't give him a lot of credit in practical matters. He shrugged. Not that she was way wrong.

Swallowing his pride, he dialed Nancy's number.

"Sorry to bother you. I was on my way over, but my car won't start. Do you think you can pick me up?"

He heard the lilt in her response. "No problem. I'll be there in about ten minutes. I've got battery cables, if you need a jump."

He grinned at the image of her jumping him. Battery cables? "Maybe, I don't know. It's a Triumph, you know."

"Right. One of those little, tiny foreign cars. I remember now."

Her sarcasm gnawed at his ego, but he bit back his words and only said, "Yes." He could visualize her shaking her head in that knowing manner of hers.

"I may not be able to help you. I don't know if domestics can jump foreigners. We'll figure that out later. Time's a-wasting. I'll get Mal and be on my way." She paused a split second. "You know, Bayfield, if you're going to manage northern winters you really have to get a four wheel drive vehicle. How did you make it through last winter?"

"I walked."

"Oh. Even a dogsled would be better than that," she quipped. "I'll be right over."

Matt hung up the phone and looked out the window at his Triumph in disgust. Why did it have to choose this day to let him down? It didn't matter what Nancy Crane thought about his mechanical abilities.

And now she was supposed to teach him how to cross-country ski. He'd never been on skis in his life. Cold weather had had no appeal to his parents when he was a child and he'd always been able to avoid the cold and any sports associated with it – until coming to Blackthorn and falling under Crane's spell.

Why had he ever agreed to this outing? Admittedly, she was good in bed, but that good? Yes, damn it, yes! And she had a brain and a sharp sense of humor that he appreciated, when it wasn't directed at him.

What had Carol Macy said at Thanksgiving dinner? "Bayfield, you've got to loosen up. Don't take life so seriously. Maybe you should get laid more often."

He couldn't help it. He'd blushed profusely at his colleague's comments. Her partner had squeezed Carol's arm encouraging her. They'd invited him over for Thanksgiving, no doubt, because they thought he had no other plans and had taken pity on him.

That wasn't fair, and he knew it. They were good friends, happy together, and they genuinely wanted him to be happy. The only thing wrong was they thought he needed a woman in order to be happy. That equation had never worked before; there was no reason to expect it would now.

But Carol knew him too well. She'd pushed her blonde hair from her face and lifted a wine glass in salute. "Well, I declare, Elizabeth, I do believe our Professor Bayfield is getting laid."

He remembered her gleaming teeth as the woman considered the possibilities. There had been nowhere for him to hide. He couldn't have said a word if his life had depended upon it.

"It's that nicely shaped Ms. Crane, isn't it, Matt?"

He'd glowered, but Carol Macy was not in the

149

least intimidated. "Don't be coy," she'd said. "I'll bet she has a body to die for. Yes, you look a little more beat than usual. This is marvelous – Matt Bayfield screwing around with a student!"

He knew he'd gone as white as a sheet and thankfully Carol realized she'd pushed him too far. Very quickly, she backed off. "I'm sorry, Matt. It's just that you've always been so prim and proper. I really think it's great for you and for her. And it's not like she's one of your students. Is she?"

"No, of course not," he'd stammered.

"Then, no problem," she'd replied, holding her open palms upward, grinning broadly.

"Right, and here comes the *no problem*," Matt muttered to himself, watching a red Jeep Cherokee pull into his driveway. Such was Nancy Crane's idea of a practical winter car. Parked next to his Triumph, the Jeep made his car look like it was built for a midget.

Matt stood at the top of a long gradual incline and peered down the trail that fell slightly away from him and curved out of sight into the woods some hundred yards ahead. He swallowed. This couldn't be worse than balancing on rings or any number of floor routines he used to do in gymnastics. Still it was unfamiliar, and the morning had hardly gone well.

He avoided looking at Nancy, comfortable and raring to go. Malaki was already halfway to the turn where he sat looking back to see if anyone was actually going to follow his lead. Matt groaned. The woman had nearly made him undress. His parka wasn't good enough. Layers, she'd demanded, for he'd die from heat exhaustion if he wore his heavy coat. He doubted that, but went along with her advice. Now, in addition to his long-johns, he had on a shirt, a sweater, a sweatshirt and a windbreaker. He wasn't cold, but he wasn't sweating either.

And his car wasn't fixed. She'd consulted with someone who said she could do damage to one or both cars if she tried to jump it. There was one car he wouldn't mind doing damage to. He'd thought the Triumph made a good conversation piece, but not the way Nancy had hooted when she saw it.

"Are we waiting for the wind to come up or the sun to set?" Nancy jibed, swishing her skis back and forth.

Ignoring her, he looked down at his skis frozen in place and frowned. She really was beginning to annoy him. Few people had gotten under his skin the way this sexy snow bunny had. He doubted she was even trying.

There she stood in some kind of thin, red snow suit from neck to boots, her black hair tied back in a ponytail and ski goggles that made her eyes loom as large as her lips. She might have had on as many layers as he did, but they didn't hide a chest and butt that could cause a four alarm fire in any healthy man's body. And he was in prime health. Was it possible to make love in the snow? Shuddering, he moved his feet back and forth while holding his ski poles tight.

"No better time than now," he retorted. "Why don't you show me the way?"

"Good," Nancy said, sliding in front of him. "It's an easy stroke. You squat slightly, move forward with the left leg, lift your right hand and place the pole such. And then repeat – right leg, left hand. And so on."

She stopped fifty feet in front of him on the left hand track. Matt stood in the right hand track. He did as she said, starting with his left and then his right. He bent too far to the left and then overcorrected by leaning to the right. Wobbling, he stood up straight, but didn't fall. The beaming smile Nancy gave him warmed his blood. He wasn't about to fall. He tried again. It was smoother this time.

"Nothing to it," she said, as he approached her. "Let's get going. You'll love it, I know you will."

Nancy moved fluidly ahead of him. As they entered the woods, Matt began to feel much more at ease. His strides were not long, nor were they necessarily smooth, but they were reasonably efficient. He was keeping up with his guide. The main difficulty was staying focused on what he was attempting to do with his legs and arms rather than on the rhythmic movement of Nancy Crane's rear end. How could a woman so completely clothed be so damned erotic?

They had gone about fifteen minutes into the woods when Nancy stopped and waited for him to catch up. When he came to a halt beside her,

Matt was surprised by his heavy breathing and rapid heartbeat. "Whew! I thought I was in better shape. You're right, this is a workout!"

"We can rest a bit. A lot of exercise experts say cross-country skiing is one of the best cardiovascular workouts available." She stuck her tongue out at him. "Apparently even better than jogging."

"Apparently," he agreed, between ragged breaths.

"But you're doing fine, Bayfield. I didn't see any spills. You'll need to fall so you can learn how to get up."

"We don't have to rush that."

"It'll happen. Happens to all of us. Sometimes one ski slides over the other without warning. Sometimes you over lean on a curve. It'll happen. But you have better balance than most beginners. How do you explain that?"

"About a dozen years of gymnastics."

Nancy whistled low. "That explains a lot!"

A wisp of a smile formed on her lips and her eyes turned darker. He'd sure like to know what she meant by that comment. He'd bet anything she was remembering back to the night they'd spent in his bed. He had to agree they both had demonstrated a lot of balance and stamina.

"We better push on, if you're ready," she said, interrupting his thoughts.

"Sure." He followed as she led the way. Further ahead roamed Malaki.

They paused every fifteen minutes or so.

Fortunately, he felt less winded each time, though he knew he'd ache like hell the next morning. Cross-country skiing sure tapped muscles he never knew he had.

They stopped at a small clearing off the main tracks. Nancy had already removed her skis and was setting out a picnic lunch from her backpack. Matt shook his head; he'd never picnicked in the snow. Weren't picnics for beaches?

"Here you go," she announced, "sausage, cheese, crackers, a split of wine, apples and chocolate bars – and water."

"I'll be so stuffed I won't be able to get back," Matt complained, struggling to step out of his skis.

"Nonsense, this takes a lot of energy." Nancy handed him a knife and he set to cutting himself a large piece of sausage.

"It's so heavenly out here," Nancy said, looking up at the snow covered trees, "and so quiet. It feels like there's no one within miles of here."

"It is quiet." He looked around, taking in the pines and spruces heavy with snow, the animal trails, and several large boulders probably left over from the glacier. "This is better than I expected," he admitted, following Nancy to one of the boulders. There she brushed off the snow making a seat for the two of them.

"I never get enough of this," she said, unzipping her outer jacket. "There's always another case to work on. Or emergencies come up. Sometimes I wish cell phones were never invented."

"That's the way I feel when I'm on a dig. I don't want to be bothered with anything else."

"So you must travel to some spectacular places. Are you moved by what you see? By nature?"

Matt cut off another hunk of cheese before answering. "Sure. I'm not immune to nature."

"I didn't mean it that way."

"No, I know you didn't. Most people, however, would be surprised by what moves me. Sometimes it's the natural world – sitting on the edge of a lake in Scotland, for instance, where the early morning fog can be utterly eerie. Then I'm not sure if I'm more moved by the natural or the unnatural."

Nancy drank from her water bottle. "What do you mean?"

"It's hard to explain. The Celts celebrated mysteries and magic in ways quite foreign to us. Sometimes I have the feeling they left spirits behind to lead me to those mysteries and then other times I feel like they are thwarting my efforts at understanding their ways." He shrugged, slightly embarrassed at having revealed so much. "I'm sure it's all nonsense and childhood imagination."

"I'm sure it's not," Nancy retorted. "I may not be so aware of the possibility of other times or other dimensions, but I share some of the same feelings. How can you not, when you hear a loon calling to its mate at dusk? Or when you're in the woods and a buck stands twenty yards away staring you down?" She rose to her feet and stood in front of him. She placed a hand on each of his shoulders. "You are a very mysterious man, Matthew Bayfield," she whispered, leaning in to him.

He could feel the heat of her breath on his lips. Her eyes were wide open watching, gauging his response. He cupped her butt between his hands and pulled her body tighter against his. Even with all the clothes that separated them, he reacted immediately. He didn't know if she could feel his erection, but it certainly strained against his long-johns.

She snaked a hand between them to squeeze him. So much for whether she was aware of his arousal. Her lips brushed his and then crushed them. His hands roamed roughly over her buttocks desperately seeking something more.

Abruptly, she backed out of his grasp and pecked him on the lips. "Whoa," she gasped. "I don't think you're ready for lovemaking in the snow. And this is a little too public for me."

"You've done it in the snow!"

"Of course. Don't look so shocked. Properly prepared, it's fun." She pulled her jacket zipper up. "I'll bet you've done it on a beach."

"So, it's probably eighty or ninety degrees warmer."

"But you had to contend with all that sand. Yuck!" She leaned over and lightly bit his nose. "You hang around me long enough, professor, and sex in the snow will seem mild."

Matt busied himself helping clean up the

remains of their picnic while trying to keep his thoughts and body in check. He guessed anything was possible. He'd never skied before. He never dreamed of having a picnic in the snow. But sex! Matt glanced over at Nancy who stuffed what remained from their lunch into plastic bags and into her backpack. If he hung around her long enough, he might not be able to recognize himself.

Were all cops so adventuresome? He watched her bend over to place a foot on the ski and her butt naturally rose into an inviting pose. Her hips rotated slowly and Nancy, as if knowing exactly what was going through his mind, turned her head and winked at him. Feeling like a kid caught with his hand in the proverbial cookie jar, Matt hurried to his own skis.

Chapter Eight

"You can cook!"

"My many talents seem to overwhelm you, Bayfield," Nancy replied dryly. "It doesn't require a lot of skill to cook stew in a slow cooker. I cut all the veggies and meat before I left this morning, put the pot on low and *voila*, we have a meal. Umm. It is good. Your kitchen looked well used. So do you cook?"

"I do," Matt said, reaching for a dinner roll, "but I don't own a slow cooker. Sounds like a fairly simple way for preparing a meal when you don't have a lot of time to spend on it."

"That's right." Nancy pointed a knife at her guest. "Bet you didn't think cops could cook either." Matt shrugged. "Have you ever known a cop before?"

"Not really. We had an FBI agent working on his masters when I was in the graduate program, but we were hardly buddies. Never had one cook for me before. Or," he smiled easily, "never shared my bed with a cop. So what do you know about sociologists?"

"Fair enough." She nodded. "Not much. Never shared my bed with one before either." She picked up her wine glass and ran her tongue around its rim before taking a swallow. "I will confess I never expected a professor to be such a considerate lover."

"Bayfield, you look embarrassed. That was a compliment." She removed a foot from its slipper and rubbed it against Matt's inner calf. Her foot rose to his thigh. He held her wide-eyed stare while he reached under the table and stroked her leg, her ankle and her toes.

He was too good at this game. Reluctantly, she pulled her foot a way from his fingers. They had all night, maybe even the whole weekend.

He didn't seem miffed at all. So it was to be her call. She rose to clear their dinner plates. It didn't surprise her that he helped scrub the dishes and put them in the dishwasher. After the counter was cleared and cleaned she leaned against it and asked, "So would you like a little Irish Cream? We could put one of those store-bought logs in the fireplace – it's fake, sad to say – and just be cozy."

"I'd like that a lot. As long as I can hold you and touch you now and then. And I love Irish Cream."

"Good. I don't have a robe for you, but it would help if you'd slip off your pants." She poured the after dinner drink into two juice glasses. "I'm going to the bedroom and get out of my underwear. I'll put the sweater back on and maybe put on a skirt that you might find more attractive and accessible than these jeans."

Matt chewed on his lower lip. The bulge in his pants was quite evident. "You like to tease, don't you, Nancy Crane? You're a woman of many disguises. I'm never quite sure which one I'm talking with or romancing."

160

Sticking out her tongue, Nancy said, "I love to tease and to play out my fantasies. But unlike some women you may have known, I deliver on my promises."

She backed up against the refrigerator. Matt placed a hand on either side of her head, leaned down and lightly kissed her nose. "And you are full of promise, Ms. Crane."

Nancy ducked away from his arms and said, "Why don't you start the fire, and I'll take care of a few things in the bedroom." Heading down the hallway, she tossed back over her shoulder, "Don't forget to take those jeans off."

"How could I forget?" was his muted response.

- o -

Minutes later, Matt sat on the living room couch transfixed by the fire and the woman who lay curled on the couch with her head resting in his lap. His right hand had snaked up under her wool sweater and cupped a firm round breast. Now and then his forefinger grazed a nipple and Nancy emitted an encouraging moan.

Matt settled back against the cushions. This was comfortable, almost too damn comfortable. Never had a woman made dinner for him. Usually, he'd take a date to dinner and maybe to a play or concert afterward. Then there would be the rush back to his place or her place. The sex would be too rapid fire and he'd be left wishing she'd go home or he would.

This was different. Nancy appreciated a slow sex play that he also liked, not that they hadn't made love fast and furious with more passion than he thought possible. He glanced down at her. Her eyes were closed. Yes, this was different.

He froze. This was a dangerous woman in his arms. She not only carried a gun, she filled up his senses. No woman had ever come close to doing that. Yet, he and Nancy Crane were so different, so opposite. And then there were precious moments like this. He shut his eyes and sipped some Irish Cream.

When he reopened them, she brushed her fingers against his chin. Playfully, she ran a forefinger around his earlobe. "Why so serious, professor? What are those wheels in your brain churning about now?"

Matt shrugged. "I don't know. Guess I didn't think it could be this good with a woman."

"I know what you mean," she purred.

"So how do you explain it?"

Nancy shifted her weight a little and worked a hand inside his sweater until she was caressing his nipple. Together they maintained the same pace – he feathered her nipple while she feathered his. He nearly forgot he'd asked a question.

"Maybe it's because we know we're just lovers for a time. You're going your way climbing that academic ladder and I'm going my way. Maybe that frees us up to be present in ways we wouldn't be if we had to decide *is this the one*. Or dealing with those silly questions of *what is he really after*?

Or *why doesn't she say she loves me?"*

Matt chuckled. "You may be onto something. Though I can't say I've ever really been in a so-called serious relationship. Of course, you were. You were married. That had to be pretty serious." Matt clamped his jaw shut to keep from rattling on. He didn't have to know about her prior marriage.

He watched Nancy's eyelids close and felt bereft when she withdrew her hand from beneath his sweater. She sat cross-legged beside him; his hand was no longer warmed by her breast. With a determined look, she reached for her half filled glass.

She sipped thoughtfully. Finally, without looking at him, she said, "Yeah, you could say it was serious. I was married for five years."

Her voice dropped in pitch. "He was a cop. My family loved him and I thought I did too. We never seemed to have the time to consider having a family." She looked at Matt. "Yes, cops do have families.

"Now, I suspect it was more than lack of time that stopped us from having kids. I think Frank knew he didn't have the emotional makeup for being a father."

Nancy placed her hand on Matt's thigh, stroking it absently. "When my father was killed in the line of duty, Frank was so gung-ho about making him into a hero, and he was, but Frank never grieved the death of my father. After a few weeks, he thought I should be done grieving too.

Finally, I told him I wanted a divorce."

"I'm sorry."

"Don't be," she responded, squeezing his thigh. "I believe everything works out for the best in the long run. If I had done what Frank wanted I would be an emotional basket case, and," Nancy beamed him a broad smile, "I wouldn't be sitting here with you knowing how well a woman can be loved."

"It takes two people," he whispered. "Believe me, I know. So why did you want to be a cop?"

Nancy lifted her glass and finished the Irish Cream and then laid back down again resting her head on his lap. She turned and wet the length of his arousal through his under shorts. "You sure you want to hear my life story?" she teased.

"Yes," he said, covering his erection with a hand.

Not to be deterred, Nancy swirled her tongue around his thumb and pulled it into her mouth. She made exaggerated slurping sounds, sucking it thoroughly before releasing him. He waited, unwilling to be detracted by her playfulness.

"Okay," she said, rubbing her head against his crotch, "if you can wait, so can I. Where was I?"

"I think you were about to tell me why you chose to be a cop."

"You sure want my life story, don't you? Oh, all right. Well, it wasn't my mother's idea. My dad was a cop and my two older brothers were cops. My mother thought I should be a teacher or a nurse. Me, I wanted to be like my brothers and my

164

dad. I'd been a tomboy from the time I could toddle."

"That doesn't surprise."

Nancy grinned. "No, I suppose not. I did a criminal justice major in college and joined the Milwaukee Police Department right after graduation. Went to Stevens Point after the divorce. If you want to experience cold shoulders, try staying on the same force as your ex. It doesn't work."

Abruptly, Nancy stopped talking and turned to face him. She grazed his lips with hers. "Um," she said, "you taste good, you smell good." She turned and nestled in his lap, facing the fireplace. He rested his chin on her head and wrapped his arms around her.

"Having a fake log is pitiful. It's like looking at a charade. I don't want to look back," she continued. "It's a waste of time. Why don't you show me how you love a sex starved woman?"

"Did you have anything particular in mind?"

"This will do for starters." She guided his hand beneath her skirt. The heat of her inner thighs welcomed him. She skimmed his fingers over her slickness.

Matt closed his eyes, listened to her tiny moans, and let her lead the way. Two of her fingers pressed on his until he entered her. She sighed as if deeply relieved. Gently, he probed her offering. He moved deeper, marveling at her slippery heat. Would he ever get enough of this woman?

She turned her head and kissed his arm.

"Damn, you do that so good," she mumbled. "You have the patience of a cat."

He smiled but said nothing. She arched her back, taking him in further. His pinky slipped in to join the other two. She started to rock back and forth. Her fingers brushed against her clit. Matt matched her pace and then took her to a new plateau. She flung her free hand around his neck trying to reach his lips. Instead, he leaned over and laved her ear.

"Oh, my God," she screamed. She scraped her fingers over his roughly. "Now. I can't wait any longer."

Together, they plied their fingers, bringing her closer and closer to what she desired. Her buttocks strained against his loins. Suddenly, her fever pitch broke. She keened softly and melted against his body.

He'd never experienced a woman's orgasm so intensely, so personally. It was like her orgasm had become his.

He flexed his fingers.

"Don't move," she whimpered, placing her hand over his. "But don't go away either. Just be with me. Stay inside me for awhile. I don't want to be alone."

Pain shot from behind Matt's eyes. How could she imagine being alone with him sitting right there? Nancy curled up holding his hand tight to her body. Soon, Matt heard soft breathing sounds; she'd fallen asleep on his shoulder. She was a woman of many faces. She'd never be boring. Matt chuckled to himself. How many times had he made love to a woman without even seeing her totally naked?

- o -

The next morning Nancy strained to open her eyes. Her lumpy pillows seemed the same, but something was different. "Ah shit," she muttered, realizing the only thing she had on was the sweater she'd worn the day before.

And then it came back to her. She sniffed. Coffee was brewing. Thank God for miracles, of any size. She had the vaguest memories of being carried to bed. He'd pulled off her skirt, but gave up on the sweater. Clearly, he'd stayed the night. But then she had the wheels.

She rolled over and hugged a pillow. What was she going to do with him? She'd never expected the remote Professor Bayfield to be so kind and understanding. How could she have fallen so soundly asleep? It must have been the Irish Cream.

Her eyes sprang open. She'd nearly spilled her guts to him last night. A little liquor and a little kindness had almost made her re-live horrors best locked away. Had she been that relaxed? Nancy closed her eyes and vowed to keep her guard up around Bayfield. She wanted a lover, not a shrink.

She threw her legs over the side of the bed and roughly ran fingers through her tangled hair. Without bothering to visit the bathroom or put anything else on, she strolled out into the living room to find Bayfield sitting in front of the fireplace, drinking coffee, with the newspaper doubled over in one hand and scratching Malaki between the ears with the other. Neither male looked up when she entered the room.

"You two seem to be getting along marvelously," she drawled, heading for the coffee.

She rushed for her cup of morning sanity. She poured herself a mug full of black coffee and took three large swallows before padding back into the living room.

Matt looked up from the paper. His smile was broad. "I never thought a woman could look so lovely in just a sweater."

Frowning, Nancy glanced down at her sweater. Realizing that was all she had on, she decided to make the best of it. "It's a new fashion for lovers. Thought you might appreciate it."

"I'm not complaining in the least."

Nancy plopped down in a soft chair across from him. She pulled the bulky sweater down, providing a modicum of modesty. "You'll have to wait a little longer. I've got to get my caffeine quota going and then maybe we'll see what we can get up."

"Take your time. Up is not going to be a problem, though."

Grinning, Nancy said, "I can tell." She placed two hands around her mug leaving him with a full view of what ever he might desire to look at. "So I assume Mal's been out and fed."

"Of course," said Matt too smugly. "He's quite adept at giving me instructions. If he wants food or water, he stands by his dishes. If he wants out, he stands by the door. If he wants his belly scratched, he straddles my leg. And if he wants his ears scratched, he puts his head on my thigh."

Nancy peered into her steaming mug. When she lifted her head, she fought back tears. "Thanks for last night."

"What do you mean? It was wonderful for me too."

He seemed sincere. Nancy didn't know if she'd ever be able to figure the man out. "I left you hanging, for one thing. Thing two, you carried me to bed and made no demands."

"Of course not." Matt looked hurt. "Who do you think I am?"

"I don't know," Nancy whispered. "Thing three, you stayed with me when I needed you." She cleared her throat. "I really appreciate that."

Matt shrugged. His eyes were full of questions that went unasked. Nancy shook her head. "Maybe some day, but not yet."

"Okay."

"So what have you been working on?" she asked, changing the subject. "Looks like the crossword."

"It is. One of my worst habits," Matt said, crossing his legs at the ankles. "I can't seem to walk by a crossword puzzle. This one's quite easy, but it did get me to thinking about something you said recently about the rapes."

169

"What's that?" Nancy tucked one leg under her torso and leaned forward.

"You said something to the effect that most of the rapes occurred right after my Celtic lectures."

"Yes, that night or soon after."

"I'm afraid what I've identified may simply muddy the waters." Deep in thought, Matt chewed on the end of his pencil.

"Go on."

"The rapist could be gearing his attacks to an ancient Celtic or pagan calendar, in tandem with the lectures or apart from them."

"I don't understand, Matt. Lay it out in black and white."

"Okay. My lectures coincide roughly with the movement of the sun and the changing of the seasons. I thought that would heighten the interest in the lectures."

"So how many changes are there?"

"Eight. Imbolc or Candlemas – February second; Spring Equinox – March twenty first; Beltane – May first; Summer Solstice – June twenty-first; Lammas – August first; Autumn Equinox – September twenty-first; Samhein – October thirty-first; and the Winter Solstice – December twenty-first. Some of the dates may shift a day or so given the specific year." He looked at her intently. "What do you think?"

Nancy leaped to her feet and began to pace retrieving the dates of the rapes from her memory. She came to halt before the fireplace, which pleasantly warmed her backside. "It's remarkable, with an exception or two. The first rape was February fifth..."

"That discrepancy can be explained," Matt interrupted. "We had blizzard conditions here from the second to the third. It took a day or so to clear the walks. I gave that lecture on the fifth of February."

"Even though your notes say the second?"

"Yes, the lecture notes would have been done in advance of the planned lecture."

"All right. The next rape took place on March twenty-first and that was followed by one on May first. Both of those coincide with the calendar you're talking about."

"Yes."

"But there was no rape June twenty-first or thereabouts. And there was a rape on August first, but no lecture."

"Right."

"You may be onto something. No rape on a given date may simply mean there was no reported rape. It may be coincidental – the link between the lectures and the rapes." Nancy creased her brow. "Maybe I've been looking in the wrong place all this time."

"Doubt that you can rule the lectures out as a link yet. But I know I am complicating matters a bit."

Nancy grunted. "That you are, professor." She just wasn't ready to think about how much he was complicating her life. "And then there was a rape on September twenty-third and October thirty-

171

first. On some of these dates, the rape actually occurred early the next morning. So why would some one choose his timing according to an ancient Celtic calendar?"

"There are still many serious pagan believers today who continue to celebrate the movement of the sun and the change of the seasons. Early Christians took over a lot of those practices. Halloween or All Saints Day coincides with Samhein. Christmas is close to the Winter Solstice and while Easter varies, it does revolve around the Spring Equinox. Did you know that Easter and the Easter bunny are named after a Celtic goddess?"

"No!"

"Yep. So there could be a multitude of reasons for choosing to rape according to that calendar. Those were high points in the Celtic year, often occasions of great celebration and reportedly of sexual excess. Actually, the sexual practices were often ritualized."

Nancy walked back to her chair and sat down. "Ritualized? So do you mean this guy is acting out some ancient ritual while he's raping innocent women?"

"Perhaps. Or at least his understanding or twisted understanding of those rituals. There are probably more rumors about the excesses than there are facts. Some historians report, if you go far enough back, there were some Celtic groups that practiced human sacrifice. How widespread such practice was is quite debatable. The Celts and Druids didn't write their own histories. That reporting was usually left to historians of the conquering Christian Romans who mostly wanted to convert the pagans. But it is fairly widely believed that a cult of the head, for example, did exist."

Nancy grimaced. "Hopefully, this guy doesn't know about that. You're not going to lecture about that are you?"

"As of this moment, such references will be scratched from my lectures."

"Good. We don't want to give this creep any new ideas. He's doing enough damage as it is. Wow, Matt. This is helpful, I think." She scowled. "I know this isn't how you planned to spend your morning, but I'm so glad you got up early and worked a puzzle." She gave Matt a bright smile. "So what are you doing the rest of the weekend?"

"Didn't have any plans, really."

"Good. Why don't we hang together? I want to pump you on more details about each of these celebrations." Nancy stood and brushed her fingers lightly through the dark curls covering her mound. "Actually, I'd liked to pump you in a lot of ways."

"Sounds like a superb plan, Ms. Crane."

"First, I've got to throw on some clothes and take Mal out for a potty break and a little exercise. You took the early shift, go ahead and work on your crossword."

When Nancy emerged from the bedroom she saw Malaki sitting at the door with his leash between his teeth. She laughed and snapped the leash onto his collar. "Now, Mr. Mal, if we run into your friend, Mrs. Lindenhammer, I don't want you begging. Begging isn't good for you."

"Bye," she shouted over her shoulder.

"Bye, I'll be here when you get back."

"You better be."

- o -

Matt looked up from the file drawer he'd been bent over to see Nancy leaning over his office desk, displaying her enticing bare rump. They'd come over to campus so he could retrieve some materials for his Monday class.

He quickly closed the distance between them and wrapped his arms around her, then wasted no time accepting the invitation and sinking his length into her waiting cleft. He rubbed his nose back and forth across her thick ponytail, inhaling her scent, loving what it did to his nostrils, to his lungs. Could you get high on a woman's scent?

He leaned over further and flicked her ear with his tongue; she cocked her head sidewise encouraging him. He laved her ear with care, all the time keeping his shaft fully encased in her tight sheath. Her upper torso lay across his office desk while her feet remained firmly planted on the floor. Her panties hung on his chair; her skirt was flipped up over her back. Her rear fit snugly against his groin. It was a scene he'd never forget; it was a Sunday morning to be remembered and cataloged in his erotic memory file.

174

She squeezed him from within. He grunted, methodically stroking her at a languorous pace. Matt kissed the base of her neck. And then he froze.

Footsteps in the hallway advanced toward them. They weren't alone. There was only one office beyond his. He stifled a cry and held onto Nancy tightly. He felt her tense. Neither of them moved.

The knock on his door caused him to jerk against Nancy. Perspiration clouded his vision. He shook his head at Nancy's arched eyebrow. She reached soundlessly for her purse sitting on the corner of the desk.

Maybe thirty seconds elapsed. The doorknob turned. Thankfully, he'd had the good sense to lock it when he and Nancy had entered. Another fifteen seconds. Footsteps could be heard retreating back down the hallway. They heard the fire door at the end of the hallway slam shut.

Matt let out a long held breath; Nancy began to giggle. Her gleaming white buttocks wiggled back and forth rubbing his groin. How could it be? He was harder than even before the interruption.

"Come on, professor. Don't hold back now. This may be a once-in-a-lifetime opportunity." Nancy shifted her weight forward and back on the balls of her feet, demanding more.

Matt blinked. They hadn't been discovered. And there wasn't any threat or consequence that could keep him from fulfilling Detective Crane's wish. He reared back and slammed his body against her. He pulled nearly out and slammed in again.

"All right," she gasped. "Faster."

The sound of skin slapping against skin served to heighten the intensity of the experience. Nancy gripped the far edge of the desk and mewed his name. The sounds, the texture and sight of her buttocks in his hands unhinged him. Standing on his tiptoes, Matt drove powerfully in and out of the dark-haired woman until his explosion made more effort untenable.

Was that his howling he'd heard? He had some remote awareness that Nancy had climaxed along the way; she might have come ten times, for all he knew. In the minutes or hours it took to fulfill her wish, he'd lost track of anything but the force that pulled him deeper and deeper into her heat.

Gradually, the fog lifted and he found himself slung over Nancy's back heaving, struggling for breath. Worse, there were tears in his eyes. They were tumbling down his cheeks. He brushed them aside hoping she hadn't noticed. Too late. Her neck was already wet. What the hell had happened? What the hell was happening to him?

He'd just made love to a woman, a student – no, make that a cop – in his office – had nearly been discovered – had the most massive orgasm of his life, and now he was crying his eyes out.

Dully, Matt gave Nancy credit for not chattering about it. She just lay there apparently as spent as him. Matt kept his forehead at the back of Nancy's head for what seemed like several long minutes. At last, reluctantly, he shifted his weight, breaking their joining. If he could, he would have remained in her forever. He'd never experience such security, such peace, such completeness.

Slowly, he reached for his swivel chair and fell back into it. Nancy turned and faced him. She lowered her skirt and pulled on her panties. "There may not be words to describe that."

Matt shook his head.

"Do you know who was out there?" Nancy sat on his desk rather than taking a chair.

Shrugging, Matt guessed, "Maybe Carol Macy. She's sometime in on Sundays. Or a security officer." Feeling his pulse slowing back down, he flashed her a smile. "Hell, it could've been the president."

"Right. If it had been Aunt Joan, she would have stayed out there and applauded."

"You think someone knew we were in here?"

Nancy nodded. "I'd make a wager on that. I'd say our boot tracks aren't dry yet."

Matt watched Nancy give him a blank expression. He was learning more and more about her nuances. She was trying to hide something. "You don't think it was Carol?"

"Might have been. Sounded more like how a man walks."

"Oh. Probably security then."

"Probably."

Her response seemed much more noncommittal than the situation required. He glanced down at the floor and smiled softly. Soon maybe he'd have enough energy to put his pants back on. He met Nancy's steady gaze. She was concerned about him, that much was clear. "So why was it so powerful?" he asked, gulping in more air.

Nancy leaned over and ran a forefinger across his lips before responding. She nodded. "It was massive. I don't know why. Maybe because it was your office. Maybe you were conquering something from your past. Maybe pent up adrenaline and energy at escaping discovery. After surviving a dangerous situation, I've seen cops behave as if they could lift a twenty story building." Folding her arms, Nancy continued, "I know one thing. I'm glad I was part of it."

Her lips spread into a broad grin. "I appreciate your tenderness, but I'm glad to know you have a rough side to you, Bayfield. I think I could depend on you in a fight."

"Don't know about that."

"I don't know about you, but your office is starting to feel cramped," Nancy quipped. "How about getting your pants on so we can go back to your place?"

He smiled sheepishly. "I think I can manage that now."

"While you do that I'm going to step down to the ladies room we passed on the way in." Nancy shoved her feet into her waiting boots, threw her coat over her arm, picked up her purse, unzipped it, unlocked the door and cautiously stepped out into the hallway.

Matt hurried to locate his briefs and pants. He

brushed back his hair with his hands. He hesitated. She'd walked out of his office with her hand in her purse.

"Oh hell," he groaned. The gun. Who did she really think had been at his door?

They held hands walking across the parking lot and down the sidewalk toward his house. They hadn't spoken a word since they'd left his office. Should he be angry, or flattered? There would never have been such a close call if she hadn't led him on.

Matt winced. Confession was good for the soul. Propriety was the last thing on his mind when he'd seen her naked invitation. She was a vixen, a minx, a goddess rolled into one sexy package. And he couldn't get enough of her. And she'd only laugh or giggle if she became aware of his discomfort with their sex play.

"That was outrageous back there," he said aloud.

"It was, wasn't it?" Nancy chortled. "Don't whip yourself, Bayfield. You went over the edge. You ought to do that more often." She held his hand tightly and swung their arms matching their stride. "Don't tell me you've never fantasized about making it with a woman on your office desk? It must be a classic male professor fantasy. Maybe even a female professor's fantasy."

"Just because you can imagine doing something, doesn't mean you do it," he replied gruffly.

179

"That's another point on which we differ, professor. If I can imagine it, then I want to try it. Reality might be better than the fantasy."

They made their way to the park separating the campus from the street where Matt lived. Walking along in silence, Matt tried to come up with a different topic to talk about but he couldn't shake the images of what had happened in his office, or the sheer terror he'd felt when he'd heard the footsteps in the hallway, or when he'd no longer been able to restrain his frenzied drive toward climax.

He'd been certain he'd hurt Nancy while hammering her against the desk, but she didn't seem to be suffering any negative aftereffects. He kicked at a stick on the walkway. Maybe she was right. Maybe he just didn't like losing control. It didn't do any good to deny that he'd succumbed to a base desire for sexual domination that he'd never realized he possessed.

Nancy pulled him to a stop. She put her hands on his lapels and drew him down toward her puckered lips. It was a caress more than a kiss, and it softened his heart immediately. Nancy Crane was not only a woman of passion she was also a woman of immense compassion. And it was that feeling that now threatened to overwhelm his body. Again, he felt close to tears. What the hell was wrong with him!

She broke off the kiss and leaned back in his arms. "There's nothing to feel guilty about, Matt. We're both consenting adults. I loved what you did for both of us back there." She kissed him lightly again. "You spend so much time figuring out how to meet my needs it shocks you to know you have some very powerful needs and responses, too. I doubt I'll even be sore in the morning. But if I am, it was worth hearing Professor Bayfield howling his gratitude to the four winds."

Before he could reach out and grab her, Nancy broke away and sprinted up the knoll overlooking his house. Matt laughed at the ponytail bobbing in the wind and ran to catch up with his lover. Damn, he hoped she *was* sore in the morning! *He* sure would be.

- o -

At seven o'clock, Nancy threw back the covers, struggled out of bed and walked stiffly toward the bathroom. Matt had an early class to teach so she'd returned to her place the night before. She glanced at the mirror and did not find the bags under her eyes flattering in the least. Maybe she was getting a little old for non-stop lovemaking. They'd mellow out eventually – or break it off entirely. More likely both.

Resolving to enjoy it while it lasted, Nancy twisted so she could see her buttocks in the mirror. No bruises, thank goodness. Bayfield would never have forgiven himself if he'd bruised her.

Nancy smirked. "Hell, what a ride." She'd

never guessed Bayfield could lose control that way. She'd finally put a serious dent in his armor. He'd never explained the tears, and she wasn't about to ask. It seemed they both were determined to hold onto some secrets.

The phone rang.

She rushed to the kitchen. It couldn't be him. He'd already be at the college.

"Hello." Why did her voice sound so weak? Maybe because she didn't want to face the real world yet.

"Hi, Nancy, how was your Thanksgiving?"

"It was fine, Mother. How was yours? Didn't you go to the Caribbean?"

"Yes, we did. We left a week and a half ago and got back yesterday. It was splendid. I can't wait until you meet Jack. Your brothers adore him."

Nancy closed her eyes. She doubted her brothers adored Jack; they might tolerate him, but adore him? Not hardly.

"You are coming to the cabin for Christmas, aren't you, honey?"

"That's the plan. I probably won't get in until Christmas Eve. The case I'm working on here could break just before then. If that happens, all bets are off."

"Oh, I do hope you can make it. The family is only going to be there Christmas Eve and Christmas Day. Everyone is so busy this time of year it's hard to get together at all. Jack is taking me to Paris afterwards for a delayed Christmas gift."

"Really?"

"Yes, he is so sweet and generous."

Nancy tried not to gag.

"I do hope you can come and please bring that professor of yours."

Nancy's heart dropped to her toes. "What?" she squeaked.

"Come on, Nancy Ellen, I'm your mother. You didn't know I'd find out? Your aunt sounds so thrilled for you. You'd almost think *she'd* found a man."

Nancy smothered her response. What about the Trillium police chief? *Don't go there.* She'd always learned if you couldn't defend yourself, it was best to go on the offensive. "I don't like people, even favorite aunts and mothers, talking behind my back. It's tacky."

Laughter greeted her ears. "So it's true. I'm so pleased, Nancy. So do bring him. You'll have the cabin to yourselves by Christmas night."

That was tempting, definitely tempting. Bayfield had no plans. His parents were on a year long sabbatical in Australia. She and Matt had planned on spending much of the vacation together after she got back from Wisconsin.

Nancy did a little jig. This could be great. She stopped. But would he agree to come along and meet her family? It sounded like it would be for less than twenty-four hours. He could handle that. She flinched, imagining the grilling her brothers would give him.

"I'll see what I can do, Mom. He's kind of shy,

but maybe I can get him to come."

"I know you'll do your best, you always do. So what's this young man's name?"

Nancy smiled. "His name is Matthew Bayfield. Do you want me to spell his name? You can tell Henry and Nathan I've already done a thorough background check on him."

"I'm sure you have." Her mother groaned. "But you might as well go along with it. They think they have to protect us women folk. I guess Jack passed the test. I'm sure your Matthew Bayfield will too."

"If you have time to bake your famous custard pie, Nancy, why don't you do two? The daughters-in-law are bringing most of the trimmings. And I, of course, will be responsible for the turkey."

"I'll try, Mom."

"Okay, I've got to dash off now. I just hope you're not overpowering that professor. I've never known you to go for shy men before. Anyway, goodbye."

Chapter Nine

Nancy braced herself, lowered her revolver a fraction and aimed for the heart.

She squeezed the trigger; a sizeable jagged hole suddenly appeared on the target exactly where she'd aimed. Quickly, she crouched and aimed for the head with the same result. She lay prone, picked out a different silhouette and fired two shots with similar results. Her lips formed a thin line of satisfaction. She regained her feet, double checked her weapon and placed it in her shoulder holster.

"Excellent shooting, Detective Appleby," Chief Bacardi praised. "I'm glad we're on the same side."

She nodded at Trillium's lanky, mustachioed Chief of Police. "Thanks. You've been holding up your end in good form too," she said, cocking her head toward Bacardi's targets.

"The first couple shots were a little off. I've been behind a desk too long," he groused. "Didn't take long for it to come back to me. Sort of like riding a bike, I guess."

The chief guided Nancy away from the range toward a small canteen off the main entryway of the Minnesota State Patrol Regional headquarters building. "It's good to get away from the office. I'm glad the State Patrol has this range within driving distance. Let me buy you a cup of coffee,

Detective."

Holding the door open for her, he glanced around the small cafeteria and said, "Looks like we have the place to ourselves this morning."

"Okay, but I should be buying you the coffee. It was my idea that we meet and talk about the rape cases."

"I was about ready to call you; I've got some stuff that might be somewhat useful. And," a small frown crossed his face, "I've a few more questions for you."

Nancy bit her tongue. She should've reached out to the chief before this, but she preferred to work alone, and she'd been so busy with Bayfield that it had been easy to put off this meeting. There was no reason to distrust Bacardi. He was a good cop; her gut told her that. He'd suggested they meet at this place so she wouldn't have to show herself at the department. Clearly, he was doing what he could to keep her undercover, at least for the moment. But she wasn't too eager to hear his questions – she doubted she had adequate answers.

After ordering, they carried their coffee cups to a small metal table with two chairs in the far corner of the canteen. Even if anyone came in, it would be quite clear that the two of them desired privacy.

"So what do you have?" Nancy inquired, running a finger around the rim of a coffee cup.

"Don't get your hopes up. I don't have much." The chief pushed his chair back and reached into his coat pocket drawing out a sheaf of folded papers. "We did a check on known convicted sex offenders in the area. We were particularly interested in learning about guys that might have moved in during the last couple years and or had some association with the college."

"Good. Did you come up with any?"

"We have five living within a fifty mile radius of Trillium."

"Really, that seems like a lot."

Chief Bacardi shrugged. "Maybe it's easier for the state to send these guys to the north woods than to organized city neighborhoods. Anyway, three of these guys have ironclad alibis. They were not in the area for one or more of the rapes. One guy works for a local computer services company and seems to be doing fine. He lives just east of Trillium on a forty acre homestead."

"Did you talk to him?"

"Yeah, we had a couple officers talk with him. Claims he had nothing to do with them, and that he has good alibis. We're still checking them."

"How old is the guy?"

"Forty-two. And he does fit the height and weight description. We're keeping tabs on him, but he doesn't seem very fearful or resentful that we're contacting him. He comes across like it's his civic duty to cooperate."

"What about the other guy?"

"Candidate two – probably too strong to describe these guys as suspects – is forty-eight, five-nine, hundred and seventy pounds. He works for the private garbage firm that has the contract with the college."

Nancy shifted toward the edge of her seat. "He's got access."

"Yes, both men do. The college contracts with the first fellow's computer firm."

"Candidate two checks out?"

"So far. He did seem more reluctant to talk to us. Told my officers they were hassling him. Even threatened to bring in a lawyer. But again, the guy claims to have been home with his wife each night a rape took place."

"Convenient."

"Right."

"Can I get pictures of those two?"

"Sure thing. I have a folder in the car with pictures, descriptions of past crimes, and the reports from my officers."

"Good. This may be helpful."

"Or they may be blind alleys." The chief tugged on the corner of his moustache. "We've run the names of all males associated with the college. Nothing popped up immediately. So we're looking again."

"Does that include the men working on the campus police force?" Nancy inquired lightly. She was walking on shaky ground, but she had to know how far she could trust Bacardi.

He leaned back, his eyes sparkling. "President Williams said you were tough and persistent. Guess she was right. Yeah, we're running those names too. Nothing out of the ordinary yet. Is there a particular reason you're suspicious of the campus police?"

Nancy stretched her neck and blew air through pursed lips. She met his intense gaze. "Only that Chief Grimes doesn't seem to understand what constitutes rape. And somehow somebody tipped you two off about my presence."

"And..."

"Okay, as I said earlier, I've been followed by a man in a gray car – nondescript, like an undercover police car."

Chief Bacardi scrunched his mouth and narrowed his eyes. "To my knowledge the campus police don't have such a car. And for the record neither does the Trillium police."

"And you won't say who tipped you off about me."

"Nope, can't do that. You know I can't. So do you have a good description of the guy in the car?"

"No, but I think he was looking at me through a scope or a video camera."

"That's strange. Doesn't sound like what a cop would do."

"I agree," Nancy admitted.

Chief Bacardi took in a deep breath and let it out slowly. "The president wants me to make sure you're safe, Ms. Appleby."

"I hope you told her you can't guarantee that," Nancy huffed.

"She knows. But it's one of my questions for you. Just who is President Williams to you?"

"What do you mean?"

"Seems quite coincidental that she would locate a detective from a small Wisconsin community to help her with a volatile crime situation here at the college." He steepled his fingers. "I'm not questioning the need to bring in outside help. At this point, I'm withholding judgment on how the campus police have responded to this crisis. And I'm not in the least questioning your qualifications.

"There's something else though. You have a comfort level with President Williams that defies the situation and her concern for you could almost be called maternal." He shook his head. "I probably don't have the guts to ask her, but you're a cop. So I'm asking. How are you and she related?"

Nancy blinked. She rose to her feet and said, "It's my turn to buy a cup of coffee."

"Okay."

As she refilled their cups, she considered her options. The chief would know she was lying if she didn't come clean. And if anyone else found out about her relationship with the president of Blackthorn then the leak would be Bacardi. Bayfield wasn't about to tell anyone.

She retraced her steps to the table and sat down. "You're a good cop, Chief Bacardi."

He shrugged his shoulders.

"You're right. Joan Williams is my aunt. When she saw the trouble she was in with a potentially explosive crisis at the college, and given her distrust of the campus police, she reached out to her family for help. As you probably know, I come from a family of cops."

"Okay, so it figures that she'd tap you for help. I just wish she'd trusted the local police more." Sadness etched the chief's voice.

"I think she's learning to differentiate between campus police and local police. It certainly sounds like the two of you are in more regular contact since we all met at her house."

Bacardi's face brightened. "Yes, that's true enough. She's quite the dame."

The chief choked and reddened. "Sorry about that," he apologized quickly.

"Don't be," Nancy responded, "I think she's quite the dame, too. And if you want my advice, she wouldn't be offended at all to know you thought that. Aunt Joan has always put career ahead of relationships. I expect that's her single regret in life."

Glancing away and clearing his throat, Bacardi said, "Whatever. We still have to deal with these questions. Is this guy who's watching you the perp? Are you being singled out for an attack? How do we plan to stop him and keep you safe at the same time?"

"Wish I had answers to those questions. I'd wager he is the creep. Why he hasn't come after me yet, I have no idea. I've certainly given him plenty of opportunities. If I stake out the bar much more, I'll become an alcoholic."

Bacardi chuckled and quickly sobered. "I can't

provide support for all your stakeouts, however, the next time Professor Bayfield plans a lecture I want to know about it in advance. You've got to have more backup than Officer Washington. This guy hasn't killed anyone. Yet."

His words were chilling, but not ones she hadn't thought of. "I'm working on a theory with Matt Bayfield that this guy only rapes at or near the days of seasonal changes according to some ancient pagan calendar."

"Great. We got some nut to figure out. You trust Bayfield?"

"With my life." Her response was firm and quick.

"Apparently. So when is the next likely occasion for an attack?"

"December twenty first. The Winter Solstice. Matt will be giving a lecture that evening. I'll attend and then go to the Northland Bar and Grill. If we're lucky, he'll try to grab me on my way back to campus."

"If we're lucky, we'll have enough backup to break this guy before he hurts anyone else, including you. The twenty-first? That's only four days from now. You weren't going to give me much lead notice, were you?"

Nancy cocked her head to the side. "I suppose we've both been trying to figure out how much we can trust each other."

"Suspect you're right about that. Anything else you need that I can get for you?"

Nancy thought a moment. "Do you have access

to a night scope video camera?"

Bacardi scowled.

"If I had that," Nancy continued, "I could at least determine if there really is a guy watching me, and I might be able to get a better description of him."

"It may be worth a try. We don't have anything like that in the department, but I'll see what I can do."

"Thanks." Nancy rose. "I appreciate you meeting with me here and giving me an opportunity to use the range."

Laughing, Bacardi replied, "Wanted to see first hand if the reports about you were accurate. They were. You're a damn good shot. I've been in law enforcement for twenty years and I've only drawn my gun in the line of duty three times. So far I've only had to shoot shots in the air."

Nancy's brow furrowed. "Wish I could say the same. There's comfort in knowing you can hit what you aim at, but afterward it's gut wrenching as hell. I hope I never have to point my gun at another human being again."

Bacardi ushered her from the canteen and retrieved two thick folders from his car for her. "Good reading, and stay in touch. I want to talk with you on the twentieth."

"Okay," Nancy replied, "thanks again."

As Nancy returned to her Jeep, she felt just a trifle lighter than before. There was some relief knowing that another good head was working on the case. And yes, she had to admit it a little more backup was welcomed. As long as they didn't get in her way.

- o -

"I'm not so sure it's such a great idea for me to spend Christmas Day with your family," said Matt, turning the pork chops in the skillet. "They may get the wrong idea."

"We've been over this many times, Matt," Nancy complained, setting plates out on his dining table. "They are not going to haul you off to a minister or a justice of the peace. My mother and brothers respect me for being an adult capable of making my own decisions. I choose to bring you along for Christmas. Besides, it would be a waste of time to drive over there and then come back to get you. It's a five hour drive one way!"

"I don't see why you can't come back to Trillium and we could hole up here for two weeks or if you want, we could go south where it's warm."

"I don't want to go south. How many times do I have to say that?"

Matt turned in time to catch her glowering at him. He quickly shifted his attention back to the stove. It wasn't just about being with her family for a day that bothered him. It was also being on her turf exclusively for two entire weeks. Going south would allow him to warm up and they would be in neutral space. He was already having a difficult time being away from her; he couldn't afford to let her become any more important to him. His future lay somewhere to the south; it didn't matter where as long as it was a fine college or university, and it was warm.

He shook some more pepper on the pork chops and lowered the heat a notch. The trick in doing pork chops was turning them every thirty seconds or so. He enjoyed being with Nancy too much. If he wasn't careful, she could get in his way. Was good sex worth that? He tried to shake off the twinge of guilt. That wasn't fair – they had great sex, but they shared much more than that. And *that* was scaring the hell out of him.

And now he had to sit by while she set herself up as a target for some damn rapist. Tomorrow night. How the hell was he going to spend his night? Not knowing if she had caught the guy, or if the bastard had overpowered her. She'd told him Chief Bacardi was involved in the trap. That had relieved him some. Still, he felt impotent just sitting around helping her bait the trap and then being sent home to wait.

To wait for what? For this woman he was already caring too much about to return, or for a call that she was in the hospital or worse, in the morgue?

"Damn," he muttered. One pork chop was about to burn. He flipped it quickly and added more butter to the pan. And what to get her for Christmas. The gift had to be just right. Personal, but not too personal. If he saw one more store add touting the "perfect gift," he was going to puke.

How many perfect gifts could there be? None of them fit his requirements.

"Maybe I shouldn't have come over this evening," Nancy said, slipping up behind him and lightly massaging his neck. "You're as tight as a wet drum."

"I'll be okay," Matt replied, lifting the chops out of the pan and laying them on the platter Nancy had placed on the counter.

"Tomorrow is just another day, Matt. You'll do your lecture. I'll do my job. We're both good at what we do. I'll call you first thing in the morning."

"Bullshit," he roared, slamming a pan of potatoes on the counter. "You'll call me as soon as you can whether you got the guy or not. Be it three A. M. or whatever!"

"Okay, I'll call you as soon as I can," she soothed. "Once we get past tomorrow we can focus on a special Christmas holiday.

"It's going to be fun, Bayfield. Just you and me at the cabin for nearly two weeks. Sleep in. Ski. Ice fish. Screw around. We can do it all without other responsibilities. I don't know why you're holding back," she said, taking food dishes to the table. Sitting down, she added, "I'm looking forward to it. Aren't you?"

Matt joined her at the table. He looked away from her and then took her hand in his. "I'll be okay. Your calm attitude with all of this is mind boggling, if not galling."

"This is what I do for a living, Matt. I've done it

before. I usually wind up catching the bad guys. That's what I get paid to do."

"I know, but..."

"Maybe we should drop it, Matt. You're not going to somehow change my mind, and apparently I can't keep you from worrying. It'll all work out fine – trust me."

Nodding his agreement, Matt sliced into a pork chop. At least the meat had turned out the way he liked.

- o -

Nancy wrestled with her simmering rage and glared at her aunt. Had she heard correctly? Was the President of Blackburn College actually removing her from the case?

"Now don't pout, young lady," Joan Williams said. "I'm not saying the decision is made. I just don't know what to do." The silver haired woman rose from her chair and stood between Nancy and Chief Bacardi.

The grandfather clock in the president's parlor struck two o'clock. In a little more than five hours she was supposed to be sitting in Bayfield's lecture hall trying to identify a rapist. Whose idea was this? Her aunt's, or the Chief's?

"Why?" she demanded.

"I was naïve." Joan Williams walked over to the floor to ceiling window overlooking a picturesque lawn decorated for the season with little white lights displayed on the shrubs and tall pines.

197

She turned slowly to face her niece. "I didn't realize how much danger I was putting you in. If something were to happen to you, Nance, I couldn't handle your mother. Not after..."

Her aunt's voice trailed off; no doubt she was remembering Nancy's father. "This job doesn't place me in any more danger than any other detail I'm on, Aunt Joan. I'm a police officer. You've never been this close to a violent case before. It's how I choose to live." Nancy brushed strands of dark hair from her forehead. "Between you and Bayfield, I should be in some barricaded iron box watching soaps and cooking pizza."

"You know that's not what I think, and I doubt Professor Bayfield does either." President Williams returned to her seat and offered a little smile. "Though I'm pleased our Professor Bayfield is concerned for your well being."

"That reminds me to talk with you about how my mother found out about him, but we'll save that for another day. Danger is part of my job. I'm a good cop. And I've put too much into this case to simply walk away from it." She directed her distress at Chief Bacardi. Struggling to keep her tone neutral, she asked, "What do you think, Chief? Was this your idea?"

Chief Bacardi cleared his throat and glanced at President William and then back at her. "No, it's not, but your aunt has been pressing me for details. She's got to recognize the danger involved. What you're attempting to do, what we're attempting to do is no cakewalk. I can help keep you safe," he looked across at Nancy's aunt, "I can't make any guarantees."

"Of course you can't," Nancy agreed. "No one can. But I might get run over by a drunk driver when I leave here. What happens if I don't go out there tonight? Do you have a replacement prepared to go?"

"No."

"So who will be raped tonight because we didn't even try to nail the bastard?"

Joan Williams rubbed both temples with rigid fingers. "Okay, okay," she said dropping her hands to her lap, "maybe I'm over-reacting some. I just want you to be as safe as possible."

"We're doing everything we can," Bacardi interjected. "She'll have a wire. Officer Washington from the campus police will be providing backup, and I and my second in command will also be backing up Detective Appleby. I'll have other patrol cars in the area, but they won't have advanced knowledge of the stakeout. Again, we're trying to protect your niece's cover. The fewer people who know what she's up to, the safer she'll be."

"I gather you don't trust the campus police anymore than I do." President William's tone was icy.

Bacardi raised and lowered his shoulders. "I don't know. At this point, I'll err on the side of caution." He pursed his lips and tugged at his moustache. "I would like to do one more thing that may protect both of you down the line."

"What's that?" both women asked.

"To this point, Detective Appleby has been here at Blackthorn fairly much as a private detective directly responsible to you, Joan – ah, President Williams. If something goes haywire, if for example she should wind up shooting someone, both of you and the college could be liable for lawsuits."

"Damn." Joan Williams paused. "So what would you have us do?"

"I'd like to deputize your niece so she'll have the full legal protection of my department. It doesn't change anything, really."

"Except, I'd be responsible to you instead of to Blackthorn's President," Nancy said.

Bacardi scratched his chin. "I'd like to think we're partners on this case, but technically you're right."

"What do you think, Nancy?" the president asked. "Is that okay? I hadn't thought through the huge liability issue. It could get terribly messy for the college."

And that had been one of the reasons for her involvement in the first place, to avoid dragging the college through a lot of unwanted publicity. Nancy forced the beginnings of a headache to subside. She didn't find working with or for Bacardi distasteful. Truth be known, she was more upset with her aunt than with him. In any case, she'd only share any information with him that she deemed appropriate. That was always a judgment call for any detective in the field.

"It's not a bad idea, Aunt Joan. My being part of the Trillium Police Department to work on this case would provide a huge buffer for you and the college. But," she cracked, "the rape cases are the only cases I'm getting involved in."

A broad grin swept across Bacardi's face. "Agreed. I'm not looking for another full-time officer." He glanced quickly back at the president. "Of course her pay will continue coming from whatever monies you have set aside for this."

President Williams nodded amiably. "Of course."

Discouraged yet alert, Nancy huddled over her drink at the Northland Bar and Grill. This time she sat in a far corner so she would have a view of every man who came in and out of the place. There were plenty of men who fit the vague description the women had been able to provide, but none who seemed aware of her or who raised the hairs on the back of her neck.

She wore no wig. If the guy wanted dark hair, she should have enough of that to please him. She did wear it up off her neck. She'd chosen a rather demure gray sweater, a mid thigh black skirt, and calf high black boots. Three men and a woman had hit on her, but she sat alone taking in the rhythms of the crowd. The place was hopping, likely because tomorrow was the last day of classes. Tonight it was primarily a college crowd, although locals had staked out the barstools. Tobacco smoke hung like a heavy fog.

Nancy rested an elbow on the sidearm hidden beneath her bulky sweater. Just touching it was oddly comforting. The wire running up her back was not. She'd used them in surveillance many times, and never had liked them. They compromised her movement and made her feel more vulnerable. And she didn't like the idea that others, even though they were the good guys, could hear her breathe or cuss under her breath. But it was an invasion of privacy she'd grown to tolerate. On a couple occasions, a wire had actually saved the day, if not her life.

She looked out a window toward the parking lot. Light snow continued to fall. They'd received three to four inches already; the weather report had indicated another six possible. Would bad weather change the plans of their rapist? Her walk back to campus would be more strenuous, but the fresh snow would make for a very pretty scene. Was Bayfield watching the snow come down?

The professor had been on edge this evening. He was sharper with student questioners than normal, and he'd tried to avoid making direct eye contact with her. Brittle, that was the descriptor she'd use for him. She studied her drink. Would he break under the pressure? Neither he nor her aunt had been close to an undercover police investigation before; how could she convince them that ninety-eight percent of the time everything turned out okay? Actually, the most difficult part of the job was fending off boredom.

The door to the bar opened and a single man

stepped inside brushing the snow form his shoulders and hat. He stood in the shadows. Nancy strained to see better. He'd come looking for someone. She couldn't make out his eyes, but saw his head sweep across the entire bar. Was it her imagination or did he pause momentarily when he spied her? Or was he looking at the table of people in front of her?

The lights flickered and then went out. "Shit," Nancy muttered. The crowd hooted and laughed. A large candle was lit at the bar. The three waitresses hurried from the back room with smaller candles, placing one on each table. The small flares of light initially blinded. As Nancy's vision adjusted, she peered over the tables, past the bar to the entry way. The man was gone.

There were still no empty seats at the bar. The same people sat on the stools as before the lights went out. Nancy looked at the people at each table. No one had left and no one had joined them, she was sure of that. The curious man in the entryway had left. She couldn't remember a sudden draft of cold when he stepped out into the darkness. But he must be outside, somewhere.

Had his partner not been here to greet him? Had he gone home? Or was he waiting? Waiting for her?

Nancy checked her watch: twelve-fifteen a.m. "Okay, guys," she whispered, "time to put the bait in the trap." They still did not know whether the attacker left the bar after his victims and followed them or whether he was lying in wait somewhere between the bar and the campus.

She dropped a dollar bill and some coins on the table and shrugged into her coat. Pulling on thin gloves, she reached into the deep pocket on the right side of her coat to check the position of her second small revolver. There was also a blade concealed in her right boot. She wasn't traipsing into the dark unarmed. And there was backup out there.

She drew a deep breath and began making her way toward the exit. Fortunately, the wire wasn't recording her heartbeat.

Stepping out into the darkened parking lot, Nancy stopped long enough to get her bearings. The parking lot lights remained off, but in the distance she could make out lights reflecting in the clouds likely coming from the campus. The college probably maintained a backup generator. That was where she was headed. She would retrace the steps taken by the victims as they headed back to their dorms. Her car was there in a parking lot near the lecture hall. It would be a good mile and a half walk.

Under normal circumstances about half of that distance was fairly well lit. Tonight, none of it was. There would be two quarter mile stretches through clumps of woods where she would be most vulnerable to attack. The rapist had abducted each of the victims either in the bar parking lot or in those two wooded areas.

"Let's get on with it," she muttered, knowing Chief Bacardi was listening.

She walked deliberately, not too fast, but not slowly either. It was cold. She pulled up her coat collar to shelter her neck. At the half mile point, she met a couple huddled together. Young lovers. She envied them, but remained alert. There was nothing but darkness and night sounds in the initial wooded section. A dog barked a little further down the walk. Nancy hesitated and then walked on. A half mile from campus, the walkway again went through a quarter mile wooded area.

Nancy's pupils dilated trying to make sense of the shapes and shadows ahead of her. Even in the dark there were shades of darkness. She was nearly out of the woods when she saw a dark shape twenty yards in front of her. It was human and it weaved. She stopped, her fingers curled around the gun in her pocket. The figure became dimmer. It was walking or stumbling away from her.

"Possible contact," she whispered and stepped forward slowly not wanting to pass the phantom in front of her.

The lights of the college stretched out to meet them. The figure was encased in a dark coat and hat; she figured it was a man. Right size. Nancy pressed the situation by passing him. He wobbled when she came up beside him, but made no attempt to grab her.

She walked on, not quickening her stride. The drunk had likely come from the same bar she'd been at, though it had been impossible see the man's features. There was no reason to stop him, and the attacker might still be ahead waiting for her.

The last quarter mile was uneventful – a couple of guys jogged by her, momentarily providing a startle, but nothing else. They'd come up blank on the twenty-first of December. She wondered what Bayfield would make of that.

Nancy ignored Chief Bacardi slouched low in a car across the parking lot. Shuddering slightly, she unlocked her car and started the engine. She waited for the heat to come on. The cold had been more biting than she'd expected. Before backing out, she looked down the knoll toward the woods. Where had the tipsy man gone?

She didn't think he'd followed her all the way back to the campus. Maybe she should have stopped and questioned him. But on suspicion of what? There still was no law against walking while intoxicated.

What if she'd been standing there questioning a drunk while the attacker grabbed another victim? She'd done the right thing. So why did she have the nagging feeling she'd just been snookered?

- o -

He chuckled softly and disappeared into the protection of darkness and falling snow. Did she think he was stupid? Did they have any understanding of how gift giving to goddesses had to be done? That Professor Bayfield thought he was the expert.

There had been no celebration of the Summer

Solstice; he'd been down with pneumonia. Didn't they have any sense for balance and harmony? How could he be expected to give anything at the Winter Solstice if he couldn't at the Summer Solstice?

He sobered against the stiff wind. Did Detective Appleby think she was invulnerable to his gift? No goddess could resist the gift of his Robyn. And she was a goddess. Maybe more dangerous than the others, but certainly he knew now what the universe had been trying to tell him.

This woman definitely merited the title "goddess of Beltane." She'd make the gift giving more challenging. He wondered if she played chess. If so, he was a worthy player, a worthy mate.

The irony was that she thought she was hunting him. None of the others were that eager to receive his gift. But she'd have to wait her turn. Not before Beltane.

Chapter Ten

Tight lipped, Nancy guided the Jeep cautiously over the icy highway south toward Duluth. It was Christmas Eve day; she should be bubbling with Christmas joy. Instead, she worked mightily to keep the car on the road against a buffeting southwest wind.

Beside her sat Matt Bayfield with one white knuckled hand on the door handle and the other on the dash. At least he wasn't about to take over driving. She'd driven in worse conditions than this, and if their luck held they'd stay ahead of a predicted major storm. If not, they could be in serious trouble. The south shore of Lake Superior was famous for heavy lake-effect snow – two to three feet could fall in a matter of hours.

By the time they reached Cotton, the road was wet but not icy. Nancy inhaled deeply and pressed the gas pedal harder. They were ahead of the cold front.

"Cotton. Strange name for a town less than a hundred and fifty miles from the Canadian border," Matt observed, leaning back in his seat appearing much more relaxed.

"Suppose so," Nancy replied. "Hadn't really thought about it before."

"Maybe it's named after Cotton Mather, the Congregational preacher of the late seventeenth and early eighteenth centuries."

209

Nancy puzzled out the centuries before responding. Right, late sixteen hundreds and early seventeen hundreds. Why couldn't Bayfield simply say that?

Leaving one hand on the steering wheel, she dropped the other to her lap and bent her neck back, rotating it gently first one direction and then the other. Sixty miles of ice could be a pain. And so could riding with a guy who would prefer to be a thousand miles away.

That wasn't entirely true. Bayfield wanted to be with her; he just behaved as if he was hunkered down to run a gauntlet. And some of that pain was likely still residue from her work two nights ago. The good news: the guy hadn't raped anyone. The bad news: they hadn't caught him.

She'd gone back after daylight to retrace her steps from the bar to the campus parking lot. Fresh snow had continued to fall throughout the night, making it impossible to determine if the drunken man had left the walkway or not. She'd hoped to find something, anything. Nothing.

She pounded the steering wheel and glanced over at Matt who was staring at her. "Sorry," she grumbled. "Wasn't Cotton Mather related to some guy with even a stranger name?"

"Good memory, detective. Increase Mather was his father."

"God, how would you like to go through life with a name like Increase. Was he supposed to be big? Or maybe he was expected to populate half of New England."

Matt chuckled. "Maybe he did."

They drove on in silence encountering no problems with the hills of Duluth or the bridge connecting Duluth with Superior. The hardest part was keeping to the speed limit. Superior seemed to stretch on forever with a speed limit of twenty-five or thirty. She kept an eye on the speedometer; Wisconsin cops prided themselves on nabbing speeders. She could likely talk herself out of any ticket, but she didn't want the hassle or the time required to do that.

In Ashland where the road came back to the lakeshore, Nancy marveled at one of her favorite views of Lake Superior. She'd been by this stretch of highway at times when the lake roared its waves across the road making clear to all who dared pass that they did so at the will of the lake.

"It gets colder than a freezer here in the dead of winter," Bayfield said, scowling at the lake.

"That it does. These people relish the winter – the colder the better. The more snow the better."

Matt shook his head and hunkered back into his parka.

A few minutes later, Nancy piped, "Wish we had more time. We could stop and make a contribution to the local Indians."

"That we could," said Matt, twisting in his seat to get a look at the Bad River Casino. "Looks big."

"It was just a spot in the road a few years back. They must be doing okay though. There's construction going on most of the time now. You can hardly go twenty-five or thirty miles in this state without running into a casino."

"Must be profitable."

"Maybe. Don't know how much of the money gets down to the locals, but it's likely a boost to the economy. You been to any of the casinos in Minnesota?"

"Yeah, a couple times. but I'm not big on machines." She caught his grin out of the corner of her eye. "Craps is my game."

"Really!" She couldn't have been more surprised.

"Used to make a couple pilgrimages a year to Vegas. Of course, I like the ponies too."

Nancy cocked her head to look quickly at Bayfield to see if he was pulling her leg. "Why should that shock you?" he asked, grinning slightly.

"You just don't seem the type. I guess I've got more to learn about you."

"No doubt. So how far are we away from your cabin?"

"Another hour or so." She glanced at her side mirror and the dark clouds behind them. "The storm is still coming. I'm glad we left when we did. We could've been snowbound in Trillium for Christmas."

"Maybe I should have gone out before you and let air out of a tire or two."

Nancy dragged a hand through her hair and grimaced at her passenger. "You're going to be just fine. No one is going to eat you."

His lips turned upward.

"Well, at least *they're* not going to," she added hastily.

- o -

Hooding his eyes, Matt tried to gird himself for the trial ahead. She was from a family of cops. They'd probably be on his case from the moment they saw him. At least her family wouldn't be at the cabin for long.

Nancy had become quite animated, once the road had cleared of ice, acting as tour guide. Not too long after passing the casino she'd announced that they were entering Iron County, the county where their land was located. It was a big county, she promised. Then at Hurley they'd turned south. She'd said the next town, nearly thirty miles away, would be Mercer. Then his tour guide had grown quiet.

Was she having second thoughts about bringing him along for this Christmas sojourn? How many other guys had she brought to the cabin since her divorce? He hugged himself tightly and shrugged the tension from his shoulders. Why should that matter to him? His being along was a matter of happenstance. They were in the late stages of a tryst and he had nowhere else in particular to go.

He imagined his parents, in Sydney, would lift a glass of wine to toast him on Christmas Day and would then proceed with their normal routines. That was about what Christmas had been for him

213

for as long as he could remember. They'd exchanged gifts on Christmas morning. It had always been a sedate time, forced cheer occasionally. The gifts were typically books that he usually enjoyed reading.

Santa had never been part of his family's Christmas ritual. The jolly old elf was only for those who required such a crutch; the same had been true of God. The Bayfields had no need of holding onto such myths.

Even though she was quiet now, he'd seen Nancy Crane bubble with anticipation as she planned for Christmas. The car was loaded with presents, Christmas cookies, and two custard pies. He remained uneasy, but curious about how her family celebrated the holiday.

Thank goodness for sociological curiosity. A sociologist could learn something from any experience, even a family celebration. He did worry about the gift he'd bought for Nancy. He'd given up on being personal, but not too personal when he realized his gift to her would be opened in front of her family members. A book on Celtic myths and lore would have to do.

Had she gotten him something? Of course she had. He wondered what? Chuckling to himself, he realized this Christmas was already different. He doubted Nancy Crane would give him a book.

The car slowed. He caught view of a road sign announcing Mercer city limits, population one thousand, seven hundred thirty-two.

"We're getting there," Nancy said. "The cabin is

about five miles out of town."

The town, Matt observed, consisted primarily of a main street and a cross street of businesses. Bars, cafes, snowmobile and boat dealers, bait and fishing equipment stores, tourist souvenir shops, and realty buildings lined the business strip. A bank and a couple gas stations were also visible. There were no stop lights. Quaint. Northwoods. It looked pretty much like much of northern Minnesota.

"There. Over there," Nancy clucked happily, "is the world's largest loon. Aren't you impressed?"

"Can't say I've seen any larger," Matt replied dryly, looking at a twenty-foot-plus structure depicting a loon. "So someone's checked out all the other loon statues around the world and determined that one to be the biggest?"

"Doubt if anyone's gone to all that much trouble." Nancy shook her head without looking at him. "It's the idea that counts."

He nodded and let the subject drop. Just out of town they passed a grocery store with late Christmas Eve shoppers filling most of the parking spots. Further down the road, to his surprise, was a sizeable two story motel.

"Place seems to be doing well," he said. "Didn't expect to see such a fancy hotel up here."

"It does," Nancy agreed. "Like so many northern Minnesota and Wisconsin towns it's either feast or famine. They pray for lots of snow around here. Snowmobiling is a huge tourist industry as long as the snow is adequate. Of course, there's fishing year around. Lots of people come up from southern Wisconsin and Illinois."

Nancy turned right toward the setting sun. The road was curvy and trees stood so tall that at the horizon they seemed to merge. "The area has become quite expensive, especially lake property."

"Your property isn't on a lake, right?"

"Nope. It's an eighty acre parcel that a river cuts through. The river empties into the Flambeau Flowage – fishermen come from around the world to fish the area. If the land hadn't been in our family for generations, we would never be able to afford it today. Still, it's not as expensive as lake property, but then neither are the taxes."

Nancy breathed deeply through her nose. "Here we are." She turned down a long snow covered lane. At its end was a plowed circle and on the edge of the circle stood a very sizeable farm house.

"Hardly a cabin," he said.

"Everything up here is called a cabin, even million dollar homes. I've always loved this house. It was built in the early nineteen hundreds and was a home for loggers and for a farmer or two since then. It was a logging ancestor of ours who built it, and the house and land have remained in family hands ever since."

The front door of the house opened and an older woman waved vigorously and five children rushed out around her waving and shouting at Nancy.

"Might as well get out. We've been spied."

Nancy winked at him. "You'll do fine, Bayfield, just be yourself. Remember, by tomorrow at this time we'll have the place to ourselves."

Stepping out of the car, Matt tried to remember her advice and words of encouragement. He felt, before he saw, two sets of eyes riveted on him. A dark haired girl and boy, maybe six and ten years old, stood quietly with arms folded waiting. Matt cleared his throat and said, "Hi."

"Did you bring presents?" the girl asked, pouting at him.

Nancy rescued Matt while hugging three other children, a boy and two girls probably ranging from five to ten. "We did indeed bring lots of presents," she shouted. "Something for everyone."

The girl who'd asked the question smiled broadly. "So who's him?" she wanted to know pointing at Matt.

"That's Matt. He's a friend of mind. You'll like him."

"Boyfriend?" inquired the boy, not smiling at all.

"Yes, Michael, he's my boyfriend."

"Good," he said, very seriously.

Matt cocked his head at the kid who was already dashing around the car to give his aunt a hug.

"You guys," Nancy said, conspiratorially. She had each of the kids' attention. "I want you to meet Matt Bayfield. He's a teacher and is an expert on witches, ghosts and things that go bump in the night."

217

Each child, with the exception of the dark-haired boy who'd asked who Matt was, took a step backward, their eyes rounding. There was hushed silence. Matt knew the silence wouldn't last.

"Matt," Nancy said, getting his attention. "I want you to meet my nieces and nephews. This is Michael and his sister Tracy, and this is John and his sisters Mary Beth and Alicia."

Michael shook his hand while the others held back and murmured, "Hi."

"Do you really know about witches and ghosts?" Alicia asked. "I've read about them. Sometimes they scare me, but my dad says they don't even exist."

"I feed monsters," chimed in the youngest of the group.

What can of worms had Nancy opened this time? He glanced quickly at Nancy who leaned against the car suppressing a laugh. He had absolutely no experience with kids. "Maybe we can share a story or two later," he grumbled, opening the side door of the Jeep.

Malaki leaped out of the back seat nearly knocking over two of the children. Why hadn't he thought of letting Malaki out sooner? He was clearly a hit. The dog and the children all leaped and jumped about and ran around in circles.

"Come on, kids, help us carry in presents and food," Nancy cried. The oldest niece and nephew responded. The others could not be pulled away from Malaki's antics.

Having made it by the children, he found the waiting adults less intimidating. Matt wasn't at all surprised to see that Nancy's family was a hugging family. Everyone had a hug for Nancy and then they stood politely back for her to make the introductions.

First was Nancy's mother, Ellen, who looked a lot like her sister, the President of Blackthorn. She had the same silver hair and regal nose, but she had at least another twenty to thirty pounds making her not quite plump. Her smile was friendly and welcoming; Matt liked her. Her fiancé was next. The guy reminded him of his father – outwardly glib, but very much in control of the situation.

Then it was the older brothers and their wives. The oldest, Henry, had to be six two and two hundred and twenty pounds, an athletic type with sharp eyes. His handshake, while strong, was not as bone crushing as Matt had expected. His wife, Alice, was petite by any standard, but next to her husband she appeared Lilliputian. Her smile was engaging. Nancy probably found her to be a fun companion.

Last was the middle child, Nathan. He was stout and had his mother's nose, though rather than regal, on him it appeared hawkish. He had all the right words of welcome, but Matt had the feeling they weren't particularly sincere. His wife, Kathy, was equal to Nathan in height, but she was as thin as a rail. Maybe some would call it a model's body. In any case, Matt didn't prefer his women that thin. She too, though, was welcoming, and she seemed to mean it.

Apparently, family members had gotten their marching orders. Nancy's companion would be greeted in a friendly manner, at least for the time being.

The evening meal was a buffet of cold cuts, cheeses, breads, veggies, nuts, and eggnog. Much of the evening was spent calming the children down or revving them up about Santa and most of the adults and even the children, with the exception of the youngest, shared stories of special Christmas memories.

Matt enjoyed listening to the stories. He laughed at Nancy's mother telling a childhood memory of thinking Santa was only leaving her coal when she mistook the delivery man – dressed in a red coat, no less – for Santa. His eyes misted when Nancy shared a story of her father bouncing her on one knee while reciting from memory "Twas the Night Before Christmas."

He became anxious when he realized there were only three others remaining who had not yet shared a story. Nancy's family was a fun family to observe, but he didn't fit in with them. What could he offer for a story? He knew they'd expect one.

When it was his turn, the words came of their own volition. "One of my best gifts was a book called, *The Flight of Dragons*. I was eight years old. It was a rich and wonderful book and had lots of detail about exactly how dragons fly – using the same gases that they use to breathe from. It sure was high adventure for me – we hardly even went to movies, and we had no TV."

"No TV!" Michael said, aghast.

Matt smiled at the boy and continued, "That book was probably the seed that began my quest for more knowledge of ancient cultures and myths."

"Without that book, you wouldn't be sitting here with us tonight." Nancy's voice was unusually quiet and he couldn't read the soft expression on her face.

"I suppose you're right. Every little step along the way shapes us in one way or another. But," he turned to speak to the children, "I want you to know this was a fun book. I couldn't stop reading, and I finished it by bedtime on Christmas night. Of course, I started rereading it the next morning."

The children applauded and were joined by the adults. "I want to get that book, professor," Michael said, coming to stand before Matt. "It sounds exciting. I especially like books about the Knights of the Round Table."

"Me too," Matt replied, absently brushing back a lock of hair from the boy's forehead. "I expect in my library I have just about every book written on the subject that's available to the public."

"Really!" The boy's eyes grew huge. "I'd sure like to see that library."

"It's big," Nancy chimed in. "I can tell you that. Maybe you'll get to see it sometime." She glanced at the clock over the fireplace. "Now, it's time for our Christmas Eve ritual. Who wants to choose the first song?"

"Me! Me!" cried the girls, leaping to their feet and waving their arms.

"Okay, what will it be, Alicia?"

"Jingle Bells! Jingle Bells!"

"All right, gang, Jingle Bells it is."

Bewildered, Matt watched Nancy rise to direct her family in song. She was good with the children...and with everyone. Clearly, all the family members had expected her to take charge and lead them through this Christmas ritual. They must have sung a dozen songs and carols, some he'd never heard before.

He leaned back in his chair and closed his eyes and listened. Even above the noise and the off key voices, he could pick out Nancy's lilting pitch like the goddess of the lake singing her song of hope.

After *Silent Night* was sung, Nathan read the traditional biblical account of the Bethlehem story. To conclude the evening just as the clock hands approached midnight, Henry, as his father had for so many years, read *Twas the Night Before Christmas*. The children sat attentive and bug-eyed, except the youngest who was sound asleep on her mother's lap. By the time Henry turned the final page, the adults discreetly dabbed at their eyes.

Nancy, who had come to sit on the floor in front of Matt, rested her head on his knee and gently squeezed his hand. Matt couldn't remember a more serene family moment.

To his surprise, Matt woke early the next morning well rested. He glanced over at Nancy's travel alarm. Six-forty-five A.M. He'd been told the night before that the children couldn't be expected to wait past seven to come downstairs. Christmas morning at his house had seldom started before ten. They'd always waited to exchange gifts until after breakfast. This family could never wait that long.

Nancy was already out of bed and apparently downstairs or out with the dog. It had felt strange going to bed with her knowing her family was scattered across the other bedrooms, but then her mother had made no particular justification for her fiancé joining her in her bed, either.

Nancy had giggled at him before drifting off to sleep. He'd lain stiffly beside her, unwilling to respond to any overtures. She'd whispered in his ear, "That's okay. I can wait."

Hurriedly, he dressed and descended the stairs to the living room where most of the family was already gathered. A pleasant fire of real logs burned in the fireplace. The noise level was already ear-popping with the children chattering and begging to open their presents early.

Nancy saw him enter, waved him to a seat next to her and held out a coffee mug, which he gratefully accepted. He greeted all the smiling faces with a nod. At least, he wasn't the last one to arrive. Five minutes later Nathan walked into the room and settled next to his wife to the cheers and applause of all the children – young and old. Matt glanced at the clock on the mantel; it wasn't quite seven, but no one seemed to mind that.

Handing out the presents started in a fairly calm manner. For the first round everyone, even the children, waited for each person to open a present and say thank you.

After that, things deteriorated into a free-for-all. The oldest child, who had handed out the presents, opened an electronic game and was lost to the gathering. Another child stepped into the vacancy, but picked only her own presents. And from there things went down hill quickly.

Parents chastised and then shook their heads. Nancy and her mother shouted encouraging words to the children, fostering further anarchy. Matt kept his feet tucked under his chair and his hands folded, trusting that the chaos hitting the family would eventually subside.

And it did, once the nieces and nephews were occupied with dolls, electronic games, trucks, or robotic toys. He had had no idea such a sophisticated range of toys existed.

Henry took over handing out the remaining gifts to the adults. Matt was surprised to receive a crystal Christmas tree ornament from Nancy's mom. It was the first such ornament he'd ever owned. He didn't tell Nancy's mother he never bothered with a Christmas tree. Nancy had been shocked that he hadn't decorated for Christmas, but he'd been adamant about not wanting to mess up his place, particularly since they weren't going to be there anyway.

He watched carefully as Nancy unwrapped the present from him. She attacked the wrapping just like the kids had. When she saw the book on Celtic myths and lore, she laughed gaily and glanced across her shoulder at him.

"I love it," she said aloud. "How romantic," she jibbed softly, just for him to hear. "I'm sure there will be stories of warriors and goddesses, of lust and love." Nancy looked at her mother. "I may yet find some of the stories grandmother was so fond of telling us."

"You may at that. Your grandmother was very enamored with her Welsh heritage."

"Maybe we should take a trip to Wales and the Isles," Jack said. "I was talking to the professor last evening. He knows of several places where digs are ongoing. I've always wanted to volunteer and try my hand at one."

"Marvelous idea, darling," Nancy's mother replied. "Maybe Matt can be our trip consultant. Better yet, maybe he and Nancy might want to join us."

Matt couldn't help it. He felt his ears turning red under the stares of all the adults in the room. What was he supposed to say or do? He had no idea. He turned to Nancy. She smiled.

"Maybe someday," she said evenly.

Whew. He was off the hook. Henry's eyes sparkled as he handed Matt a present. The tag said to Sir Knight Matt from the Goddess of the Snow.

225

Matt hunkered down and removed the bow and then slid the tie from the wrapping.

"Hurry up, Bayfield. Other people still want to open presents," Nancy chided, poking him lightly on the thigh.

Not to be deterred, Matt took his time with the wrapping. He peered into the box and frowned, not certain what he was looking at. He lifted it up. It was some kind of jacket and pants.

"It's to keep you dry in the snow," Nancy said.

"Oh." Then he remembered it was on the same order as the red suit she wore cross country skiing. She'd said it was great material for keeping the body dry and protected from the wind. "Thanks," he said, grinning at last. "Sounds like I'll need this before the week is out."

"You bet. It'll come in quite handy. Trust me."

Matt nodded. When had he last heard her say that? It generally meant trouble, embarrassment or both. He watched her redirect her attention toward her mother who was unwrapping a gift.

"Nancy Ellen Appleby," the woman shrieked, holding up a wood carving of what Matt assumed was a duck and three ducklings. "You shouldn't have. This is lovely. I'll put it on the mantel at home."

Matt's ears strained and then collapsed. Nancy Ellen Appleby. Appleby. He looked at her. Glacially, her head turned toward him. She could not have been more ashen if she'd seen a ghost. He watched her wet dry lips before whispering, "It'll be okay, Matt. I'm sorry. I'll explain later."

Matt forced himself to remain in the chair. He wanted to dash out of the house and gulp in some of that cold air she was so fond of. Maybe that would slow his heart rate some.

He didn't even know her name. She hadn't trusted him enough to tell him her damn name. What had she taken him for? Surely, she knew he had nothing to do with the rapes. What else hadn't she told him?

He closed his eyes. It didn't matter now. Nothing mattered.

The rest of the morning and early afternoon passed smoothly enough with Matt existing in a kind of altered state. No one else seemed to notice, except Nancy. She knew, but thankfully she also knew enough to let him be. It surprised him how well he could carry on conversations with perfect strangers while his insides hemorrhaged.

After dinner, the women turned to cleaning and packing. A weatherman had predicted the storm, which had stalled over Duluth, would reach the Mercer area that evening. Everyone except Matt and Nancy were hurriedly preparing to head south before the bad weather arrived.

Matt slipped outside and took Malaki for a stroll. It was going to be his misfortune to be marooned in snow banks as high as the house, according to the Applebys, with a woman who didn't trust him enough to tell him her name.

He and the dog walked a half mile into the woods and then turned back toward the house.

All the way, he'd been whipping himself for lousy judgment. He should have known better; he *had* known better. Somehow he'd allowed himself to fall under the spell of the mysterious woman. She'd looked too much like the Celtic goddesses of his dreams – dreams he rarely admitted, even to himself. Yet there she was as if appearing out of the mists of Avalon.

Matt kicked at a clump frozen snow. Why couldn't she trust him? He'd already become too fond of her. There was a kind of warmth about Christmas, the way her family celebrated it, that he longed for. Or was it just *her* warmth that clouded his ability to be rational?

But no more. His mind was clear and his own again. He'd insist on returning to Trillium as soon as the roads were clear. Then he could get on with his life, absent a certain female detective who played a game he wanted out of as quickly as possible.

Large snowflakes already swirled about before a growing wind. At the edge of the woods, Matt brought Malaki to an abrupt halt to prevent stumbling into an animated conversation between Nancy's brothers. The cars were loaded with packages and suitcases.

Nathan leaned against his SUV and dragged deeply on a cigar, letting smoke curl out of his nostrils. "Felt damn funny last night knowing we had strange men in the house."

"Yeah," Henry agreed, "but Mom and Sis would've batted ours ears but good if either one of us said anything."

Nodding, Nathan said, "The wives would've been down on us too. Impotent, that's what we are. In our own family. Impotent!"

Henry laughed, lightly punching his brother on the shoulder. "That may be a little strong, given all the little Applebys running around here." He shook his head. "Oh, I know what you mean. But I expect it's for the best. Mom's not that old. Hell, she could live another thirty years or more. Too long to live alone."

"Suppose you're right. The guy's not my type, but he seems to care for her a lot."

"And she for him. As far as Nancy is concerned," Henry heaved a deep sigh, "it's about time. Oh, I don't imagine she's exactly been a nun since the divorce, but in five years time she's never brought a man to meet any of us."

Matt's breath caught in his windpipe. Could that be true?

Nathan ground the cigar butt in the snow. "She's always been on the wild side." He chuckled. "Hell, we trained her well. But it's good to see her relax some and enjoy life. She's had a rough go these past several years."

What else wasn't she telling him? And why should he care? Was he really the first man she'd brought home? But that was happenstance. Wasn't it? She certainly hadn't made a habit of brandishing her lovers before her brothers.

"He just better not hurt her," Nathan said.

"I'm more worried the other way around,"

Henry countered, "I hope she doesn't maim him or scare him off. He makes a nice contrast with Frank. I think this guy's more her type."

"Really?"

"Really. There's a feminine side to our sister that the professor is drawing out. He treats her like a woman, not like a cop. She wasn't nearly as combative with either of us. And she even seemed to enjoy working in the kitchen."

"Nancy?"

"Uh, huh."

"Maybe the guy's a miracle worker."

Aghast, Matt watched the two men lumber back toward the house.

A miracle worker? Hardly. He was drawing her feminine side out? Maybe. In any case, he hadn't disgraced himself with Nancy's brothers. They'd hardly talked to him, but apparently they'd been busy scrutinizing.

He bent down to scratch Malaki sitting at his side. "So now what?" he muttered. "Mal, I need some advice. I was ready to go toe to toe with your mistress, but now I don't know. What's been troubling her so much these five years? Her father killed, a divorce – that should be enough. But I'd bet you a bag of dog biscuits there's more. Ms. Crane – no, Ms. Appleby is turning out to be one complex chick."

Mal growled softly and took a step toward the house pulling on his leash.

Matt stood beside Nancy in the doorway of the

farmhouse and waved at her family until they were out of sight. He turned as if to retreat to the living room. Nancy grabbed his arm stopping him and tucked her arm through the crook of his.

She looked up at him with tears in her eyes. "I'm sorry, so sorry," she said, biting her lower lip.

Unable to withstand the pain on her face, Matt looked away. He walked to the living room and plopped down on the couch. Nancy followed but remained standing. She folded her hands at her waist; her shoulders slumped. Matt had never seen her so remorseful. "Why didn't you just tell me your name?" he asked, trying not to sound too accusatory.

Nancy shrugged shifting her weight from foot to foot. She shook her head and turned her palms face up. "I never thought about it," she confessed.

"Never thought of it?" Matt couldn't help sounding incredulous. "How could you forget a thing like that?"

"It's not an excuse, but I can get so completely into a role that I sometimes forget who I am." She could not interpret his silence. "I imagine a part of me wanted to forget. I was your Ms. Crane; you were my Professor Bayfield. It was fanciful. There was an unreality about us that felt good. Maybe I didn't want to burst our bubble." She slumped to the floor in front of him.

"The bubble is certainly burst now."

"I know." She dropped her gaze. "So now what?"

"I don't know." Matt thought back to the

conversation he'd overheard between Nancy's brothers. What else was she holding back? What wounds did those sad eyes conceal?

This wasn't the time to push, or the time to be the bully – though he'd sure like to stay angry with her. He'd like to make her feel guilty about not trusting him. But then given what she'd just said, maybe she didn't trust herself. What he'd really like to do was make unhurried, uncomplicated love to Nancy Appleby.

He breathed deeply and held out a hand. She reached for it and he squeezed her fingers between his. He couldn't totally ignore the tears streaming down her face, but he knew she wasn't ready to share more of her story. "So where did the name Crane come from? I sort of grew to like it, though Appleby is a fine name too."

"It's my grandmother's maiden name." Nancy rubbed her eyes with her knuckles and managed a wan smile. "Although tiny, she was a giant of a woman. I often use her name when I'm undercover. It's sort of like a blanket of protection and strength – I've come to treasure it a lot, actually. Like I'm wrapped in one of her quilts."

"Then it's appropriate. You know you don't have to worry about me telling anyone your real name."

"I know," she sniffled. "It was never a matter of not trusting you. Can you forgive me?"

Giving her a wicked smile, Matt rose and drew her to her feet. "That might require some time and any number of acts of penance, but I think I'll probably find it in my heart to forgive."

Nancy hugged him tight. He breathed the scent of her hair so deeply he thought he might float. Her tongue played at his neck just above the sweater collar. "Maybe we ought to go upstairs so I can begin doing penance." She snickered against his chest, "I wouldn't want to risk a change of heart."

Chapter Eleven

Nancy looked over her shoulder at Matt and broke into a wide grin.

He was still following some thirty yards behind her. He looked like an oversized, waddling blue frog in the new ski outfit she'd given him for Christmas. First time snowshoers were seldom graceful. Satisfied, she waited for him to catch up. Bayfield was turning out to be a great sport after all.

She warmed, remembering she hadn't even worn him out doing penance the night before. Over fourteen inches of snow had fallen during the night; they'd watched it fall and blow before a stiff wind at intervals during her various acts of contrition. She'd never realized penance could be so much fun.

This was an invigorating crystal clear morning. The late morning breeze, although frigid, was tolerable and complemented the fresh snow sparkling like a field of diamonds. Mr. Arrington, their neighbor, hadn't come by to plow out the driveway yet. He would get to it when he had the time. They were in no rush.

It would take them much of the day, unless Bayfield could keep up better, to prepare a cross country ski trail. A lot of folks used snowmobiles to do that; Nancy liked doing it the old fashioned way, with snowshoes. It was a lot of work, but it was much quieter and provided for some excellent exercise.

Matt, breathing raggedly, plodded to a halt behind her. He had every right to look tuckered. They'd already packed over a mile of trail. There was still another half mile to go on the way back to the house. One segment of the trail would be ready for skiing.

"This is harder work than I ever imagined." Matt grabbed his knees and gasped for air. "And it has to be harder for you breaking trail."

"It's fun. You'll feel some burning in the hamstrings and may have some hip pointers by the time we're finished." She looked out across the open meadow. "I love it here. Look, you can already see where the deer have come and gone. Their trails always remind me of that kid's game in the snow, Duck-Duck-Goose."

Matt shook his head, leaning on the ski poles for support. "Never heard of it."

"Probably not a popular game in sunny California. It's a form of tag but all the players have to stay on paths in the snow that look like deer trails."

"Okay. How much farther do we have to go?"

"Another half mile or so for today. If you're up for it, we can ski this afternoon. Or we can wait until tomorrow. I may come out later and break more trail. Of course a problem we have with grooming our own trails is dealing with the wind. We could come out here tomorrow morning and all of this work might be drifted over. Sometimes I can't even find the track I was working on."

"But if you like snowshoeing, it doesn't really matter?"

"That's right. So how do you like it?"

"At first, I thought it was the craziest thing I'd ever tried, but once I sort of got the hang of it, it's really great. I don't have the speed you have, but I can already feel the tightening on the muscles. And you're right, it's magical being out here without a sound other than birds and your own breathing. I'm not saying I'm a fan of winter, but hanging around you is at least making it tolerable."

"We're going to make winter more than tolerable." Nancy gave him a wide grin. "We're coming up on a grove of spruce that's very well protected from the wind. Follow me!"

- o -

"This is one of my favorite places, no matter what the season," Nancy said, nearing the grove. "No matter the time of year, there's something awesome about these big old spruces. I sit under them in the summer and it's the coolest place around. If it rains, no problem; they are a giant umbrella. In the winter, the wind hardly penetrates and soft needles provide a springy bed."

Matt didn't doubt this place was special one bit. The clump of spruce had the look and feel of the kinds of groves he'd read about and seen in

Ireland and Wales.

He followed the woman bedecked in a red ski suit breaking a path through a four foot snow drift running some thirty feet in length. Beyond it were the spruces where the snow might have been only eight or ten inches deep, but even that was hard to tell given the bed of needles and boughs the snow barely covered. It was as if they'd entered a white cocoon isolating them from the world they'd just left behind.

Nancy bent down and released the snowshoe bindings and Matt followed suit. As they moved to the center of the spruce grove, Matt's throat tightened. It was like being in the middle of an ancient dance of stone, only this dance was composed of spruce trees. He didn't have a vocabulary imaginative enough to fully describe the place or his feelings about being here and being here with Nancy Appleby.

"I can see this place has already drawn you into its mystique," Nancy said softly. "I'm pleased. I've been coming here ever since I was a little girl. Some of the trees on the edge weren't any bigger than I was. But they've matured."

"And so have you."

"Yes, in some ways, but I still like to dream little girl dreams when I sit under these boughs – of a knight on a great steed coming to rescue me."

"You do have a vivid imagination."

"This is my favorite tree," Nancy crawled under a huge spruce that had to be very old and stretched out on spruce boughs that shifted with her weight. Had the boughs fallen that way, or had she arranged them? She held out her hand inviting him to join her.

Without breaking the silence, he stretched out beside her. The bed of boughs flexed accommodating his weight.

They lay there with their heads tucked up against the tree trunk. Without saying a word, Nancy pointed above them. It was uncanny, but through the boughs he saw a patch of blue sky. Was that the canopy of heaven so many of the ancients had talked about?

This was a charmed place, almost surreal. There was no wind. The layer of snow on the boughs added to the illusion of having a blanket of warmth. Maybe he'd crossed into the non-ordinary reality of the shaman. He caught a glimpse of Nancy out of the corner of his eye. There was nothing ordinary about that woman either.

"So," Nancy said, "has my knight recovered enough from snowshoeing to make love to his damsel?"

"You don't look particularly distressed."

"I'll only be distressed if you don't make love to me within the next five minutes."

"Well," said Matt, his voice thickening, "a knight can't let that happen. But I'm not sure how to begin. You seem to be under a lot of wraps."

"No problem. Ski clothes are made so rescue teams can easily get to broken legs and such. Secondarily, they're made for minimal exposure for winter lovemaking." As she made the last comment, Nancy began unzipping the zipper down the side seam of one pant leg. Then she did the same to the other. When she had them parted she flipped down the front flap. "*Voila!* The target is in sight."

"I'll be damned."

"These long johns aren't coming down until I see you're prepared, Sir Knight. Your zippers work the same way. And now you know why it works best to only have long johns under the ski outfit."

"Yes, I understand." Matt knelt to unzip the side zippers on his pants. The boughs beneath him sprang up and down with the shifting of his weight.

His nostrils flared when Nancy reached cold fingers inside his long johns to claim his erection. The sudden chill from the cold only made him harder.

"Men have it easy," said Nancy, pushing her thermals down around her ankles. "It may not be pretty, but it'll work. Hurry," she demanded, "the sooner you cover me the warmer we both will be."

He guided his shaft to her crevice. Nancy lifted her hips, aiding his entry. Matt closed his eyes tight, not believing her heat, not believing what they were doing, not believing they were lying there encircled by trees flocked with heavy snow. The grove had become a feminine vortex, and he reveled in it.

"Are you getting cold?" he murmured at last.

The question must sound inane, but he desperately had to hold onto what was real for fear of being transported to a place from which he could not return. Cold was real.

Nancy giggled. "Hardly. You're generating enough heat for two women. So are you convinced people can make love in the snow?"

"Absolutely." He nuzzled her neck and felt her pull away.

"A tip, Sir Knight. We don't want to get each other wet with a lot of kissing. The air is colder than you think. I'm not up for ice crystals on my neck."

"Oh, sorry."

"But I am up for more action from where you see that steam rising between us."

Matt's eyebrows arched at the little wisps of steam rising from where they were joined. That image ignited him to a slow steady movement in and out of her body. With her legs more encumbered than usual, she joined him in this dance among the spruce by flexing her abs and raising her hips to meet and encourage him. She giggled again. He stopped. "What now?"

"I couldn't help but wonder what your students would think if they could see their professor now."

He plunged harder. He wanted her to focus on them, not on his students. Her eyes blinked open and closed; he had her complete attention. The spruce bough bed acted like a mighty spring, making deep penetration easy. With satisfaction, he watched Nancy's eyes go wide and her mouth contort.

"Go for it!" she howled. She grabbed his butt, adding more strength to his thrusts. The spasms started low from some hidden place in his body and then rose, propelling his loins, pushing him until he spilled without finesse into Nancy's body. He collapsed on her gasping for air. She clutched him tightly.

"Winter," he said between deep breaths, "is becoming quite tolerable."

- o -

Several days later, Nancy sat at the kitchen table reading her Christmas book on Celtic myths. Matt sat across from her cranking out a course syllabus on his laptop. She was amazed at how quickly the man could type. She couldn't think that fast, and if she could, her fingers would never be able to keep up.

The two of them had become quite comfortable with each other on this trip. Any early doubts about the wisdom of spending the vacation together had been long forgotten. She hadn't felt like she had to entertain him every minute of the day. He was quite capable of doing things by himself and had requested occasionally some alone time to work on his next semester courses. They skied or snowshoed daily. With the driveway plowed, they would go into town later in the day to buy groceries for the remainder of their stay.

At that moment, Matt looked up from his work. "What's wrong? You look sad."

She brightened. "Didn't mean to disturb you. I just realized we only have three days left before we have to head back to Trillium."

"It has been real nice here. Laid back. You've stretched me every which way with these winter sports. I'm having a much better time than I predicted – plus..." His voice trailed off. "Plus just getting to know you."

"Even the silences. You're easy to be with. Most men aren't."

"Sounds like a voice of great experience."

Nancy felt herself blush. "I don't know about that, but most men I've known want to be on the move all the time, or plopped down in front of the TV, or at least they want to be in charge."

Matt looked thoughtful. "Guess I'm not most men. Hope that doesn't disappoint you too much."

"Not at all."

"Good." Matt punched several keys and Nancy heard the familiar tones of his computer signing off. "So," he asked, with a quirky smile, "woman of great experience, how many men have you made love to in the spruce grove?"

Nancy burst out laughing and closed her book. "I was wondering if you'd ever ask. You were the first."

"Come on." Matt scowled in disbelief.

"It's true. My ex wasn't into outdoor sex at all.

243

And you're the only other man I've brought here."

She couldn't read his facial expression – surprise, elation, distrust. "I'm honored," he said at last. He bowed his head and then looked up meeting her gaze. "Will you ever stop surprising me?"

"Maybe not," she replied, ducking away from his intensity. *Careful,* she cautioned. H*ave fun, but don't lead him on. This has been a good break, but as soon as the rape case is solved Professor Bayfield will go his way and you will go your way.*

"So...I've been meaning to ask you about the rapist," she asked. "Why do you suppose he didn't strike when we expected him to?"

Matt's brow furrowed. She wasn't certain he knew why she'd deliberately switched the conversation, but he surely knew she had.

"Could be any number of reasons, I suppose. I have wondered about that. Maybe it was simply the bad weather, though I expect not."

"Me too. This guy seems more driven than to be easily deterred by bad weather. A blizzard maybe, but not a simple snow storm."

"I expect the reason can be found by looking back to June, when there was no attack."

"How so?" Nancy leaned forward on her elbows, her chin resting in her hands.

"Balance. Harmony. Polarity. All fundamental Celtic concepts. Whatever happened to cause him to miss in June made December impossible – he had to maintain universal harmony and balance."

"You mean, by not attacking in June, if he did

so in December there would be an imbalance," she said, swallowing hard.

"Exactly. The universe would be out of whack because the Summer Solstice is exactly half way around the calendar from the Winter Solstice. They hold each other in balance, in harmony."

Nancy leaned back in her chair. "It fits. This guy is a control freak. Can you imagine how much control it must take to rape only at certain times and then not to rape because of the needs of the universe? I don't know which is scarier – the fact that we're dealing with a serial rapist, or that we're dealing with a guy who is so in control of his own urges."

"What happens if he snaps? If he loses control?"

Nancy shuddered. "We've got to catch him before that happens.

Nancy held up a small wood carving of a loon from the shop display case for Matt to see. "It'd look good on your office desk." She saw him wince, but she didn't back off. "It could be a memento of this trip, and you would remember me whenever you look at your desk."

Matt started to speak and then stopped.

Nancy continued, "Of course, you may already think of me when you look at your desk." She sighed longingly. "That *was* one to remember. Well, I'm buying you the loon, whether you want it or not. Is there anything else you'd like while we're here?"

Shaking his head, Matt said, "Not a thing. Do they actually sell all this stuff?"

"Tourists are always looking for souvenirs and novelty gifts. You'd be surprised at the volume of business "Loons R Us" does. You can get everything from key chains to scented toilet paper, from scarves to heart shaped panties, from first class reprints to replica Coca-Cola signs. Surely, there must be something here you desire."

"Think I'll simply savor the experience," he said dryly, shying away from a display of men's pajamas in loon print.

The bell over the front entrance jangled. Nancy looked up and beamed.

"Nancy!" a woman shrieked.

Holding out her arms, Nancy embraced her long time friend, Laura Metell.

"How have you been? Did you come up for Christmas? When do you have to leave? Why haven't you called?"

When Laura ran out of breath, Nancy said, "I've been great. Yes, we came up for Christmas. I'm sorry I haven't called." She glanced at Matt. "I've been pretty busy."

Laura followed her gaze and seemingly for the first time noted the presence of a man standing by Nancy. She stepped back, pushed her glasses up her nose and stared hard at Matt. "Oh wow," she said at last, "you've got a beau."

Nancy gave Matt credit for not running. She wasn't sure when she'd last heard the term beau, but then that was Laura. They'd known each other for years, ever since Nancy spent much of her childhood summers with her grandparents at the cabin. She and Laura used to hang out together. They'd compared notes about boys and shared their dreams. Laura had wanted to travel the world and be a geologist. She did work for the Department of Natural Resources, but she could probably count on both hands the number of times she'd been south of Madison. Laura seemed happy, though, with her husband and three kids. Nancy always had a twinge of jealously around Laura, especially since the divorce.

"So how are you, Laura? You look great."

"A few more pounds, but not bad. Kids are doing well in school. Fred? Fred is Fred. Nothing outrageous, but dependable."

Nancy heard Matt clear his throat. "Oh, let me introduce Matt Bayfield to you. Matt, this is Laura Metell, an old friend."

"Pleased to meet you," Matt said, shaking the woman's hand. "So you live around here?"

"Yep. North of town a few miles. So are you from Point?"

Matt frowned and Nancy jumped in, not wanting to go into why she was temporarily away from Stevens Point, "No, Matt's from Trillium, Minnesota. We met through a mutual friend. So, maybe we can get together yet while I'm here?"

"I doubt it. You won't believe it," she said, conspiratorially, "but Fred is whisking me away – we're leaving the kids with the grandparents – to Branson. Celebrating our tenth wedding anniversary. Can you believe it?" Laura preened. "We're leaving this afternoon. I just dropped in here to give my cousin an extra key to the house."

"Wow! That is big news. And romantic, too."

"I hope so. We'll be gone ten days, but a fair amount of that time will be spent driving."

Nancy saw worry lines forming on her friend's brow. "So what's bothering you?"

"It's going to sound strange. I just hope Fred and I have enough to talk about for ten days alone. We've never done anything like this."

Smothering a giggle, Nancy replied, "It'll work out. You don't have to talk non-stop, you know. Sometimes it's good just to be with someone."

Laura glanced quickly at Matt. "Yeah, I suppose you're right. It's just that usually Fred is just old dependable Fred, and then all of a sudden he shocks the bejeesus out of me."

Laura checked her watch and yelped, "It was good to see you both, but I have to run." She rushed toward the cashier, handed her a key and shouted at Nancy, "I don't want him to leave without me. See you next time you're through."

When they stepped out of the store onto the sidewalk, Matt chuckled. "Maybe that loon is an appropriate memento."

"How so?" Nancy grinned, placing her arm through his.

"Loony. I'm beginning to wonder whether you and all your friends aren't just a bit loony."

Nancy tugged at Matt as they strolled down the sidewalk stride for stride. "And does that bother you?"

"Not in the least. It's rather refreshing, actually."

- o -

"Damn, Bayfield, you're a good shot. Who would've ever guessed?" Nancy said, peering through binoculars toward the bull's-eye target a hundred yards away. "You've got five shots within an inch of one another just a little to the right and above the center of the target. Are you sure you've never shot a rifle before?"

"Never. Beginner's luck, maybe." Matt flipped on the safety and emptied the chamber and then handed Nancy the Remington two-seventy bolt action, her favorite deer rifle.

They stood inside a sandpit located on the north side of the Appleby farmstead. It was where Nancy's dad had first taught her how to shoot a twenty-two rifle. She and her brothers had often tried out new guns or tuned up old ones in this protected space.

She laid the rifle down on the army blankets they'd spread out on the ground and began to break down the arm rest Matt had used to help steady the rifle. It had been fairly ideal shooting conditions, but she'd seen many people screw it up. Surprisingly, he hadn't backed away at all from the recoil.

She saw triumph in his eyes. He hadn't wanted to come along with her while she practiced shooting. Reluctantly, he'd joined her and more reluctantly he'd risen to her goading him to give it a try. From his looks, he might be more amazed by the results than she was.

Once Nancy had the range cleared, she walked out and retrieved the target Matt had been shooting at and placed a similar target a hundred feet from the shooting position. She handed Matt the target. He whistled lowly when he saw the cluster of bullet holes. "No man or beast," she said, "would have survived those placements."

He folded the target and put it in his back pocket. "I expect shooting at a target is a lot different than shooting at something that's alive."

"Or at someone who is trying to shoot back." He flinched, but said nothing. "So, Bayfield, why were you perusing a book on guns when I found you that day in the bookstore?"

Matt pulled his cap lower over his eyes. "Oh that. I was trying to figure out why a stunning young woman would be carrying a gun in her purse. Thought there had to be some appeal. I never thought of the obvious."

"May not be so obvious. I think more women carry guns than most folks realize. Anyway," she said, reaching into a canvas bag. "We're going to try something different now. A little more challenging." She pulled out a smaller case, opened it and hefted a revolver. She laughed at Matt's eyes widening; he took a step backward.

"That's not your service revolver?"

"No. I could get in trouble letting you use that.

This is a spare. Sometimes I use it as a backup. We're not supposed to do that either, but there are occasions when you don't want to go into an area without a second weapon. Here, hold this while I get some ammo."

Gingerly, he wrapped his fingers around the handle of the pistol. Out of the corner of her eye, she saw him nearly drop it. A lot of folks never expected a handgun to weigh so much.

"I'm not sure I'm up for this," he protested, when she stood back up with a handful of bullets. "A rifle is one thing; a pistol is very different."

"Nonsense." She dropped all but one shell in her pocket. "I'll just put one bullet in at a time. You'll do fine."

She took the revolver back and shoved a bullet in the chamber. "Now the trick here is to brace yourself, because this little sucker packs a bit of a wallop."

Nancy placed her left foot in front of her, raised her arms and pointed the gun toward the target. "Flex your joints – knees, elbows, don't lock them in place. They need to absorb the recoil. Sight down the barrel using the iron sight as you did on the rifle. And as before, squeeze. Don't pull." She did as she instructed. The firing of the gun was accompanied by a whoosh and a loud report. A sizeable hole appeared at the target's center.

Nancy took a replacement target to the hundred foot marker and again retraced her steps to Matt. "Didn't look so hard, did it?"

"You're a pro."

"That's right, and I'm also a licensed instructor. So listen carefully. Here we go." She made sure the safety was on before slipping in a fresh cartridge.

Nancy handed him the gun and he took it tentatively. "Take a couple deep breaths," she advised.

He did as she said. "When you're ready, get into the stance I showed you. That's good. Flip off the safety, sight down the length of the barrel and squeeze."

The gun went off and Matt staggered backwards. "Holy shit! That's more than a little recoil," he said sharply, glaring at her in disgust. "You could've done a little more to warn me about that."

Nancy repressed a laugh. "I could've talked to you about it for an hour, but until you experienced it you wouldn't have known what I was talking about. Now then, it doesn't look like you damaged the target at all on that one. The key is to relax into the shot. Yes, you have to hold the gun steady, but don't tense all up like you're trying to cling to the tail of a runaway tiger. Hand me the gun and I'll reload."

"Here we go again," she said shortly.

Matt aimed the gun barrel at the target. "Don't forget to breathe," she said.

She admired the sheer determination etched on his jaw.

Again the gun fired. Matt stood his ground.

"Much better," Nancy praised. "That wasn't so

bad was it?"

"Felt smoother." Matt peered dubiously at the target. "Is that a hole? Did I put that hole in it?"

"Do you see me holding a gun?" She was pleased to hear the glee in his voice. If nothing else after this day, he wouldn't be afraid of guns. She wanted him to respect guns, but not fear them or shrink back every time he saw her weapon.

Matt handed her the revolver and jogged out to retrieve the target. "Not dead center, but at least on the target," he shouted, holding up the bull's-eye for her to see.

"Very good, for a second try. If you had a guy coming at you with a gun, you certainly would have stopped him."

Matt immediately sobered, slowing his stride. "I don't think I want to think about that. This seeing if I can hit a target is kind of fun. But beyond that..." He shook his head.

Smiling, Nancy put a hand on his shoulder when he joined her. "That's all right. I'm not trying to turn you into a cop. Just thought we'd satisfy some of your curiosity and give you a little window into how safe what I do really is."

"If that's what you intended, I'm not sure it worked. Guns are as dangerous as I expected them to be. I may have more respect for what you do, but I still worry about the nutcases who can be found on the other end of a gun."

Unsmiling, Nancy knelt to recase the revolver. "We've probably done enough for one day. You're right, of course. In my line of work, you never know who will be on the other end of a gun. But I did hope you'd find this useful."

Scooping up a couple tote bags, Matt said, "I'm glad you showed me this side of things, of your life. I'm just not sure I'd ever want to shoot anything." A wisp of a smile worked across his lips. "Of course, I wouldn't mind competing with you in shooting targets if the rewards were substantial enough. And then you'd have to give me a load of points to begin with given the discrepancy in experience."

"That could likely be arranged, Professor Bayfield," Nancy replied, trudging out of the sandpit toward the trail leading back to the house. She was pleased he'd at least tolerated this part of her. Guns, to her, were about as basic as breathing.

Somehow, she expected, Bayfield had just passed a test she hadn't even known she'd set up. "You know why you're good at this, don't you?"

"Tell me."

"You have slow, steady hands."

- o -

Matt nuzzled the back of Nancy's neck. Without dislodging himself from her heated core, he nibbled on her shoulders. Her moans gratified his senses. They'd initially made the kind of fierce love Nancy seemed to like best, but now it was his turn to lead them at a more leisurely pace through an erotic maze. This was their last night at the cabin; he wished it could last forever.

They lay like two spoons cupped and joined. He wrapped one hand around a breast while softly teasing Nancy's aroused clit with the other. She pressed against him, demanding more. Ignoring her demands, he eased in and out of her tight channel only to pause again. He brushed her dark hair aside and leisurely grazed an earlobe. The sounds coming from her lips were those of surrender. At last, he felt the tension ebb from her body; she was receiving what he had to offer without trying to get him to move faster or harder.

He seated himself deep and stayed there, not twitching a muscle nor yielding to his own rising pulse. How often had his give and take lover ever allowed herself to simply accept what a man had to offer? Nancy whimpered; he pursed his lips and hummed along her spine. She stretched her arms out in front of her, not interfering at all with his ministrations.

"You're so delicious," he whispered. She mewed a soft response.

He brushed a finger pad against her engorged flesh relishing her quivering hips and legs. He flexed his hips against her buttocks and began a steady cadence. He couldn't delay their pleasure much longer. Soon he was slamming against Nancy's rear and she gasped for breath. Still, she remained passive, receiving. She was the dark-haired goddess yielding her flower; he was the supplicant piercing her with adoration.

She uttered unintelligible sounds. He lost any sense of rhythm or finesse. "I'm lost," he cried out.

"I want to fill you." He shook violently, emptying himself into her depths.

Nancy's body quaked against his and then quieted. He held her close, certain that this time they traversed the outer edges of the universe together.

Tears slipping from Nancy's cheek onto the back of his hand brought him back to a fragmented reality. He inhaled and exhaled shallowly for fear of disturbing her.

"Just hold me," Nancy murmured. Her body continued trembling against his. He heard choking sounds and then Nancy, unable to contain herself broke into a mournful wail. Matt laid his cheek against her back and cuddled her.

Sobs wracked her body. He felt every heave, every constriction. For whatever reason, Nancy Crane Appleby needed to cry. He recalled the night at her apartment when she'd asked him to hold her and then she'd fallen asleep. Would she trust him enough this time to put some words to those tears? It was pure hell not having any clue what was going on.

He lost track of time. The sniffling halted.

"Could you hand me a tissue?" Nancy asked quietly.

Matt carefully dislodged himself from her and rolled over to reach for the tissue box. Nancy took the opportunity to pull herself to a sitting position against propped pillows. She accepted the box without meeting his eyes. She blew loudly into the tissue. He tried not to chuckle. Nothing feminine about that.

She placed the box on the bed beside her. "So, I suppose you're a little curious about all of that."

"A little, but you don't have to tell me."

She placed her fingers in his palm; he stroked them softly. She pulled back. "That's what starts it," she accused.

"What?"

"Don't be hurt. It's just that when…you love me so tenderly, I get all mushy. I start remembering things I don't want to remember."

"Oh." Matt didn't touch her, but hoped she'd clear up the confusion.

"Don't get me wrong. I love it when you go so slow and love me so thoroughly. No one has ever cared enough to take the time. I feel like some kind of treasure you're exploring that you've discovered on some far off desert island."

Matt chuckled. "You may not be so far wrong about that."

Nancy didn't chuckle. "Deserts are also known for mirages. Once I thought I was in a caring relationship. I think I told you my ex wasn't very supportive when my father was killed." Nancy swiped at her eyes. "There's more to the story than that." She looked at him, checking to see if he was listening.

Matt nodded his encouragement.

"I had a miscarriage shortly after my father died. I was only three months along but my dad was so looking forward to the baby. Frank seemed relieved by our misfortune. The baby hadn't been planned and he'd never been thrilled about the idea of being a father. When I first told him," Nancy swallowed hard and paused, "he wanted me to abort. So we could wait a few more years."

Matt recoiled. Had someone slammed a fist in his gut? Nancy's contorted features pulled at his heart; her words were nearly too much to comprehend. What kind of asshole would deny his wife a baby? The bile wasn't from fear; it was from a fierce need to protect. That was a need he didn't even know he possessed. "You don't have to relive it," he said.

"It's okay," she muttered, "I want you to know. I need you to know. I moped around for a couple months. I'd lost purpose, and Frank was constantly in my face about getting over it. How can you turn a switch off and get over the loss of your father and of a baby you hadn't even realized you wanted until you were pregnant? And how I wanted that baby." Nancy reached for another tissue.

"We laughed at Laura the other day, but I'm really very jealous of her. She has three fantastic kids." Nancy grinned a little. "And while Fred might not do much that's outrageous, he's dependable and loves Laura more than anything in the world.

"The final straw came when Frank dragged himself home after a swing shift and a stopover at one of the guy's places for some beers and a little loving on the side. Threw it in my face when he got home. Likely too drunk to know what he was saying, he might as well have handed me the divorce papers. He swore he never did want the damn baby and that he was happy we didn't have to be bankrupted by some damn kid. By the time he hit the bed snoring, I was reaching for a suitcase."

Nancy crawled out of bed, threw on a robe, pulled its sash tight, and took a seat in a chair opposite from Matt. "So Bayfield, you're involved with a more emotionally unbalanced woman than you thought."

"I haven't seen or heard anything that'd suggest that." He looked squarely at her.

She folded her arms under her breasts; her nipples grew taut in response. "I think it's your tender lovemaking that triggers all of this baggage." New tears emerged. "But I don't want you to stop, unless you want to."

Matt was taken back by Nancy's fragility. Was he getting in over his head? Maybe she did have more baggage than he wanted to deal with. Wasn't this his cue for a polite exit?

"So is that why you come up with so many outrageous ways to have sex? So your partner won't really touch you?"

"Whoa, Sigmund," Nancy joked and then quickly sobered. "You may be right, although I enjoy sex most any place, most any time."

"I'm not complaining."

Matt breathed a little easier when Nancy stuck her tongue out at him. "Soooo…where do we go from here?" he asked, not liking the catch in his voice.

Rubbing her forehead, Nancy said, "Continue as we are, I guess. Unless you want out. I'd understand. I'm not saying I'm looking for more than what we have, but I will admit it scares the hell out of me that I've just shared my darkest pain with you. I feel more naked, more vulnerable."

Matt slid off the bed and knelt before Nancy. He placed her hands between the two of his, relieved that she made no effort to withdraw. "You scare me, too."

Her eyes rounded.

His lips curled up at her surprise. "Truthfully, *we* scare me. When you asked me to come over here for Christmas, I was uneasy about being introduced to your family. I should have been more afraid of what might happen if I spent two weeks with you."

"So what happened?" she asked in a husky voice.

"I'm not sure yet. At least I don't want to risk naming it, but I'm not ready for you to walk out of my life either. That I know."

Nancy met his gaze and nodded.

Overcome from exhaustion, Matt rested his head in Nancy's lap. Her fingers weaved in and out of his hair soothing his frayed nerves. Her scent flooded him with promise.

The next morning Nancy sat alone among her spruce friends in the grove. It had always been a place for thinking and for sorting out feelings.

Why had she shared so much of her pain with Matt? His gentleness made it possible. But why? Idly scooping snow into a pile with her gloved hands, Nancy tried to study the situation objectively. She'd never told any man the things she'd said to Matt. She wasn't a woman who needed to bare her soul to a man.

Yet, she'd certainly done that.

Nancy smiled softly at the sound of a pair of ravens calling back and forth overhead. She'd always enjoyed watching the large black birds frolicking in the sky. Mates would play with each other, often swooping into big dives or doing barrel rolls as if to show off. And then there was the incessant chatter whether they were next to each other or a great distance away. It was sounds that allowed them to stay in touch with one another.

She shook her head. It was difficult even for her to acknowledge how much she still grieved the loss of her baby. Not only that loss, but also the loss of knowing her husband had thought the baby was a mistake that should never have happened. And then his relief when she'd miscarried.

She shuddered. That was the past. Why the hell couldn't she leave it there? And why the hell go and dump that crap on Matt?

Again she heard the distant call of the ravens.

Her fingers trembled, but not from the cold. No, it couldn't be. She wouldn't allow that to happen. She'd been in love once, and look how that worked out. Nancy Ellen Appleby knew better than to fall in love again.

Nancy crossed her legs in lotus pose and drifted into meditation seeking stillness, affirmation and direction.

Much later, she slowly opened her eyes. Her body felt like it had turned to jelly. She took several deep breaths. She shrugged. So it was okay. Her world had not shattered just because she'd shared her darkest secret with Matt. And he hadn't run away, at least not yet.

She rose to her feet humming a tune. She was okay, and that didn't necessarily mean she was in love. She was just okay for having named a heavy burden that had been weighing her down.

Love? That was a mystery she'd have to solve on another day. It was enough for now to simply be okay.

- o -

At the kitchen table, Matt stared unblinking at the blank computer screen. He knew Nancy had gone to the spruce grove, and he knew why. She regretted telling him about the miscarriage and about the asshole of a husband she'd been married to.

He didn't know how to help her feel all right about telling him. It wasn't like he was going to repeat her secrets to anyone else. Everyone had a secret or two and he honored that.

Wiping dust from between the keys of his laptop, he was stymied about what to do next. Would Nancy go on as if nothing important had been shared? Would she cry again when they made love? Would she want to make love again? And what about that "gentle" nonsense? Did it always have to be fast and furious? Sometimes he wondered if the sensational sex they shared didn't serve as some kind of smokescreen.

But what were they hiding from? From each other? Or from themselves?

Chapter Eleven

"So, Professor Bayfield, it has come to my attention that you are not entirely satisfied here at Blackthorn College."

The president's words were not accusing. So why did Matt find himself cringing inside like a fly caught in a spider web? And who was the white-haired matriarch's information source? Nancy? Maybe.

He took in a deep breath, held it and let it out slowly. Dealing with President Williams – with any college administrator, for that matter – required considerable finesse. If they thought you were good for the institution, they'd flatter you, dangle a lot of incentives, and guarantee little to pry a commitment out of you. Typically, processes worked so slowly at a college or university that promises made or inferred by one administrator, in order to be fulfilled, would have to be carried out by that administrator's successor. And in that transition there was room for a lot of slippage. He'd been around academia all his life. In this instance, he had to be as cautious with the aunt as with the niece.

Matt settled back in the leather chair in the president's office across from an identical chair in which she sat. Clearly, Joan Williams had no need to use the large oak desk as a barrier or as a symbol of authority. Her raised chin evidenced more than enough authority.

Tread cautiously. "Blackthorn was not my first choice when I left graduate school," he said honestly.

"No, I don't suppose it was."

"The town is woefully small and the winters are awful."

"I imagine the winters can become long unless you adapt to winter sports."

Was she playing with him? Her niece thrived on winter sports. The president's poker face gave no hint of what lay behind her interest in his satisfaction with Blackthorn. He forged ahead. "I was hoping to get an offer from a more prestigious school, but I must admit I've been rather surprised at the intellectual curiosity and creativity of the students here at Blackthorn."

"I am pleased, Professor Bayfield, that you remain open to surprises." President Williams idly brushed at the sleeve of her dark blue dress. "Top notch academics must maintain an open mind, or they risk ossifying and missing out on crucial discoveries."

Matt waited. It was time for Joan Williams to play another card. He'd given her an answer. He sure wouldn't want to play high stakes poker with the woman. His spine tingled just a bit. Maybe that's precisely what they were doing, only she hadn't yet told him what the stakes were or what the ante limit was.

President William wrinkled her brow before continuing. "You have excellent student evaluations. I'm impressed. You may not be where you want to be, but you've nonetheless committed yourself to educating our students."

Although pleased with her assessment, Matt kept himself in check. What was the woman really concerned about? Was it the college, or was it her niece?

"I'd also rate your recent work on the impact of Celtic myths in our own time a solid contribution to the field. I'd be surprised if the journals you've submitted to fail to accept your submissions."

"Thank you. I've enjoyed working on them." Obviously, she'd done her own research on his file. So, the question remained, why?

President Williams stood and leaned against the oak desk. "Shall we get on with it?" She smiled knowingly. "You're wondering why I asked you here. Well, I'll tell you. I'm wondering what it will take to keep our creative Matt Bayfield here at Blackthorn. Don't look surprised. If you're not sending out your vita to other schools, you're stupid. And I don't think you're stupid."

She gave him a withering look. "No, you're young, bright and ambitious, and you don't believe Blackthorn has enough to reward you properly. I suspect money is not the issue as much as creative opportunities and academic challenges. Am I right so far, professor?"

Matt crossed his legs. "I suppose so."

"Good. Because I want to explain an opportunity here at Blackthorn that may interest you. And I'd like to solicit your support, if you

267

decide to remain with us."

President Williams picked up a folder from her desk and sat back down opposite him. She opened the folder and glanced at it briefly.

"Blackthorn has received a National Science Foundation grant," she said with a faint smile, "to pilot an interdisciplinary social science team to explore how faculty and select students from various disciplines may study and work together to advance the knowledge base at the undergraduate level in a particular area of joint interest."

Uncrossing his legs, Matt leaned forward. The key words had been *interdisciplinary* and *advance the knowledge* at the undergraduate level. He believed there was much more room for stimulating education for undergraduates if faculty were committed to interdisciplinary teaching approaches. No single department, however, would take scarce funds to support interdisciplinary efforts. You'd have to be at a large research university with a commitment to interdisciplinary work to pull that off. He gave the president a puzzled look. "I don't understand what you're saying."

President Williams smiled regally. "Oh, you understand. You just don't think a small school tucked away in northern Minnesota can attract the necessary funding." She hesitated. "We have the funding – at least for a pilot effort. It's been a pet project of mine along with the Dean of Liberal Arts. Now that we have it, we need someone equally committed to interdisciplinary effort to help us get the project off the ground. Are you interested?"

Matt blinked. She'd clearly played one of her aces. Was he interested? The experience would be helpful wherever he went. And if they could pull this off at Blackthorn, there would be any number of schools around the country who would be interested in him. "How long is the project?" he asked.

"It's a three year commitment. After that, who knows? We may seek more funding, or we may be able to fold components of the project into ongoing efforts. What we're after here, in large part, is to change the attitudes of faculty. A college, particularly an undergraduate school, cannot afford to have its departments deteriorate into small fiefdoms waging turf battles over scarce resources. It does a disservice to the college, faculty and students alike.

"And we want to enrich the undergraduate learning experience. Students exposed to this program should have extremely high rates of acceptance in graduate schools, and that will in turn result in a larger pool of quality applicants for Blackthorn."

President Williams closed the folder on her lap. "We need a coordinator, Professor Bayfield. We do not want an older, entrenched faculty member entrusted with this task. The project would be quickly undermined before it got off the ground. We would be inundated with committee meetings.

No, we want a relatively new, bright individual for the job. We want you. What do you say?"

Matt tried his best to breathe. On one hand this opportunity was incredibly challenging, but how could he continue to do research and publish if he took on an administrative role as well as that of teaching? "What about summer research?"

President William nodded agreeably. "You will have support for your summer research. I hope you'll use the grant, in part, to expand that research. Take several students from different disciplines with you. It could be a summer dig abroad. Students will find it appealing, and your data bases will be enlarged. Of course, we'll cut your regular teaching load in half. You will be adequately compensated for taking on more administrative responsibilities. But this is a three year commitment. I wouldn't want to have to break in a new faculty member every year."

"No, of course not."

"If you do as well as I expect you will, Professor Bayfield, I have no doubt this undertaking will greatly advance your probability of promotion and tenure here at Blackthorn, if you choose to stay."

Ignoring those implications, Matt said, "I'd be a fool not to be interested, President Williams. I'm honored that you'd think of me. How long do I have to think about this?"

"Twenty-four hours."

"Twenty-four hours!" He tried to erase the surprise from his face.

"If you don't want the coordinating position, it's imperative that we find someone who does as quickly as possible."

The determination on Joan Williams' face looked vaguely familiar. What the hell. He didn't have anything else nearly as attractive as what Blackthorn was offering. He could be in the field another ten years before having this opportunity, if then. "There's just one more question I have to ask before making my decision."

Joan Williams emitted an unladylike grunt. "My niece has nothing to do with this offer. We had you in mind for this position before you and she became – what do they say – an item."

"Then I accept." Matt exhaled and grinned. The downside was three more northern Minnesota winters, but he'd survive.

"Good. That pleases me." President Williams clasped her hands in her lap. "Now then, Professor Bayfield, what *are* you intentions regarding my niece?"

Matt felt like he'd been hit by a bowling ball. When he first received a call from President's Williams' secretary to set up this appointment, he figured it had to do with Nancy. But the discussion about the interdisciplinary task force had numbed his senses.

Alarms bells were going off everywhere: in his stomach, his brain, his heart – even his nose twitched. Classes had been back in session for almost two weeks. He and Nancy had found some time in their busy schedules to spend time together – but "intentions?" That word carried a lot more weight than he was ready to think about. "What do you mean?" he managed to stutter.

"For a bright young man, you can be fairly dense at times. I love my niece and I wouldn't want to see her hurt."

"Me either. I wouldn't want to hurt her at all." He stared at the president. "So why did you ask her to come here in the first place? She is in danger, you know."

"Of course, I know." President Williams stood and walked to a window looking out onto a snow covered lawn. Keeping her back to Matt, she said, "I've always known Nancy lived with potential danger on a daily basis. When I asked for her help, I thought naively she'd come and interview people and puzzle this thing out. I never thought she'd turn herself into a target for the rapist." The older woman's shoulders drooped. "Guess that shows you how much I know about police work, or about my niece."

Surprised by Joan Williams' display of emotion, Matt chose not to interrupt the ensuing silence.

At last, President Williams turned to face him. "I admit I've placed her in danger, and I don't like that one bit, but I also know she's been trained to handle the situation. Frankly – and please, Matt, I'm not talking to you now as President of Blackthorn College – what frightens me more is the danger you may unwittingly pose for her."

Matt scowled, not knowing what to say.

"Nancy's been through a lot in recent years.

She's headstrong and adventurous." Joan Williams peered at him and Matt winced. "I can see I'm not telling you anything you don't already know. But there is a side to Nancy that most people don't see. She's emotional and can be quite easily hurt. She may appear so strong to be self-sufficient, but she's not. Nancy has needs, and I'm not certain you can meet them."

"I'm not certain I can either, but I have no intention of hurting her."

"Of course, you don't. I shouldn't be meddling. Nancy would have a fit, if she knew."

"That she would," Matt replied, smiling easily. "*We* may know she's not self-sufficient, but that doesn't mean Nancy knows."

"You may be right about that." President Williams strode to where Matt sat and extended her hand. Matt stood and shook it. "Thank you, professor, for agreeing to work with us on what I believe will become one of the more important curriculum undertakings here at Blackthorn in recent decades. And forgive a concerned aunt for prying."

"No apology needed, and I am looking forward to the interdisciplinary project."

Matt walked out of the president's office hoping he hadn't made a huge mistake. The redefinition of his job would strongly enhance his marketability. Three more years at Blackthorn wasn't all that bad. Even the winters were becoming manageable. He huddled in his parka against a stiff late-January wind. He didn't want to know the wind chill factor. With renewed vigor in his stride, he headed toward his office.

Halfway across the quadrangle, he paused briefly to watch students chipping at huge blocks of ice. Only two days remained until Winter Fest, a joint celebration between the college and the town to mark the coldest time of winter. The focal point of Winter Fest was an ice sculpture competition.

He tilted his head to the side and studied two huge twenty-by-twenty foot ice blocks, but it was too soon to discern a shape. Most of the pieces would be a tribute to the northland or to its voyageur heritage: loons, bears, trappers. From time to time, a college group would throw in its own tribute to Mickey Mouse or on occasion a well disguised ice erotica piece slipped by. It was difficult for him to imagine how or why men and women would spend hours chopping away at ice.

He walked on, mulling over Joan Williams' comments. Nancy had needs. That wasn't news. Didn't everyone? Still, Nancy Appleby was turning out to be an unusually intriguing woman. He liked her, a lot. But when she'd successfully solved the rape cases she'd go back to Wisconsin. Maybe they'd see each other now and then, but that would be that. Matt tightened the hood of his parka.

Nancy had needs. He didn't want to think too long on that topic. But another question swirled in his brain like the blowing snow across the sidewalk. What were Matt's needs vis-à-vis

Nancy? No, he didn't want to go there, either.

- o -

Nancy sat next to Matt at the Winter Fest Ball trying to shake a foreboding mood. They shared a table with Carol Macy and Elizabeth Donne, both of whom were delightful. The four of them had spent a raucous afternoon touring the ice sculptures and craft displays and snacking on fry bread and hot dogs.

Everything from beaded necklaces to elaborate metal display pieces to woven blankets to handmade canoes were available for purchase. Many artists demonstrated their craft-making on site. Matt had been intrigued with the man who carved wood sculptures using only a chain saw. It was about the last thing she could imagine Matt ever doing.

Late in the afternoon, she and Matt had gone back to his place to get ready for the ball. She shivered at the memory of their lovemaking. Maybe it had been due to spending a half day in sub-zero temperatures, but making love with Matt had been particularly warm and tender.

Nancy closed her eyes. Was she fooling herself? Since when had what they shared become lovemaking? Calling it hot sex had been self-protection. Could she risk opening her heart?

Was that the cause of the chill creeping through her body? It had started in her toes. Now, it rested behind her eyes. Tuesday would be Imbolc eve.

275

Would he attack again? Certainly, he knew they were after him. Maybe he'd fled the area. After all, he hadn't raped at the Winter Solstice.

She shook her head. Every instinct in her body told her he hadn't left. Her skin crawled. Her eyes sprang open. The rapist was in the ballroom. That was as certain as the sun rising in the morning.

Carol's laughter jarred Nancy's attention. She scanned the crowd. Over three hundred people packed the college gym. The dim lighting established an atmosphere more appropriate for a dance than for a basketball game. About the only way she'd identify the guy is if walked up and introduced himself. But that didn't mean he wasn't there leaning against a wall, sitting at a table, or dancing. Was he picking out his next victim?

Underneath the table, Matt squeezed her thigh. She looked over at him. "You okay?" he asked.

She nodded and shrugged. "I'm back. Sorry about that. You want to dance?"

He tilted his head and listened to the music. "Sure, why not. It's a slow one. You've worn me out on the fast pieces."

Matt made a pathway to the dance floor. She moved into his arms and rested her head on his shoulder. She liked the familiarity of her breasts crushed against his chest and his fingers resting on the rise of her buttocks. They weaved slowly along the perimeter of the dance floor. This was very good. Her aunt had insisted they attend the Ball. She knew Matt had questioned the propriety of coming since he was a professor and she was nominally a student. But Aunt Joan had said "Balderdash" and declared that the new interdisciplinary academic coordinator better be there, and he'd better not ignore her niece. So here they were.

Was her aunt playing matchmaker? She should know better, but then her aunt might have romance on the mind.

Surreptitiously, Nancy peeked over Matt's shoulder at the president's table. Next to Aunt Joan sat Chief Bacardi. Apparently, he'd been invited to the president's house for New Year's Eve. Nancy hadn't heard about any other invitees. Next to Bacardi was Chief Grimes and his wife, who was as plump as her husband. She was laughing with the person next to her.

Although Nancy didn't know most of the others sitting at the table, she assumed they were trustees and their wives. She did recognize Mayor Johnson and his wife Elma. Apparently, the mayor coveted a trustee position when he retired from politics.

Of the twelve trustees, ten were expected to attend tonight. That had been important to Aunt Joan. Winter Fest was a town and gown affair and she wanted as many trustees and faculty present as possible. She'd explained to Nancy that maintaining good community relationships was especially imperative for a small college located in a small community. That was why at least half the trustees were area residents, with the rest

277

scattered from around the country. It was another reason why her aunt preferred the rape cases to be dealt with as quietly as possible. The local trustees would likely revolt if the rapes attracted sensational media attention.

"You still seem far away," Matt murmured, in her ear.

"I can't shake the idea that the rapist could be here watching us, or selecting his next victim."

Matt squeezed her tighter. "I thought that might be it. You may be right, but he could be anyone of a hundred guys. Don't let him rob you of your evening, Nancy, or you'll be his victim."

"Suppose you're right. I'll try to perk up. How much longer do we have to stay?"

"We need to do the obligatory stopover at the president's table, then we should be able to leave."

"Good. I can't shake this mood and we can check up on Mal. He doesn't like being left alone too long. And we've been away from him much of the day."

"Seems like I remember seeing him about three hours ago." Nancy pinched Matt's shoulder. "Okay. We'll go."

- o -

The Blackthorn College mug shattered against the stone fireplace. Who the hell did she think she was, parading around with that idiot professor? He was an imposter. He only studied about the ancient ones. In order to know something, you had to experience it. You

278

couldn't just study it.

If Nancy Appleby wanted to know about Celtic practices, then she needed to come to him. He'd show her. He pressed his thumbs against throbbing temples. No, not yet. She couldn't come to him yet. It wasn't time. She had to wait.

He gasped for breath. Patience. He sank to a lotus position before the blazing fire and watched the flames leap about. She would be his at the Beltane fire, but not before.

There was another to be taught on Imbolc. He smiled to himself. The small, slender raven haired co-ed he'd been following would have to suffice. He'd nearly asked her to dance. But that would've been too risky with the detective watching.

Still, the co-ed would do. She was a natural brunette. He had a video to prove that. It was time to plant new seed, and he'd picked fertile ground in which to plant his.

He spat into the fire and crossed his arms. Detective Appleby thought she knew his patterns by now, but it was a new season. She'd be in for more than one surprise before he revealed the true nature of things to her. By Beltane she'd be so eager, she'd be easy prey.

- o -

Slamming the apartment door behind her, Nancy marched to the bedroom, threw off her coat and pulled her turtle neck roughly over her head. She plopped on the bed and bent to unzip her boots. She saw herself in the mirror and gagged.

279

The heavy makeup cracked. The auburn wig looked like a wig. The false contacts caused her eyes to sparkle wildly. Was there nothing real about her?

She clawed at her bra. There. She breathed. There. They were still real. Her nipples pebbled. Were they responding to the cooler air? To her visual inspection? Or to her heightened sense of danger?

Again, she'd failed to attract the rapist. And now all she could do was wait. Would he strike on Imbolc? Had he already raped? Was he even now tormenting a young woman while she, the hotshot detective, waited in the security of her apartment?

She couldn't think like that. She swiped at a glob of mascara. It wouldn't help anyone to get down on herself.

She'd gone to the bar after Bayfield's lecture and done her job. It wasn't enough. The bar hadn't been crowded. Maybe the frigid weather kept patrons away. She hadn't sensed the rapist's presence. Maybe he had fled the area.

Nancy finished undressing and took a long hot shower attempting to wash off the façade and her nagging worries. She climbed into bed and tucked the covers tightly under her chin. The flannel sheets provided warmth and comfort, but that wasn't enough. They were a poor substitute for Matt Bayfield. She drifted.

The phone rang. Immediately alert, Nancy peeked at the clock and dashed for the kitchen phone. It was six minutes after four a.m.

"Hello."

"It's Officer Washington. I'm at the hospital ER. He struck again. Worse this time. You're probably gonna want to come down here right away."

"I'll be right there."

Nancy hung up the phone and wheeled toward the bedroom. With practiced efficiency, she pulled on a pair of slacks and a sweater over longjohns. She checked and rechecked the safety on the Berretta Tomcat before tucking it in the side holster under the bulky gray sweater.

Without bothering to make coffee or grab a banana, Nancy Appleby rushed out into the early morning darkness.

Nancy avoided staring too closely at the tiny dark-haired woman lying in the hospital bed. She must have been easily overpowered by a six foot man.

The co-ed watched Nancy through blank eyes; she wet her lips and then asked, "Who are you? Another cop?"

"Yes, I'm Nancy Crane. And I want to find the guy who did this to you."

"You're a little late."

"Pardon me."

"I found him first." The woman emitted a dry laugh. "Or he found me first."

Nancy nodded and glanced at Officer Washington and Chief Bacardi for direction.

"This is Sarah Jane Anderson," Chief Bacardi

said. "She was walking back to campus around eleven p.m. from the grocery store on Seventh and Adams when she was attacked from behind."

"From the grocery store?"

"Yes, the grocery store. Don't know why that surprises everyone so. Students have to eat too." Sarah Anderson glared at Chief Bacardi. "And I can tell my own story. Please don't try to spare me. I lived through it; I certainly can tell you about it."

Nancy took out her notepad and waited, admiring the young woman's spunk. The bastard might have raped her, but he hadn't stolen her resolve. Nancy tried to control her own heartbeat. The rapist had become even more dangerous by altering his plan of attack. This woman hadn't been near the bar. She'd only been coming back from a grocery store.

"I don't know what happened to my groceries," Sarah lamented. "His car couldn't have been far away. Once he covered my mouth, I assume duct tape, and blindfolded me, it didn't take long for him to dump me into the backseat of a car."

"He put you in the backseat?"

"Yes. It was a four door. He drove for what seemed like a long time. Can you hand me that water cup?"

"Sure." The young woman closed her eyes and with effort sipped through the bent straw. How could the woman be so calm under the circumstances – or was she still in shock?

"Thanks," Sarah murmured. "So he drove to

some place. I don't know where. Then he pulled me out of the car and threw me over his shoulder with seemingly little effort and started walking. He must have walked for another fifteen or twenty minutes. All I could think of was I'll do anything you want, just don't kill me. And I tried to listen so I might recognize something."

"Did you recognize anything?"

"Nothing that will help much. An owl. Some wolves a considerable distance a way. Mainly just night sounds that you would hear in the woods or near a lake."

"You sound like you're a good observer."

"I've grown up in the woods and I've taken a course on observation skills from Professor Bayfield."

"Oh." Nancy's stomach somersaulted at the mention of Bayfield's name. "I didn't mean to interrupt you."

"That's okay. Somewhere along the way we come to what must have been a hut or a cabin. He opens a door. Places me gingerly onto a cot or a small bed and proceeds to strip me. He leaves the blindfold on but does remove the duct tape. I'm crying some, but I'm also begging for him not to kill me. I ask him what he wants and he gives me an hysterical laugh."

"*You'll do*, he said. *At least you've got dark hair. I like dark hair*."

"I heard him removing his pants. He placed my hand on him; he was large. He said he didn't want to hurt me, and he was sorry about my groceries.

283

As if they mattered at that point. I asked him if he wanted to be in my mouth, figuring if I could make him come that way it would be best. He said *sure*."

"He got me up on my knees and I took him in my mouth. It didn't take long before he seemed about ready, and then he pulled back and laughed. He mocked me. *Thought I didn't know what you were trying to do, bitch. I'll be done with you when I'm good and ready and not before*."

Sarah closed her eyes and wet her lips.

"He proceeded then to rape me," the young woman continued. "I don't know how many times, I lost count and consciousness after four. I never knew a man could last that long.

"When he was done he must have waited for me to come around. Then, he thanked me and helped me put my clothes back on. He taped my mouth shut, tied my hands and carried me back to his car. Then he drove me here. Can you believe it? He rapes me and then takes me to the hospital."

"That does sound pretty weird," Nancy responded. "I know you probably want to rest, but can you answer a couple more questions?"

"Sure. It's worse when I stop talking. When I do that, I'm flooded with my own thoughts and memories."

"Is there anything else about the cabin that you recall?"

Sarah wiggled her nose. "It smelled like fish."

"Like fish?"

284

"Yes, almost like a fish house." Sarah's eyes widened with recognition. "That's what it was!" she exclaimed. "I've ice fished with my dad and brothers for years. It was a damn fish house. Why didn't I think of that before? Not that it would've made any difference."

"That's very important information, Sarah. A fish house." Nancy rocked back and forth on the balls of her feet. There had to be hundreds of fish houses in the area, but at least it was something. "He never beat you or threatened you with a weapon."

"No. He seemed only to use enough force to subdue me and get me to comply with what he wanted. I'm sure I have some bruises, but I don't think his intent was to harm me in that way." Sarah's voice shook. "Bruises he left me with are much less visible."

Nancy nodded and paused before asking, "Anything else?"

"This may sound odd, but I really think he thought he was doing me some kind of favor. When he was in me, he kept muttering about it being a time for seed planting. And that he had a gift worthy of a goddess. Only I don't think I was the real goddess. I think I was his pretend goddess."

Nancy frowned. "What makes you say that?"

"The man seemed to be going down several paths at the same time. He was raping me. He would say he was planting his seed, but he also babbled about some goddess of the bell who would have to wait. But that it helped that I had dark hair. I was too small, but he forgave me for that."

"He never mentioned a name?"

"Not clearly. I thought I heard Dick Apples, but that makes no sense at all."

Nancy's skin crawled; she avoided eye contact with Chief Bacardi and Officer Washington. Dick – detective. Apples – Appleby. Was her cover blown? If so, the rapist must be obsessed with her.

Nancy blinked. If that was the case, so be it. She'd get her man. Sooner or later.

"At least I'm alive," Sarah whimpered, glancing down at the sheet covering her frame.

"You did what you had to do, Sarah," Nancy said. "You did right. And what you've shared with us may help us stop this guy from attacking again."

"I sure hope so." Brightness flared briefly in Sarah's eyes. "I'd like to see the guy get his." That brightness flickered out. "I'm afraid of what my fiancé is going to do."

Nancy stroked the co-ed's fingers and noticed the diamond ring. "If he's the right man, he'll be there for you no matter what."

Sarah squared her shoulders and smiled weakly. "I guess it's better to find out if he's the right man now than later."

Squeezing Sarah's hand, Nancy nodded. "Thanks for talking with us. You look like you could use some rest. If you think of anything else call us."

"I will." The woman's fingers tightened around Nancy's. "Thanks for listening."

Chapter Thirteen

Matt sat on his couch staring hard at the fire in front of him. It was difficult to concentrate on what Nancy had just recounted. She'd talked about her interview with the latest rape victim. Malaki, lying in front of the fireplace, twitched as if he were dreaming about chasing rabbits.

If only life was that simple. Was he that different from the dog? Hanging with Nancy at times was little more than a frustrating chase. He tried to keep up with her. She could be so focused on her work that whatever time was left for them was squeezed out like it was the end of a tube of toothpaste.

The fire crackled and spat sparks. Malaki stood and shook his coat and then resettled. This should be a serene moment; a time for soft caresses, sharing dreams, gentle lovemaking. Yet he was forced to analyze the words of the latest victim.

He wasn't insensitive about the horror occurring on campus, but they needed to get away from it once in a while. His house was no sanctuary. He longed for the peaceful spruce grove outside of Mercer.

He mulled over Nancy's latest story. The fire drew him into its inferno. He'd never been in love before. Matt's heart skipped a count. Where the hell had that come from? Good God. Was he falling in love with a cop?

What they had was special. He'd never known anyone like Nancy. She tapped him, body and soul, in ways he hadn't conceived possible. But was he ready for love? That meant long term relationships, committed relationships.

They could work it out. He was at Blackthorn for at least the next three years. Nancy could find a job in the area. Chief Bacardi would love to have her on the Trillium force. They could make it work.

But what about Nancy? He resisted looking at her. What would she do if she could read his mind? She'd made it clear she wasn't looking for anything long term. She lived dangerously and wanted a good time. Was he merely goodtime Matt?

Yet she'd shared pain with him that she seldom shared with anyone. Even her brothers thought this relationship was different.

How to proceed? If there was a map for how best to move forward, he hadn't discovered it. He'd have to move slowly. Maybe they should talk about a committed relationship. That should be easy because neither of them was involved with anyone else.

"Have I lost you?" Nancy asked. "So what do you make of what the latest victim told us?

Matt pulled his gaze away from the fire. "Sorry, guess I got caught up watching the flames. Actually, much of what you said is consistent with a guy obsessed with Celtic rituals. The planting of the seed certainly fits with Imbolc. Doubt if she could've come up with anything to divert him from that part of the plan. Has there been a reference to hair color before?"

"Not really. There was one, a blonde, who complained about him putting something on her head. Maybe it was a wig."

Matt draped a leg over the opposite knee. "But there have been women with auburn hair as well as dark brunettes?"

"Yes, I double checked. One auburn, one blonde, and the rest dark brunettes or black."

"Wonder if he's biased against Nordic and Scottish Celts. Maybe he's more into Irish and Welsh."

"Maybe it's just a color preference."

"Maybe."

"What about the goddess of the bell?"

"That's pretty obvious," Matt said, failing to keep a touch of smugness from his voice. "This guy is primed and waiting for the goddess of Beltane. Wouldn't surprise me if he's already picked her out. No other woman quite measures up to his image of her."

Nancy glanced quickly away to look at Mal.

"Why a fish house?"

Nancy stood and walked to the fireplace. She warmed her hands and turned to face Matt. "Privacy, I imagine."

"Do people fish at night?"

"Sometimes. But I expect this guy has access to a fairly private lake."

"Doesn't sound like your typical college

student from out-of-state."

"No, it doesn't. I'm still putting my money on a local, likely tied to the college."

"He's less predictable now."

"You think so?" Nancy's gray eyes darkened.

"He's broken his pattern by taking a woman coming from the grocery store. Once he breaks the pattern you have to wonder what he'll do different next time."

"That's bothered me a lot too." Nancy sat back down on the couch next to Matt. He placed a hand on her thigh. She flinched.

"It's going to be harder to do a stakeout," she said.

Matt's fingers tensed. "Do you ever get the impression that he knows where you are and what you're doing?"

Nancy shrank from his touch. "No!" she said, too quickly. Her voice rose. "What makes you say that?"

Rubbing her thigh, Matt said, "You're good at what you do, but he always seems one step ahead or behind or something. Do you think he knows who you are?"

"Possibly."

Color crept from Nancy's neck to her cheeks. Matt lifted his hand from her thigh. His throat constricted. "Are you not telling me something? Again? Nancy Crane Appleby."

Nancy froze.

Matt stood up and began to pace. He spun around to face her. "You're the goddess of Beltane, aren't you?"

"You're too damn smart, Professor Bayfield."

"And you're too damn secretive, Detective Appleby."

"It goes with the job."

"I suppose you're right about that, but you've chosen to involve me in this case. And you've become important to me."

He looked toward the kitchen doorway. There was no escape. "Maybe more important than I'd like. But I feel I've some right to know the kind of danger you're in. Or maybe that we're both in. If the guy is obsessed with you, he's probably not too fond of me."

The horror in Nancy's eyes was evident. Hadn't she realized the danger she was putting him in? Matt grunted. She'd been a walking crossbones danger sign since he'd first met her. So why did he love her?

He watched Nancy rotate her neck trying to release tightness. "I'm not actually sure I'm a target."

She was lying; he hated that.

"Oh, all right…he may have followed us back to my place the morning after we first made love. And he may have made a reference to me while he was raping Sarah, but we're not certain."

"Sounds like we're not certain of much," Matt snapped. "But I don't like it. You're in danger and still keeping secrets from me."

Nancy rose and wrapped her arms around Matt. He held her close.

293

"Don't worry so much," she whispered into his shoulder. "I'm a trained professional. This is what I do for a living."

"But it's so risky," he murmured into her hair.

"Everything we do is risky. I don't take unnecessary chances. I have backups." She leaned back against his arms and met his gaze. "I've done this many times before, Matt. All of this is new for you, but it isn't for me. Trust me."

That was a joke. Trust her. How could he trust her when she'd failed to trust him with things that mattered from the very beginning? She seldom shared more than she absolutely had to. Matt tried to slow his breathing back to normal. How had he gotten hooked up with a woman who preferred hiding in the dark? There were times, like right now, when she seemed as adept at concealment as the damn rapist.

How much more of this charade could he take?

She stood on her tiptoes and brushed her lips across his. "You're an expert at archaeological digs. I would make a mess of that. But I'm an expert at what I do."

"And I'd make a mess of that?"

"You could. I appreciate your help with ferreting out how this guy is thinking, but I don't want you getting in the way when it comes time to trap him. I don't want you getting personally involved."

"I *am* personally involved."

Nancy ran a finger along his tight jaw line. "I know you are, and that means a lot to me. But when things get messy, and they likely will, I can't be worrying about protecting you from the bad guy. Do you understand? Worrying about you would only put me in greater danger."

Matt's grip softened. "I understand, but I don't like it."

"You don't have to like it. You just have to respect the boundaries around my work." She ran her tongue across his lips. "Now what I'd like is to put work aside and get you inside."

Nancy withdrew from their hug and tugged on his hand. "Come on, professor. Where do you want it? Here or upstairs? We haven't tried the kitchen yet," she said, thrusting her tongue out at him. "Aren't you hungry? I am."

"No!" An electric shock jolted his brain. He had to take a stand. He pulled away from her.

"No?" she echoed.

"Sex isn't a cure-all bandage to be applied haphazardly." He took another step back. "Nancy, you don't trust me. How the hell am I supposed to set that aside and go upstairs or to the kitchen or wherever your whim takes us and screw our brains out?"

"I didn't know I was imposing sex on you." Nancy interlaced her fingers at her waist. She stared at his feet for what seemed like an eternity. At last she looked up at him. "I guess that's it then."

Matt went cold. He shrugged his shoulders. "If that's what you want..."

"What do *you* want, Bayfield? You're the one

who's saying I'm using you as some kind of sex object."

"I didn't quite say that."

"You might as well have. So what are you saying?"

"Damn it, I think I may be falling in love with you."

"What! In love? With me? You don't know the first thing about love, or you wouldn't say that." It was Nancy's turn to backpedal. "I'm too mercurial for a lasting relationship. I don't love easily. And I'm not very lovable. You're deluding yourself, professor."

"Matt," Nancy's voice softened, "I'm humbled, terrorized actually, by what you think you feel. But you've never been in love. This isn't it. I'm a cop."

"I'm going to take Mal and leave now. I'm very fond of you, Matt. You've been very supportive and helpful. And after you think about it more, if you want to pick up from where we were, I'm okay with that. If you're looking for more than a committed short term relationship, you better look elsewhere."

Matt nodded, fighting tears, not trusting himself to speak. He stood rooted in place, watching Nancy and her dog move toward the entryway. The door closed with hardly a sound.

So was that it? Had he simply been the lucky recipient of thank you fucks? He'd been supportive and helpful, but not worthy of love?

Two days later, Nancy sorted mail at her kitchen table. A squarish envelope – the kind used for wedding invitations, with her name and address printed in block letters cut out from newspapers or magazines – fell face up on the table.

Her fingers froze. Holding her breath, she reached for a knife and carefully slit the envelope open.

She managed to swallow. Her eyes narrowed, focusing on the note spelled out with pasted block letters. She read its contents silently and then mumbled them aloud as if their meaning would be more evident.

"Dear Detective: You may be good at games, but I am a master at them. I can hardly wait until we play around the maypole. Rest assured you are the chosen one. You will reign at the fire – no one else will do. Only one more pretender before you will mount the throne.

Be true to your virginal goddess self. Stay away from the professor. He who soils the virgin will suffer greatly for his transgressions.

In full armor, I stand ready to protect you from any who would defile you. Until the peals of the bel, I am your steadfast White Knight."

Nancy released a breath and with trembling fingers placed the note on the table. She braced herself. Think. Don't panic. Think. The note only confirmed what they'd already deduced: she was the goddess of Beltane.

Yet the disembodied words were more sinister than that. Their tone projected a haunting inevitability. The man delighted in teasing her, in playing a game. Nancy cringed. Matt was singled out as a rival. She'd have to tell him of the threat. If anything happened to Matt...

She hesitated. First, she'd let Chief Bacardi look at the note and see if he saw anything she'd missed.

Matt probably wasn't in a lot of danger as long as she stayed away from him, and that seemed highly likely. She hadn't heard a word from him since their fateful exchange two nights earlier.

Nancy slumped into a chair and rested her forehead on the table. She should've seen the train coming. Matt Bayfield was too sensitive to have an uncomplicated affair. He thought he might be falling in love with her – whatever the hell that meant. He either wasn't very certain about himself, or he wasn't sure of her. And he shouldn't be. He'd rushed her.

Why hadn't she leveled with him from the beginning? Maybe then he wouldn't have gotten so emotionally attached.

Nancy reached for a Kleenex and swiped at tears. Emotionally attached. Who was she kidding? She missed the man. She'd never felt more thoroughly loved than when he held her in his arms after lovemaking. She missed his humor and his penchant for sharing stories.

She blew her nose. What did that have to do

with love? Nothing and everything. She'd chided him for not knowing what love was. How about her? Had she ever really loved? Before now.

- o -

"Okay, Bayfield, out with it. You've been prowling around the office for three days like a mountain lion with a knot tied in his tail." Carol Macy paused and then with a smugness Matt detested, she added, "And I can just imagine who tied that knot."

"Go find someone else to pester," Matt said.

Carol smiled easily. "No way. I have a responsibility to protect our students from rabid mountain lions and rabid professors. Right now, professor, you are a danger to be around."

"So leave!"

"Come on, Matt," Carol said, softening her tone. "You're in pain. It's obvious you're hurting. It may help to talk about it."

She waited. Ignoring her, Matt stepped across his office and gazed unblinking out the window onto the quad.

"I know Nancy's a headstrong woman. So how did she step on your toes, or your ego?"

Matt spun around to face his friend. "She doesn't trust me. She never has. I discovered her real name by accident. She never told me we'd been followed and watched by this creep. And wasn't going to tell me she was a target for the rapist until I put it together for myself. She doesn't trust me, and she never will."

The words tumbled out. A part of him was alarmed that he'd shared his agony with Carol while another part screamed for relief and understanding.

Matt hid behind closed eyes. He didn't want to see Carol's pity or her chastisement. He just wanted her gone.

He waited. She said nothing. At last, he peeked to see if she was still sitting there.

Carol flashed an eyebrow. "Never is a long time, Matt. Maybe trust isn't the issue for her. Is it possible she's trying to protect you?"

"Protect me? I doubt it. That would require her to think about me first and the rapist second."

"My, my. We are wounded, aren't we? So what happens now?

"Nothing. It's over."

"Just like that?"

"Just like that."

"Oh, well," Carol said, brushing lint from her sweater. "I guess you two didn't have as much going for you as I thought."

"What do you mean by that?" Matt retorted, quicker than he liked.

Carol cast him a wan smile. "I thought maybe you had actually met your fair maiden. You two seemed to have such a good time together. You looked like you were falling in love."

"Humph!" Matt grunted. "Nancy Crane Appleby doesn't know the first thing about love."

"And you do?"

"Probably not. But it *doesn't* mean playing second fiddle to a rapist."

"I won't argue with that. Nancy may be letting professional stress overpower a personal relationship."

"What do you mean by that?"

"You know the woman a lot better than I do, but I can't help but think that not solving this case – and with the rapes continuing – good God, she's got to go and interview these women each time the guy strikes – she must be holding herself personally responsible."

"Too much so," Matt grudgingly admitted.

"And I understand you've been a big help to her in putting the pieces together."

"So, where are you going with this?" Matt fumed. "That I'm just some kind of professional colleague to her?"

"Not at all. Actually, if I'm any judge of relationships, I'd say Nancy is quite fond of you. At least as fond of you, as you are of her."

"I believe "was" is the operative verb. And fond is starting to sound like brother and sister."

"Pardon me, professor. Your mind might prefer *was,* but your heart is screaming out *is.* Carol raised her hand. "Don't say anything, damn it. This isn't an academic debate."

Matt rolled his eyes. He didn't want to listen to Carol, but he was unable to dislodge her from his office chair and boot her back to her own office. He glanced at his desk. The image of Nancy leaning over it and him entering her from behind came to him and was quickly follow by a wave of nausea. How had things gone so wrong so quickly?

"So she deceived you, Matt. She didn't tell you everything you think she should have told you in a timely manner. She *is* a cop. There must be a lot cops don't tell their spouses or lovers. Maybe she gets so used to wearing a mask that she forgets she even has one on."

"That's my point."

"Maybe she needs some help including a partner. Apparently, she hasn't had a serious relationship for some time. And her marriage doesn't sound like a partnership made in heaven.

"That's for sure."

"So, do you love her?"

Matt looked away and clenched his teeth.

"I didn't ask if you're lovers; I asked do you love her?"

"I told her I might be falling in love with her."

"You told her you might be falling in love. Damn, Bayfield, that's a real vote of confidence. Women aren't moved much by "might." Nuances aren't important. You either love her or you don't."

Matt held his tongue.

"So is it too risky to say what you really feel? Don't want to be the first to commit?" Carol smiled at his surprise. "Yes, I know about all of those niggling fears. So what is it?"

"Probably both."

"So you hide behind a mask, too."

"Maybe."

"I suppose we all do to some extent. But there's more to this quagmire than your inability to come clean about loving her, isn't there?"

Folding his arms across his chest, Matt glared at Carol.

"Ah, hah. A picture is coming in clear," Carol said, clapping her hands. "You're afraid."

"Afraid – that's not true."

"You're not only afraid she won't return your love. You're afraid for Nancy's safety, for her life and you don't know how to protect her. Matt Bayfield, you're hung up on that old western macho guy with the white hat. Only there's no white hat for you. Your woman holds the gun."

"Well, how would you feel if the person you loved was in grave danger and you couldn't do a damn thing about it? God, Carol, I could get a call to identify Nancy's body at a morgue."

"Whoa, you really do have it bad. Don't crawl back into your shell, Matt. What you say is possible. And I can't tell you what I'd feel because I've never been in that position. But I think if I loved that person, then I'd be talking with her directly about how I felt about her, and how I feared for her safety, and how damn scared I was." Carol rose and headed toward the door.

"That's it. You open the can of worms and now you're leaving."

"That's right. I'm not the one you should be talking to at this point." She paused while turning the doorknob. "And I think even you, professor,

303

are aware of that."

Matt listened to the soft click of the door latch closing behind Carol. He exhaled. So now what?

He rested his chin on his hand. Did he have the guts to talk with Nancy? Would she even want to listen to him?

Closing his eyes, he saw a little boy standing before his parents. Their unsmiling eyes fixed on him. They'd just told him how proud they were that he'd mastered reading the book he still held in his hands. Then they went back to their own reading. The boy turned toward his bedroom with tears in his eyes. Why didn't they tell him they loved him?

Matt's eyes snapped open. He shook his head trying to erase the picture of the little boy and his parents.

He stood, his jaw set. It might be the biggest mistake of his life, but he had to see Nancy at least one more time.

He needed her to know how he really felt about her. It'd been one thing to tell her he thought he was falling in love; it was another to tell her straight out that he loved her and he wanted them to be together – marriage or not.

He'd tell her; he had to. And if it was the biggest mistake, so be it; he would just have to live with the consequences.

But what about his fears? His feelings of inadequacy? Could he tell her about those? If they were to have a chance, he'd have to.

"Come on, Mal. Let's get out of this apartment for awhile. I'm going to go stir crazy if I have to stay cooped up much longer."

Malaki got slowly to his feet and stretched to the full extent of his body. He cast a sheepish look toward Nancy who was intent on donning her parka.

Nancy looked down at Mal, dropped to her knees and put her arms around his thick neck. He responded with his own hug and his stubby tail wagged rapidly. "Don't look so guilty, Mal. You didn't do anything wrong. I'm just in a sour mood this afternoon. I've got to sort things out, and these walls are stifling. Thank goodness I have you! Or I'd be talking to those walls."

She stood and grinned. "Talking to you is one thing; talking to the walls is entirely different."

Mal perked his ears as if waiting for her to lay her problems out for him to solve. "Okay, let's go," she chuckled.

They headed for the park where Mal would enjoy running after a stick or the ball she had tucked in a pocket. It was good to be outside. With any luck, the calm frigid day would soothe her soul.

She really was being hit from all sides. Her meeting with Chief Bacardi had not gone well at all. She'd had to plead with him to remain on the case. Bacardi had nearly freaked when he saw the note from her White Knight. Was his extreme reaction because of inexperience with these kinds of crimes, or was he getting more pressure from her aunt?

Probably the latter, because her aunt had called wanting her to quit and go back to Stevens Point. Nancy snickered. "I'm no quitter and neither are you, Aunt Joan," she'd told her aunt. The resulting silence had stretched on until she'd wondered if their connection had been broken. At last she'd heard her aunt's voice, "No, I suppose you're not. But, you must be cautious, Nancy. Your mother will never forgive me if..."

"Nothing is going to happen," Nancy interrupted, "except a rapist will be taken off the street and the women of the college and of Trillium will be safe again."

"Oh, all right," her aunt had muttered. "I've never been able to reason with anyone from my sister's side of the family. One more thing, though."

"Yes," Nancy had responded holding her breath.

"I respect your professionalism, Nancy. I know you are a first class detective, but if you let Professor Bayfield slip through your fingers – well, I can only imagine you are a very foolish young woman."

"How do...?" The soft click of the phone being hung up had been louder than a blast of dynamite.

Nancy pulled back sharply on Malaki's leash. "Slow down, damn it. We're not racing to the park." The Rottie stopped and gave her a querulous look. "Damn, Mal. I'm sorry."

At least her aunt had backed down; that was an unfamiliar step for the woman. Chief Bacardi wanted to be more closely involved, wanted to know the moment the rapist contacted her again.

Nancy shook her head. Not likely. He'd just run and tell her aunt and they'd have a replay of what just happened. And there was certainly no guarantee the president of the college would acquiesce again to her niece's wishes.

While the two of them were temporarily mollified, that still left Matt to contend with. She'd been chagrined that her aunt already knew they'd broken up.

Matt was proving to be more than a complication to her case. She had to contact him and warn him of the danger posed by the rapist. She had a professional responsibility to inform him. Would he even listen to her?

He was right. She had deceived him over and over. Was she so obsessed with the rapist that she couldn't sort out her professional life from her personal life? It had been so long since she'd allowed herself to have a personal life.

That was no excuse. At the very least, she owed Matt an apology.

Malaki tugged on his leash. "Yeah, you're right, we're here."

They approached the section of the park used as a practice field for soccer during non-winter months. Ski trails now crisscrossed it. Nancy pulled the ball out of her pocket. Malaki leapt at it.

She released him from the leash and threw the ball. The dog tore out after it kicking snow at Nancy. He leaped to smother the ball.

Nancy laughed and clapped her hands. He turned with the dull yellow ball showing between his teeth. Quickly, he returned to her, dropped the ball at her feet and begged eagerly, anticipating the next throw. Nancy did not disappoint him. They repeated the retrieval game until her arm began to tire. Mal would never give up.

He had provided a welcomed distraction from her thoughts, but once the game had ended she was again flooded with foreboding. Things would be much less messy if Matt Bayfield had been what he seemed to be – just a nice fling.

Turned out there was nothing simple about the man at all. She'd grown to really enjoy being with him. Not just the sex. Though that was super. She missed talking with him. Talking about the case. Listening to him rattle on about things Celtic. She hadn't always paid close attention, but she'd found his dedication to his work endearing. He had such a curious mind and was unafraid to try most anything. She chuckled remembering him on snowshoes. Surprisingly, he was fun to be around. Challenging in many ways, but fun.

So did that make for a long term relationship? Hell, she would be going back to Point as soon as she closed the rape cases. And Matt wanted to get out of Trillium in the worst way – though he'd really shocked her by accepting a three year assignment at Blackthorn. Still, he'd been straight with her that it was his guaranteed ticket to bigger and better things.

They might share a lot in common, but a favorite locale was not one of them.

What kind of future was really possible with Bayfield, if any? How did he actually feel about her?

He thought he might be falling in love with her? That sounded like he was hedging his bets. The more she'd gone over their last conversation the more suspicious she'd become. How many guys told a woman *I think I may be falling in love?* Maybe it was an original Matt Bayfield line. Thinking, pondering, contemplating was quite different from being. In any case, she wasn't buying it.

Matt Bayfield wouldn't know what love was if it reached up and bit him. Not a helpful image at the moment.

Nancy kicked at the snow. Why couldn't he leave the *L* word out of everything? She'd caught herself thinking about it too often. He made her feel loved. And, damn, there were times when her heart nearly exploded with emotion for him. But feeling love didn't mean they had to be in love and have some kind of meaningful relationship.

God, she hated that word meaningful. What they had shared was good. So why did he have to go and spoil it by talking about love?

What was he really looking for in their relationship? Could he ever forgive her enough to even have a relationship?

What if he wanted marriage? Nancy chilled. She'd done that once. She wasn't prepared to go through that kind of misery again.

Matt had enjoyed her nieces and nephews. What would happen to her career if she did have children? She knew other cops, female cops, who combined family and career.

Nancy huddled against a sudden gust of wind trying to block out images of children and dreams of marital bliss. Maybe it was best to let Bayfield go his way. Her life would be much easier. Catching bad guys was less demanding than dealing with inexplicable feelings.

Hanging around Matt was making her indecisive and inattentive. She didn't like being either. She could ill afford distractions. She needed a clear mind to stay one step ahead of her so-called White Knight.

But she still had to tell Matt about the rapist and the threat. Would he talk with her or look through her like she didn't exist? Would he get down on one knee and propose marriage? At this point, she didn't have a clue what to expect or really what to do.

She needed to stay in control of her feelings, of the rape case, and of whatever relationship she had with Matt. But everything seemed to be spinning wildly out of control.

"Damn, Appleby, you're getting way ahead of yourself as usual," Nancy muttered. "He probably won't even speak with you. You have a rapist to catch. Don't forget that."

Malaki dashed from her side up the hill. Startled, it took Nancy a moment before she could cry out, "Come back."

The command lodged in her throat. A familiar figure in a blue parka had crested the rise and bent over to greet the elated Rottweiler cavorting back and forth around the man seeking and receiving attention and affection. Malaki knocked the man down into the snow. In spite of herself, Nancy giggled. Seemingly unperturbed, Matt Bayfield rolled over and over with the dog as if they were making angels in the snow.

Nancy plunged her hands deep into her parka pockets and trudged toward the snow comedy. When she was halfway there, Matt stood and brushed snow from his clothes. Malaki, with his entire rear wagging, stood before the man, waiting for more play.

Matt patted him on the head and said something to the dog that Nancy couldn't hear. Malaki sat beside Matt. The two of them formed a frosty statue waiting for her to make her way to them.

She came to a halt before the two stoic males, unable to read anything from Matt's expression. He could be a damn cop, for all the emotion he displayed. Even Malaki had lost his exuberance. He just stared at her without greeting.

Nancy ignored their lack of acknowledgement. Could she say anything that'd melt Matt's frigid composure?

"You got a minute?" she asked.

311

"Yeah." Matt shrugged, placing a gloved hand on Malaki's head.

"You're not going to make this easy, are you?" Nancy paused. Seeing no reaction, she forged ahead. "I need to talk to you. I received a note from the rapist – he's calling himself my *White Knight.*" She let out a dry chuckle. Still no response from Matt. "Anyway, he made a fairly direct threat against you. You need to know you may be in danger."

"So what did he say exactly?" Matt's tone was cool, but not condescending.

"He said, and I quote, "Stay away from the professor. He who soils the virgin will suffer greatly for his transgressions.""

"I'm shaking in my boots," Matt retorted with sarcasm. "That guy is an idiot. So you really are his virginal goddess of Beltane."

"So he says." Nancy looked down at Malaki. "He claims there will be one more pretender. Then it will be my turn. He wants me to stay pure for him."

"He's going to try to kill you, you know." Matt said evenly. "The goddess of Beltane will be a human sacrifice."

"I know, but we'll get him first. Hopefully, before he strikes again."

"Right. So professionally you would have had to tell me about him and your status as the goddess of Beltane anyway. So much for secrets. So the game has intensified."

"What do you mean?"

"Sounds like he thinks the two of you are engaged in a chess game." Matt laughed thinly. "That's a joke. You're really playing hide and seek. Though you're both so skilled at hiding it's not clear who's *it*. But you got what you wanted. He's made direct contact. Do you always get what you want, detective?"

"No, I don't." Nancy stared hard at her toes. Her lungs constricted. She could use a bathroom stop, but she had to press on. This might be her only opportunity to make any kind of amends.

She fixed her eyes on his, which remained blank. "I do apologize for deceiving you. It wasn't always intentional. Maybe I am too obsessed with the bastard. Sometimes I forget how other people may be affected. And now you're in danger."

A spark flickered in his eyes. Nancy steeled herself to again withstand his rage.

"You've been a danger to me ever since I met you," he said. "About the other night, I said some things I regret too." Nancy watched him bend down and grab a handful of snow. He made a snowball while sorting out what to say next; she waited.

"I've done a lot of thinking about what happened. About us. About me, really." He threw the snowball. Malaki rushed after it. The snowball smashed against an oak tree. The dog came to an abrupt halt, cocked his head to one side and looked at the tree. Eventually, he turned around and with his head down retraced his steps to sit by Matt.

"What really galls me," Matt said, "is the secrecy and deception. How long do you think this guy has known about us? How many times has he followed us? Would you ever have come clean about that?"

Nancy's mouth twisted in a grimace. "I don't know. The fact is I didn't tell you. Maybe I was trying to protect you. Maybe I hoped he'd become jealous and finally break his cover."

"And he has."

"Yes, but now you're in danger, too. I was trying to avoid getting you involved."

"That sure as hell didn't work."

"No, it didn't, and I'm sorry for that. Your life had to be much more tranquil before I came along."

"That's true. But I'm not looking for tranquility. Would I go back and rewrite our relationship? Yes, I would change some things. Not to have met you, though, would have been a terrible loss.

She trembled, but not from the cold. "So now what? What are you saying, Matt? What do you want?"

"A part of me wants to wish you well on your case and for you to get the hell out of my life." Matt knelt beside Malaki who leaned into Matt. "But it's not that easy; I wish it were." He looked up at Nancy. "I told you I thought I was falling in love with you. I lied."

Nancy squeezed back tears.

"You see, I discovered these last few days that I care about you more than I've ever cared about

314

another woman. Any other person, really. I'm not falling in love with you. I *am* in love with you. I love you, Nancy. And I don't know what to do with you."

Relief and fear swept over Nancy in such quick succession she couldn't tell which was which. He loved her and he still wanted her – relief, she decided. That was a start. So what was the fear? *Hold on. Take your time.* Speechless, she searched his face, her eyes brimming with tears, the bare beginning of a smile playing at her lips.

Matt held her gaze. "Are you ready for an open, honest relationship? Wherever it leads? No secrets. No withholding. No trying to protect me. Tell me what you feel, what you want."

There. *That* was the fear: he was too far ahead. Her smile froze in place. If she said *no*, she'd lose him. But she wasn't ready to say *yes,* either. Could they wait it out? Where to start? Clearly, it was her turn to speak.

"I'll try. That's not much – maybe not enough. I'm scared of what I feel for you. I care about you in ways that go beyond what I felt for my husband, even in the good years. Am I ready to make a lasting commitment?" She frowned and gulped a long deep breath. "I can't. Not yet. I don't know if ever. I can't promise that. I'm sorry."

Matt's eyes softened. "I didn't ask for a lasting commitment – not yet, anyway. I asked for an honest relationship, one where you tell me if you're afraid, like you did just now. One where

315

we have a chance to sort out what we might have together in the long run."

Where was her clear head when she needed it? What could she really promise? And why did she feel so torn apart, as if she had to choose between being a cop and being in love? What had he just said? Tell him if she felt afraid. Deep breath, again.

"Okay...and thanks. I can't tell where I am with the rapist still on the loose. I feel like I can't sort myself out. I'm still scared. Scared I might lose you, scared you won't have patience to wait 'til I get it all figured out. But I know I don't want you to go away, either." Nancy paused. "That scares me even more."

Malaki chose that moment to stand and stretch. He moved to Nancy's knee and sniffed. "I expect if Mal had a vote," she patted his head, "we both know what it would be."

"Easy for him to say. But it's a start. Yes, I want to be together too. So how do we proceed?"

"Slowly, I think. Very slowly." She noticed Matt lean back. "I don't mean we can't be together." She finally smiled. "In all ways. Can we be together without you pressuring me?"

A wry smile crossed Matt's face. "That's a tough one. I want to be able to say how I feel about you, that I love you. Does that pressure you?

She smiled back. "Yes, and no. Things were so much simpler before you said that. But I'd rather have you here, saying so, than *not* here." There. She was certain about something, at least.

"So. We keep our separate places and see how things develop?"

Nancy nodded. "Are you okay being together without knowing the end of the story?"

"What choice do I have? No, I take that back: this is the choice I'm making. I doubt if we ever know the end of the story anyway. Aren't mystery and romance intertwined? So, do you want to come over tonight?"

"I can't. It's my turn at the Crisis Center."

"How about tomorrow night?"

"I'm on stakeout."

"Shit. So you tell me when."

"I want to check out the gun show Sunday afternoon. That should provide you with a little local color, if you like. Want to come along? Then afterwards," she wet her lips, "we might get something to eat and see what develops."

"You're on. Sunday afternoon."

"I'll pick you up around two o'clock."

"I'm headed toward my office. You want to walk with me?"

"Of course," she said. She wrapped an arm around his waist and he did likewise. They took several steps toward campus before being roughly assaulted by a big ball of black fur. Malaki wedged himself between his two humans.

Smiling at each other, Nancy and Matt separated and clasped hands, allowing the Rottie to walk between them.

"I've really missed you, Matt."

"Yeah, this feels a lot better."

Chapter Fourteen

"Well, what do you think?" Nancy said, grinning at Matt.

They stood at the edge of the Civic Auditorium crowd. Tables with guns of all types and makes lined the auditorium, forming half a dozen aisles. Even she was surprised by the size of the turnout. She wasn't surprised at being one of few women in attendance. While increasing numbers of women were becoming shooters, they were still not likely to come en masse to a gun show in the middle of winter. These were hard core gun folk who'd gathered today.

She'd been so busy surveying the crowd for anyone who might be the rapist that she'd said very little to Matt since their arrival. He'd appeared engrossed with what was taking place around them, which ranged from guys telling hunting stories, to hawkers trying to entice sales, to distrusting looks.

They didn't fit. She was female and Matt, in his sports jacket and sweater, looked like Joe College. She smothered a chuckle. She should have suggested other appropriate clothing for him, but this was more fun, though Matt seemed quite unconcerned by the stares. He was probably accustomed to folks trying to assess him.

"I didn't know there were so many people interested in guns," Matt said. "And I didn't know camouflage clothing was so in." Matt bent to whisper in her ear. "Does that mean all these people are into paramilitary stuff?"

This time Nancy did laugh. "Not at all. Some may be, but camouflage is used in just about every form of hunting you can think of. I expect most of these guys are into duck hunting or deer hunting or both."

"Why all the handguns then? I didn't know people hunted with pistols."

"Actually, more and more people are doing just that. But I imagine most handguns are sold to people who are into target shooting, or because they believe they're safer if they own a gun."

"Your sarcasm, detective, is noted. So you don't think people are safer because they have a firearm."

"Depends. Some wind up shooting themselves or their loved ones."

"So do you think he's here?"

"Nope, I don't think so. Might be, but I can't feel him. I think I'd feel him if he was here."

"You're getting quite mystical about this guy, aren't you?

"Maybe. I call it gut instinct. You ready to leave?

"Not yet."

"Haven't you had enough observing for one afternoon?

"I'm done observing."

Nancy didn't like hearing the cockiness that had crept into Matt's voice, nor the thrust of his chin. She groaned. She could tell she wasn't going to like what he had to say next.

"Let's go back over to that guy with the missing front teeth, the one who talked to us about hunting big game in the Rockies. He seemed like a jovial sort."

"I've heard enough hunting stories."

"Me, too. I'm not going to ask him to tell us a story. He had several Colt handguns on display. I'm going to buy one of them."

"You're going to what?" Nancy glared at Matt. She stomped her foot. "You can't buy a gun. You don't know the first thing about how to use one. You'll kill yourself."

"Nonsense, I've had some superb instruction," Matt said, grabbing Nancy by the hand and pulling her behind him through a crowded aisle toward the man he sought.

What the hell had she created? He was behaving like some sort of caveman. Had all the guns on display brought out his macho gene? Maybe he *did* belong in this crowd.

"Here we are." Matt nodded toward the guy grinning at them totally unabashed about showing off the gaps where three teeth should have been.

How had he lost those teeth? The guy was dressed in old camouflage. Bloodstains from prior hunts were evident. He wore a battered felt hat with a pheasant feather sticking out of its band.

"So, young fellow, you decide what you want to buy?" the man asked. He was friendly enough, but Nancy saw a very calculating core behind that façade. She didn't doubt for a moment he'd already made her out as a cop.

"Not yet," Matt said. "I see a couple possibles. Can I handle them?"

"Don't see why not." The man grinned at Nancy. "They're not loaded. Which two?"

Matt pointed at a Colt Single Action Army revolver and then at a Colt Python Elite. He ignored Nancy's groans, hefting each pistol in turn.

"How do they feel?" the seller asked.

"Not bad."

"Can't go wrong with either one," the man grunted. "That one's modeled after the old Peacemaker. I've had one of those since I was old enough to hold a gun." He grinned his toothless smile. "They say it's the gun that won the west. Don't know why, though."

"Why not?"

Nancy couldn't believe Matt had bit. He seemed entranced by the man and his guns.

"It's well known that the Colt was a favorite of Wyatt Earp, Bill Cody, Pat Garrett, and Wild Bill Hickok." The man coughed, looked for a place to spit, thought better of it, and swallowed. "Course, the Peacemaker was also the favorite of Billy the Kid, John Wesley Hardin, and them James boys."

"So, what's your point?"

"That gun was used by guys on both sides of the law. The gun didn't know nothing about right and wrong – or peace, for that matter."

Matt bobbed his head in agreement as if he'd

just gained an important insight into western history. Nancy absently scanned the crowd. Was Matt being naïve, or was he setting the dealer up?

"What about this other Colt?" She heard Matt ask.

The man grinned again. "Now that one is pure class, mister. Yep, one of the leading gun magazines calls it the Rolls Royce of six-guns. You can't go wrong with either gun. So which one is it gonna be?"

"What do you think, Nancy?" Matt asked, not taking his eyes off the two guns.

"You know what I think. Neither is the best choice."

He turned to face her. His bullheaded bearing made it clear he meant business. "Okay," she muttered. "Which one do you like best?"

"I'm sort of partial to the Peacemaker."

"Humph. I bet you had one that looked like it when you were a kid."

"Now that you mention it," Matt said, rubbing his fingers along the barrel of the Colt lying in front of him. "I did. I had one just like this one. It was a toy, of course, but mine in my cowboy days."

"Well, I don't need any cowboy racing to my protection."

She could nearly hear Matt's teeth grind.

"So which one do you recommend?"

"Assuming you're not getting a gun just to admire, I'd go with the Python Elite. Our friend, here," Nancy pointed to the dealer who was listening more intently than she liked, "is right. It's a highly rated weapon. Personally, I think it's more functional and easier to use. If you ever fire it at anything other than a paper target, you're going to want to do some severe damage. The three-fifty-seven Magnum is guaranteed to do that."

"That's for damn sure, ma'am," the dealer agreed. "That'd make one god awful big hole, even if you're not the best shot in the world.

"And," Nancy added, "if you ever point that damn thing at a living thing, I don't want you to confuse it with your childhood toy."

Matt nodded soberly. "I'll take the Python."

After going through less red tape than either one of them had expected, Nancy hustled Matt out the door toward her Jeep.

"What's the rush?" Matt asked. "Are we headed to your place or mine?"

"Neither. We're going to the target range. I probably never will trust you with that damn gun, but I want to at least be convinced you're not going to accidentally kill yourself, or anyone else for that matter."

- o -

"Don't you think hanging the target on your refrigerator might be just a little bit childish?"

Matt looked at Nancy who shook her head and tried to squelch a laugh. "Not at all," he said, holding up two fingers with pieces of tape stuck to

324

them. "Let me get this last corner taped. Okay..." He stepped back and admired his work.

"That was some very fine shooting. You have to admit that, detective. Five shots in the bulls-eye. No misses. So what do you think?"

Nancy ducked between Matt and the refrigerator and ran her fingers over the bullet holes. "I've been telling you ever since we left the gravel pit that you did great. Better than I expected. After you got a feel for your weapon, you were quite proficient. I wouldn't want you aiming that gun at anything you didn't want to kill."

Peering over her shoulder at the target, Matt said, "That even surprised me. The gun felt like it was merely an extension of my arm. Never thought I'd get such an emotional charge from putting five shots in the bulls-eye. Amazing!"

"I know what you mean. Just don't get too cocky about it. It took several attempts before you could group five shots like that. You were also only firing at a stationary target; it wasn't trying to shoot you first."

Matt sobered some. "You're right about that. Guess the adrenaline is still flowing. For a guy who spends much of his time buried in the dusty backrooms of libraries and museums, hitting a target like that is fairly heady stuff."

"Maybe we can redirect some of that excess adrenaline." Nancy turned around to face Matt. "Wouldn't want you to have to run out and find another target."

Casting him a seductive smile, she undid the top four buttons of her sweater. Slowly, she parted the cardigan until it was clear to him that she wore no bra.

Gasping for air, Matt watched her jerk aside the material and thrust her breasts out at him. Her nipples immediately awakened, responding to the cool air. She grinned broadly welcoming his appraisal.

"Wow," Matt groaned. "Let me just look at you." He held his hands as if he were framing her for a picture. "I want that image to sear my brain so I'll never forget. So full. So round. So sexy."

"You're pretty easy on the eyes, too, you know," Nancy teased. "Tall, dark and handsome. With a trace of mystery. No wonder the co-eds flock to your classes."

"They're interested in the subjects I teach," Matt protested.

"Right. I wonder how many of them have imagined seducing you with their breasts like this?" Nancy wiggled her upper torso, her breasts bobbing as if riding a wave. "I doubt any have such vivid imagination. But it doesn't matter. These are the only breasts that can hypnotize me. They dazzle."

He placed a palm under each and lifted them gently, brushing a thumb across each nipple. "I can't tell you how much I've missed these," he said, bending to lick each in turn.

"And they've missed you," Nancy said, clutching his head to her breasts. "I've missed you."

Hurriedly, Matt tugged free the remaining sweater buttons and stepped back, admiring his woman. "You are incredibly beautiful. I don't know why I'm so lucky to have you in my life." Nancy's eyes gleamed with impatience.

"But I'm not complaining," he added, pulling her to him. Her breasts crushed against his sweater. He bruised her lips with his, groaning her name. She teased him with her tongue, giving as much as he was taking, offering even more.

Without breaking the kiss, he moved his hand to the buttons of her jeans. Nancy scrunched and shifted, helping to work the jeans over her hips. Still not breaking the kiss, she kicked them across the kitchen floor. Panties quickly followed. He pressed her against the refrigerator, using one hand to palm her crotch.

This was no time for finesse, nor was finesse required. Pushing two fingers into her sex, he again covered her mouth with his and swallowed her groan. He explored more. She lifted a leg, giving him more access. He went deeper, as deep as he could. He felt convulsions rake through her entire body, from center to extremities.

Matt trembled, wanting more, needing more. Still without breaking the kiss, he eased his fingers out of her body and fumbled with his own belt buckle. Two more hands moved quickly to assist. Nancy dipped her fingers into his shorts, finding what she sought, freeing him.

Using his length to separate her folds, Matt

lifted her slightly and entered. He lost his own groan in Nancy's mouth. Her smile was evident against his lips, even as she suggestively corkscrewed her tongue further into his mouth.

Unceremoniously, he lifted her hips, pressing her hard against the refrigerator door. She clasped her legs around him while he supported her buttocks in his palms. Flexing back on the balls of his feet, Matt steadied himself and then plunged forward. He stroked repeatedly, with Nancy's moans vibrating inside his mouth at the apex of each stroke.

Her eyes flew open wide and then shuttered. He surged onward, nearing his own completion. Nancy broke the kiss, placed her head against his neck, gripped his shoulders tightly, and pushed downward with strength he didn't know she possessed.

Gasping for air, clasping her buttocks as if they were a lifeline, Matt erupted deep in her chamber. For some moments, he rocked gently into her. Through an erotic fog, he sensed that Nancy, too, had come again. He could still hear her screams echoing against the kitchen walls.

They held each other, afraid to let go, afraid to let the world come between them. Matt rested his forehead against hers. "I was afraid I'd lost you."

"Me, too."

"Don't imagine it's possible to remain like this for the rest of our lives."

"Doubt it," Nancy said, leaning back against the refrigerator to look at him. "You sure are right on target today. But if we stay like this much longer, either we're going to suffer from muscle cramps, or I'll get my death of cold from this fridge."

"Oh. Sorry." Closing his eyes, Matt eased himself out of her and settled Nancy back on her feet. He ignored the abrupt chill and watched her stretch before him like a well satisfied feline.

"Hope that sweater kept your shoulders warm enough," he said. "It looks like a shawl."

"Fortunately, your sweater was quite cozy, but if you can manage without the view for a while," Nancy said, moving to retrieve the rest of her clothes, "I do need to warm back up."

"Guess I'll have to manage. I'll fix us some tea," he said, pulling his pants back up over his hips. "Enough target practice for one day."

"Maybe..." Nancy threw him a lazy smile.

- o -

Freshly showered, Nancy sat cross-legged next to Matt watching the fire and sipping tea. She was completely and totally satisfied. Why had she ever doubted they could work things out? There was no other place where she'd rather be this evening. There was certainly no other man she'd want to share the evening with. This was about as close to heaven as she could ever imagine.

A log sputtered and crackled. Flames shot upward and lowered.

"I never tire of watching a fire, whether it's in a

campfire or in a fireplace," Nancy said. "There's something about fire that soothes and excites at the same time. Don't know how to explain that feeling."

"I understand some of what you mean. We often have an evening fire on our digs. There's something magical about the movement of the flames."

"I imagine lovers have sat before campfires since the beginning of time."

"Fascination with fire is not a modern phenomenon, that's for sure. Fire has long taken on sacred qualities. Rebirth, for example – the Phoenix arises from ashes."

"Yes, and a flame is a symbol for the Christian holy spirit. I think it was tied into Pentecost somehow." Nancy stroked Matt's thigh.

"What about Beltane, Matt?" She felt his muscles tense. "You've never really told me much about it. Is that where May Day came from?"

"It is, though not many folks even celebrate that anymore. I wonder why? It lost favor during the last generation or so. Perhaps it was regarded as too pagan."

"So tell me about it."

Matt hunched over and poked at the logs. They hissed and spat even more and flames leaped high into the chimney flue. "At its core, Beltane was a pagan religious festival. It was probably the most raucous festival of the ancient Celts. And for good reason. After all, they'd survived another period of winter darkness and cold. They were more than ready to welcome and celebrate the arrival of spring bringing color to the otherwise drab landscape."

"To see flowers again must have been magical."

"I suppose so. Apparently, the five-fold blossom of the whitethorn and blackthorn was most revered at Beltane."

"Blackthorn!" Nancy gasped. "As in Blackthorn College?"

"Uh, huh. Doubt the founders of the college were aware of that tradition." Matt chuckled. "Maybe the college should make more of the symbolism.

"Actually, the blossom was believed to be that of the young May-queen." Matt smiled at Nancy. "No leap of imagination is needed to know what that symbolized. In some of the lore, dances are performed where she is linked with Robyn Hode. Robyn was a colloquial name for the penis."

"Goodness, they were justifying an orgy."

"Some believe that to be the case. We don't know how widespread that practice might have been. There are indicators that families barricaded doors and windows to protect wives and daughters on Beltane. There is little doubt the festival was a time for sexual excess. Celebrants devoted the entire day to suggestive dancing around the May pole, which itself was a phallic symbol.

"Just as at Samhein, Beltane was a time for shapeshifting. Participants might dress up as animals or as mythical creatures such as dragons.

Sort of like the Victorian masked ball, shapeshifting permitted overtures that otherwise might not have occurred. Remember, all of this was done to honor the wakening of the earth. Lovers could spend the night under the stars."

"So making love in the spruce circle wasn't so outlandish after all."

"Those folks celebrated warm weather at the time of seed planting. I'm not at all certain they made love in snowdrifts."

"I'll ignore that comment. So what about the fires of Beltane? You made passing reference to them in your lectures."

"There was no single way to celebrate Beltane, or any other Celtic observance. Practices varied by culture. At least one tradition suggests Beltane meant fire, particularly an oak fire. People would dance around bonfires."

"Sort of like snake dances around bonfires at high school homecomings."

Matt looked quizzically at Nancy.

"There are a fair number of high schools in the Midwest," she said, "that still have homecoming bonfires, parades and dances."

"Really. I hadn't noticed."

"Maybe you should study contemporary customs more. What else happened around the bonfires? More sex, I suppose."

"Probably, but fire also has cleansing powers. In some places, it was expected that men and women would leap the fire."

"Really." Nancy's pulse quickened. "I hope the

bonfire wasn't too huge."

Matt nodded. "I expect most times it was a low fire. Even cattle were driven over ashes."

"But sometimes the fire was too high to escape?"

Matt scowled at the burning logs. "Probably. Folklore suggests animal sacrifice was fairly widespread."

"And human sacrifice?"

"There is some evidence that it was practiced."

Nancy examined the fire. It had died down considerably, yet tongues of orange, red, and yellow still lapped at the nearly consumed logs. "So, it's safe to assume our nemesis is well schooled on all of this."

"No doubt."

"His latest victim talked about the creep saying something about seed planting and gift giving. He really thinks he's honoring some ancient mythology."

Matt shook his head. "It's hardly a myth to him. He likely believes he's an instrument of the gods of the universe."

"What a twisted mind."

"That's right. Celtic worship helped some people deal with an unknown world that often dealt them harsh blows. But like so many attempts to understand the holy, Celtic wisdom can be savaged to justify evil."

"I wonder how in touch with reality our guy actually is. He doesn't seem to make mistakes. At least, not yet."

"I'm not a psychiatrist, but I'd guess he goes back and forth. When he's under the influence of being a pagan instrument, he may be quite out of touch. But he does seem to transform with ease. That may not always be the case."

"Damn," Nancy said, curling her fingers into fists. "I've got to get him before March twenty-first. There's one more co-ed he's targeting before me. But I'm running out of ideas. He's got to slip up sometime."

"What if he doesn't?"

"Then we'll get him at Beltane."

"How can you be so sure, Nancy? This guy may be certifiable, but he doesn't make mistakes." Matt's voice cracked. "How can we protect you from this creep? It seems like when he wants to strike, he strikes, no matter what you or Bacardi or anyone else does."

"Whoa, Matt." She gave him a piercing look. "This is part of what I didn't want, remember? You're not involved in protecting me." She pulled her knees to her chest. "Good God, you didn't get that gun thinking you were going protect *me* – did you? Well?"

Matt eyes had a pained look. "Don't know. Honestly, Nancy. I didn't buy the gun to protect you. But if that bastard comes storming into this house, I want to have some kind of equalizer. Whether you're here or not."

"Shit." Nancy jumped to her feet. "Every time I think you and I are making some progress, something like this happens. You are not a cop. I am. My job is to catch the bad guys. I appreciate and need your help in many ways. But I don't need you packing a gun. That's the last thing I need."

"Well, maybe I have a need or two also," he said, standing and confronting her toe to toe. "Maybe I don't want to feel totally impotent when it comes to protecting my woman."

"That sounds so damn macho!" Nancy's heart thudded against her chest. She wrapped her arms around his shoulders and kissed his neck. "But I can't help loving you for it. Just don't do anything stupid."

She leaned back against his arms encircling her and looked directly into his face. "I'll smoke the guy out of his hidey hole if I have to drag him out by his tail."

- o -

No more pretenders! He couldn't abide another substitute. He could only get hard for the true goddess.

He paused the machine to admire Detective Appleby's body. Such full breasts. The dark patch of curls protecting her hot spot tantalized. No one else would do.

Wouldn't they be surprised when he didn't strike at spring equinox? Maybe they'd think he left and let down their guard. The local cops would be relieved. He laughed and spat on the cabin floor. They were so stupid. Too bad that bitch Williams wouldn't get hers; it would serve her right.

The detective was the only real challenger. She was the only worthy player in the game.

The goddess wouldn't be deceived. She knew he was preparing a place for her. She'd be ready when the time was ripe for her to dance around his maypole.

He pushed the play button. The woman was insatiable. He enjoyed playing and replaying a scene where she brought herself off. He wished he could hear her moaning and crying for him. He tried to ignore that she was teasing the professor.

So the wimp had bought a gun. A lot of good it would do him. Did the professor think he was so dumb he'd let himself be trapped? As much as he hated the man for defiling the goddess, he wasn't about to blow his cover by going after the imposter. Bayfield was only a prop in his story.

Only he *knew the ending. And it was written in stone, had been for centuries. The Goddess of the Bel was different from the others. He'd take his time with her. He'd fill her with seed every way possible, and then she'd become the gift.*

Not only his gift, but the gift for the fire.

Chapter Fifteen

"I don't like it," Chief Bacardi said to Nancy, who sat opposite his desk. "I don't like it one bit. You haven't heard a thing from that nutcase in weeks. You're not holding out on me again, are you?"

"Nope," Nancy said. "There's been no contact since the note."

"Grimes thinks we got too close to the guy and he fled the area."

Nancy scrunched her shoulder. "Maybe. I doubt it."

"What does your professor think?"

"That the guy's laying low until Beltane, May first."

"Two more weeks and then he comes after you."

"That's his plan."

The chief tugged at his moustache. "Sure would like to get him before then. On our schedule. Don't know what else we can do to lure him out. The guy must have a clamp on his emotions. You've paraded before him like a pro. We've gone over profiles of men who have any connection with the college. We've tracked down any known sexual predators. We might as well run an ad in the paper asking him to please come out and play."

"It's baffling and frustrating," Nancy admitted. "You're right, I'd rather deal with him before

Beltane. But I'm running out of possible scenarios for flushing him out. He's buried deep somewhere."

"Yet, he seems to know what's going on in the community. Do you have the feeling he's playing with you? Teasing you?"

"Sure. He's enjoying this. He thinks he holds the winning hand."

"But he doesn't."

Nancy shook her head. "If only we could provoke him enough to react. He really must be wound tight."

"Don't know if he's more dangerous now, or when he starts to unravel."

"If we can get him to unravel just a little bit, he might slip up."

"Well, we can't count on that. Maybe Grimes is right, but we can't take the chance of being wrong. What's your plan for May first?"

"I'll be at Matt's lecture and then go to the Northland Bar and Grill. There won't be any need for a disguise. I expect he'll try to grab me on the way back to campus, if he follows his routine."

"Why would he follow a routine now? He didn't even attack in March. And the February victim was walking home from a grocery store. What makes you think he'll be at the bar?"

"That's makes more sense than anything else. I think he's seen me there at least a couple times, maybe more."

"Okay, we'll have you wired. Officer Washington can cover the parking lot outside the bar. I'll have a man stationed halfway between the bar and the campus parking lot where I'll be. You shouldn't be far from assistance, if you need it."

"That should work." Nancy stifled a yawn.

"You might want to get a little more rest before the big event. Oh, I almost forgot. That night vision camera you requested finally arrived. Probably too late to matter much now."

Nancy shifted to the edge of her seat. "Let me look at it."

Bacardi reached into a bottom drawer and placed the kit on his desk.

"Not very big," Nancy muttered, hefting the camera, scope and fold-down tripod.

"This is pretty hi-tech, at least for up here. Go ahead and take it, if you want. I wouldn't know what to do with it."

Nancy sat at her kitchen table with the camera components spread out in front of her. It looked like a fairly simple process, not much different than operating the typical video camera. She could record onto the memory card and immediately play it back.

She looked through the view finder. Too bad she hadn't had this earlier. She might've been able to smoke the perp out.

Now it was too late.

Or was it? If she waited for Beltane, he would be in charge and he'd have more favorable odds than she liked. If she could get him to react, to come to her on her timetable, then her odds increased.

But what to do?

She repeatedly spun the lens cap on the table and watched it fall to one side and then to the other. So much was happening. So much had happened.

The past several weeks were as close to bliss as she'd ever experienced, other than for the looming threat of the rapist. She and Matt hardly spent a night alone. She hadn't wanted to put clothes in his closet, but she did leave essential toiletries in his bathroom, and he in hers. A duffle worked just fine for carrying clothes. She'd become addicted to his gentle passion, though she could still spice it up often enough. They had found a balance.

That thought made her grin. Matt hadn't used the *M* word yet, but she knew he wanted to. She couldn't even think about marriage until the rapist was in jail.

Then what? Nancy slumped lower in the chair. What she and Matt shared was rare. She couldn't walk away from it. Maybe she could convince Bayfield that living together without the benefit of marriage was the way to go.

He wasn't likely to accept that, and did she really want to settle for less than marriage? What about kids?

Goosebumps fought for space on her arms. Kids. She slapped her cheeks lightly. She couldn't go there, not now.

There was a rapist to draw out of his hiding hole. She hated to admit it, but the guy was driving her up the wall. Why couldn't she make him budge?

Was Bacardi right? Was the guy teasing her, playing with her sanity? She cupped her hands over her ears.

Damn if she'd wait for him. Two could play that game.

- o -

Matt rinsed the supper dishes. He'd put them in the dishwasher later. He refilled their wine glasses and followed Nancy's scent to the living room.

She'd worn a particularly exotic perfume this evening. It accompanied very nicely the large loop earrings hanging from her earlobes. While she wasn't a clothes hog, Nancy was very adept with color, fabric and accessories. That skill probably helped with her undercover disguises. Would he ever tire of her many faces?

Two more weeks. Would it be a flash or an eternity? Would Beltane pass without incident? He hoped so, but he wouldn't put any money on it. And his hands were tied. Nancy wouldn't think of backing out and returning to Stevens Point. He didn't really want her to leave.

He wanted her to move into this house. Shuttling back and forth with duffle bags was tiresome. What he really wanted was marriage. He'd bide his time on that one.

Nancy Crane Appleby was too preoccupied

with her work to consider an offer of marriage. He should feel lucky she made time for them at all. She'd worked long hours trying to crack the rape cases. She'd used herself as bait, but the guy wasn't budging.

He'd watched Nancy grow more desperate day by day. She didn't like anyone taking control of her life, and the rapist, at the moment, had succeeded in doing just that. Nancy had hardly said a word at supper. She was operating on autopilot.

This entire mess had to come to an end, soon. Matt's heart missed a count. Maybe then they'd be able to get on with their lives.

When he entered the living room with a wine glass in each hand, Nancy gave him one of her bemused smiles. "Afraid I haven't been much company this evening."

"That's okay. I know you have a lot on your mind."

"Soon," she said, "soon it'll be over."

He handed her a wine glass. "You think he'll be brave enough to strike? He's got to know you'll be waiting for him, and that you won't be alone."

"He knows. That won't deter him. He's a long time resident of the area; I know that in my gut. He'll try to use that knowledge to stay one step ahead of us."

Matt winced.

"But he won't succeed. I'm good, Matt. Remember that. I'll do what I have to do to catch that creep. That's my duty. There will be no more rapes."

He nodded, wishing he could be as confident. He glanced out the front window at the dwindling light. A few patches of snow remained. Grass hadn't begun to turn green. Most everything was dull brown. This wasn't his favorite season either. Did he have a favorite season in Trillium?

Turning back to Nancy, he saw her full lips grinning broadly. She rose and hugged him. He breathed her scent deeply; his arousal was immediate. Was she wearing an aphrodisiac?

She hooked a finger in his and tugged. "Come on, professor. Let's go upstairs and let me put a show on for you."

Matt pulled his robe tighter and fluffed up the pillows. He switched off the overhead light and lit several candles, providing a romantic ambiance. He glared at the bathroom door where Nancy had retreated to prepare. Was he one of those push-me-pull-me toys like Nancy's youngest niece received for Christmas? He hated being so ambivalent. He hated caring this much. Why couldn't he just allow her to be a cop and let it be?

Because she had wormed her way into his heart, damn it.

And now what? He was supposed to sit idly by while she set herself up as a target for a crazed rapist who had singled her out as just prey. Matt rolled onto his side and then quickly back again. She'd done stakeouts before and it hadn't bothered him this much. But now the rapist knew who she was and that she was a cop. If the bastard got his hands on her he wasn't about to let her go. She'd become a human sacrifice for honoring Beltane.

Matt listened to water running in the bathroom sink and stared blankly at the ceiling. Did she love him? She'd never spoken those words, even when he had. Was she withholding? Or was she too busy being the hardnosed cop to explore her own feelings for him?

"Close your eyes."

He glanced toward the closed bathroom door and then complied with Nancy's request. He heard the bathroom door open and then Nancy padding to her sound system and punched a button.

Soft, sensual drumbeats filled his ears. The high toned lilting of a flute joined with the drumming.

"You can open your eyes now." Her voice was low and inviting.

He did. He gasped for air. Nancy stood between him and the floor to ceiling windows swaying gently to the music. Adorned in diaphanous white, she looked like a goddess – Matt smiled – like an experienced woman of the harem. A sequined headband held her dark hair in place. A wispy see-through veil failed to conceal a bold smile.

Her breasts overflowed a bra that only served to highlight shadowy nipples; tiny rings outlining the bra jingled with her movement. A matching sequined belt coiled around her waist rested just above a panty that showed more than it covered, and a sheer skirt flowed down the length of her legs. At the center of it all was a light blue stone gleaming from Nancy's navel.

Nancy clasped her hands above her head and swayed to the beat. She shook her hips and the blue stone momentarily blinded Matt. Back and forth across the room she glided and danced like a ballerina.

Matt glanced at the windows. He should probably get up and pull the curtains, but no one could see in anyway. He fixed his full attention on the gyrations of his outrageous, unconventional lover.

Nancy unfastened the veil and played peek-a-boo. She turned away from him, facing the windows, and wiggled her hips seductively. By the time she turned around, she had undone the clasp between her breasts. Again she teased. Only this time it was her nipples playing peek-a-boo. She swayed. She twirled. At last, she stopped and faced him; a bewitching smile crossed her lips and the flimsy material floated to the floor.

Without uttering a word, she retraced her steps, dancing, even leaping to the music, with her breasts swinging freely. Matt licked his dry lips. His arousal was stiff.

She twisted a nipple between thumb and index finger and then reached for the snap holding the lower veil in place. That veil parted and pooled at her feet; she stepped out of it. She twirled about and bent over displaying her firm buttocks. When she turned the next time, both hands slipped the flimsy white panties downward. Her dark curls glistened with moisture.

He sucked on his lower lip. Nancy closed her eyes and smiled, easing the panties back up. He swallowed hard. How much more of this bewitching could he stand before leaping to his feet and ripping those damn panties off her?

She turned away from him and again slid the panties down her thighs. Wiggling her butt, she kicked the panties aside and whirled to face him. She took three steps toward him, and he reached out for her hand.

Shaking her head, Nancy quickly spun around and danced away from him. She pressed against the window and shimmied her rear-end toward him. He caught her reflection in the window. She cupped a palm over her heat and began rocking back and forth on the balls of her feet. Her butt undulated, teasing, hiding her self-pleasuring.

Matt clinched his fists. His erection wavered on that precipice of pain and release.

She turned to face him maintaining a slow rocking motion. She locked her eyes on his. He saw the briefest glimmer of despair before the haughty harem queen returned. She teased herself and him with her fingers while flicking her tongue suggestively.

This was Nancy's fantasy, but it was driving him crazy. He lowered a hand to his arousal. Damn. Sorcerer or sexual goddess. It didn't matter. She was driving him over the edge, and she hadn't even touched him.

Still uttering not a word, Nancy crawled over the bed to kneel between his legs. She took his arousal deep into her mouth. The drums and flute played on.

She devoured him. There was no time to enjoy, no time for savoring. His orgasm originated in his toes and exploded through the top of his head. Then there was nothing – an absence of sensation. Her chuckle vibrated around him while he lay back gasping for air.

Regaining his composure, Matt pulled Nancy up by the shoulders. She shook her head. "I've got to clean up," she whispered. "I'll be right back."

Matt's eyelids fluttered and then flew open when he remembered they'd exhausted the stash of condoms in the bedside dresser. Stiffly, he climbed out of bed to retrieve more from the bathroom.

When he opened the door and stepped into the small room, he saw Nancy, still naked, bending over a tripod of some sort and peering out the bathroom window toward the park.

Dimly, he understood her actions. His brain convulsed. His stomach curdled. "What the hell are you doing?"

Nancy swung about to face him. Her reddening face didn't appease him in the least. "Don't get bent out of shape," she said evenly.

"What the hell were you doing – performing for me, or for some goddamn lunatic rapist?"

"I did a dance for you that I thought you'd appreciate." Her wounded voice sounded false. Ignoring their nakedness, struggling to find words to express his rage, Matt stood his ground.

"But I wasn't enough." He reached around her and tapped what he now recognized as a small camcorder rather than a scope. "I imagine this is some kind of high-tech, night vision. You can't stop playing detective long enough even to make love, or to be loved."

Nancy opened her mouth to speak. Her mouth closed tight. In that moment, she looked so alone, almost lost. Tears formed.

He wanted to throw up, but instead stormed back into the bedroom. He didn't need this shit! Not any of it. If she wanted to be super cop, so be it. He'd had enough!

Matt reached for the clothes he'd discarded only an hour or so earlier. He pulled on the pants and lurched for the bedroom door. The sounds of Nancy crying and flinging things around in the bathroom did not deter him in the least.

He plopped down on the cushioned living room chair and tried to blank out thoughts and memories. Shortly, he heard her footsteps on the stairway. She entered the room fully dressed, holding a duffle in each hand. One was no doubt for the camera and collapsible tripod. The other probably contained personal items.

She wasn't leaving anything behind. Thank God! And that was the woman he'd thought he wanted to marry. How stupid. How gullible was he?

"I'm sorry I hurt you," she said quietly, standing at the bottom of the stairs. "It probably was a dumb thing to do, but I have one more chance to flush out the bastard. If I can't do that, then he's in control."

"Control! That's all you think about." Matt spat the words out, not taking his eyes off the darkened fireplace.

"If you want to try again, you know where to find me." Her words were barely a whisper. "Maybe it's best not to try to be an "us" until I catch this guy."

"There'll always be another guy," Matt shot back, not bothering to glance in her direction. "I'm not going to be a prop for your investigations, detective. Don't wait by the phone for me to call."

"I understand. Come on, Mal. It's time to leave now."

Matt didn't get up to let her out; he remained staring into the emptiness that was rapidly replacing Nancy's presence. Why had he allowed himself to get suckered into such a crazy relationship? One nightstands suited his needs much better.

Tears filled his eyes. He settled deeper into the chair, its cushions providing little comfort. Who was he trying to kid? He was as screwed up as she was. Why the hell did the first woman he'd ever loved have to be a cop?

Wiping tears from her cheeks with one hand while driving with the other, Nancy wailed, "I really screwed up this time, Mal. How can I expect to have a relationship with a man if I can't let go of a case long enough to love him?" She shook her head trying to see the road. "But I've got to stop this creep before he gets me."

Later, at her apartment, still feeling bereft, Nancy played back the video. "Damn," she mumbled. It was fuzzy.

She watched for long minutes before she spotted movement on the hillside. The movement appeared to be one person who stepped out from a line of trees. He seemed to be aiming something toward Matt's house. Nancy swallowed hard. She was certain it was her man. She'd brought him out of his hiding hole for a better view, but all she'd gotten for her efforts was a fuzzy picture of a person cloaked in heavy clothes and a ski mask.

And what had getting that useless image cost her? She'd gone over the top. Bayfield would never forgive her this time. She wasn't certain she could forgive herself.

- o -

He played the video on the state-of-the-art large screen entertainment center. He'd chosen well. Detective Appleby was the epitome of the Beltane goddess. Such full breasts matched by full lips. And she was naturally dark haired. He didn't want any damn imposters, not for the goddess of the fire.

Carefully, he edited the video, deleting the last disgusting scene with the professor. Those images were now erased from his memory and from hers. She would come to him like a virgin. She had looked enticing in white. White was her color. He'd remember that. The goddess of Beltane deserved the best and he intended to provide her with just that.

Smiling thinly, he replayed it and paused it when she pressed her breasts against the window and looked right at him. He loved it when she played with herself. Was that a pout? Or had she blown him a kiss? It didn't matter. She'd be his soon, very soon.

Visions of his goddess dancing before a bonfire filled his mind. Then he was filling her. And then she was consumed by the flames. He stroked himself until he jerked wildly.

- o -

Nancy steadied her hands enough to tear the envelope open. She stared at the printed words and read the brief message aloud.

"Dear Goddess of Beltane. Thanks for the show, not that you had to whet my appetite even more. You are a tempting morsel. But I can wait. Waiting builds character and makes the ultimate meal that more tasty and fulfilling. Thankfully, I can push replay and caress your body over and over again. Isn't modern technology great!

"I am very much looking forward to honoring you as

351

Goddess of the Bel. Until then, I remain your faithful White Knight.

"*By the way, on Beltane – no need wasting your energy trying to find me. Rest assured, I will find you.*"

"So what do you make of it?" Nancy said.

Bacardi held the most recent note from the White Knight in his hand. He looked up and frowned at Nancy. "I'm not sure what you've been up to, detective. And this time, I don't think I want to know the details, but it looks like our guy has some fairly expensive tastes."

"What do you mean?" Nancy sat down in a chair in Bacardi's office.

"If this guy was as far away from the house as you think he was, he has to have some fairly sophisticated equipment. When I got the night vision camera for you I asked around about the stuff. Apparently, anyone can pick up adaptors for most camcorders that will work at night. But you have to be quite close to your subject. I'll bet our guy has military or police quality stuff. That costs a bundle. Could be ten grand, likely more."

"Whew. That rules out most college students."

"Yeah, much more likely someone on the outside with money and connections. Not just anyone can buy military quality equipment."

"At least not legally."

"Right."

"Can we run searches on purchases of night vision cameras?"

"Probably. But where do we start? And when

352

do we stop?" Bacardi smoothed his moustache. "I'll see what I can do. I know an agent in Duluth I can check with. He might have some ideas. I'm afraid it's going to be like hunting for that needle in the haystack."

"But if we can link anyone from this area to such a purchase we should have our guy."

"Maybe. Anyway, I'll work on that." Bacardi shifted his weight in his chair. "Doesn't look like he's coming out until May first."

Nancy folded her hands in her lap. "Looks like. Unless we can track him down through the camcorder, I guess all we can do is wait. Not my strongest skill."

"Maybe it's for the best. At least we'll have you covered then."

Chapter Sixteen

The day before Beltane. *Soon, it'll be over*. Nancy knotted her sweatpants waist-string. Her service revolver rested against her lower back. She pulled on a matching red top and stepped into her running shoes.

It had been a long, trying several days. She'd heard nothing from Matt, not that she blamed him. She'd tried to forget him and what she'd done. There wasn't any way she could undo how she'd abused him. The best that could happen now was for her to get the damn rapist behind bars and head back to Point. Hadn't that been the original plan anyway?

So why did she feel like a piece of shit? Because she'd violated his trust? That would do, for starters. Because she couldn't separate her private life from her professional life? Maybe. Because she'd tossed the love they shared in the garbage?

Stop berating yourself, girl. There's nothing you can do about it now. It happened. Life went on. It had to.

She hated waiting. Bacardi was still working the camcorder angle, but so far he'd only drawn blanks. His contact in Duluth wasn't hopeful. He claimed more night vision equipment was likely sold on the black market than through legitimate sources.

At least the waiting wouldn't last much longer.

355

She picked up her keys and hollered for Mal. As usual, he greeted her at the door with his leash between his teeth.

"You're the only positive constant I have in my life, Mal," she said. "Let's go get us some exercise."

They jogged north toward the park. At the edge of the park, Nancy groaned. Mrs. Lindenhammer was waiting for them near a clump of lilacs. Nancy wasn't eager to deal with the overly friendly lady this morning. Mal, however, pulled on his leash, in a rush to get his treat. Nancy hurried along, wishing the lilacs were already in bloom. She loved the scent of lilac.

"Good morning, Miss," Mrs. Lindenhammer said cheerfully. "And you too, Malaki." She pulled a treat from her pocket and Malaki snarfed it down in one swallow.

"Good morning, Mrs. Lindenhammer, and how are you today?"

The woman frowned. "A little troubled, I'm afraid. I was wondering if you could help me." She reached into another pocket to retrieve a piece of paper. "I received a note from my daughter who lives in Kansas. She has such a hen's scrawl and my eyes are so bad, I'm not sure I'm reading it correctly. Could you look at it for me?"

"Sure, no problem." Nancy reached for the piece of paper and tried to make out the tightly shaped handwriting.

"Welcome to my lair. It's been a long wait, but it

will be an honor to confer upon you the title, Goddess of the Bel."

A wet cloth covered her nose and mouth. In slow motion, she clawed for her revolver. Her hand never made it to her waistband. Matt! The scream never reached her lips. Darkness played with pinpoints of light. Darkness won.

Nancy groaned, trying to pry an eye open. Her head throbbed. Awareness gnawed at the edges of her brain. Her muscles slackened. She'd been kidnapped. She'd been such a fool.

She cocked an eye open.

"It's about time you joined me. Wouldn't want you to miss the festival." The wiry man laughed. His demonic laughter chilled Nancy to her bones.

She glanced quickly about her surroundings. She was lying on a couch in what was likely the den of a cabin. Her wrists were bound tight with rawhide. Mrs. Lindehammer's clothes sat on a folding chair. The air smelled faintly of lake water and fish. Malaki appeared quite contented sleeping on a braided rug. There was no apparent immediate means of escape, but she wasn't giving up. She had to find a way.

Again, the man laughed. "You can try, detective. I would think less of you if you didn't, but there's no way to escape your destiny. You are the goddess of the Bel. We've both known that for some time now, haven't we?"

Wobbling, Nancy sat up. "Who are you? Where? Why?"

"Just like a cop. So many questions. I appreciate a curious mind, Ms. Appleby, particularly when it goes well with a gorgeous body like yours."

Don't cringe. Keep him talking. What time is it? Nancy glanced at the wall clock. Four o'clock. She'd been out for six or seven hours.

"No need to worry about the time, my goddess. All will come to pass in due time. We have much to prepare before midnight. Beltane awaits us.

"Nor do we want to rush. We both need to relax in order to enjoy ourselves. I'll answer your questions. I don't want your curiosity to get in the way of your enjoyment. When it's time to plant my seed, I want your complete attention. When it is time to pay homage to the fire, you will need total concentration in order to avoid the pain. So, would you like something to drink?"

Nancy shook her head. "Who are you?"

"Ah, yes, the basic question. Who am I? I've spent nearly fifty years sorting that one out. We've never been formally introduced. The president didn't see fit to do that at the Ball. The stuck up bitch. My name is David Grimes. Does that have a familiar ring to you, Ms. Appleby?"

"You're related to Dennis Grimes, the campus chief of police?"

"Unfortunately, yes. He's my older brother. Incompetent, but quite malleable. He's like a sieve when it comes to information."

Grimes walked to his desk and picked up a sheet of paper. It was official Blackthorn stationary. "I've been under your nose much of the time, detective." He pointed to his name on the letterhead. David Grimes appeared in the list of trustees.

"So you were in the inner-circle."

"The only inner-circle is the damned president and Bacardi. I hadn't counted on the two of them teaming up. That made keeping track of what you were up to more difficult, but I managed."

Nancy's fought to stay alert. *Keep him talking. As long as he's talking, he's not doing anything else.* Had he drugged Malaki? The dog hadn't moved since she'd awakened.

"You were clever, I'll give you that. I'm curious – how did you select your victims? You seemed to know them."

His smile curdled her blood.

"I did. I can show you later, if there's time. I have quite a video collection. You screwed up Samhein for me, by fleeing with that goddamn professor."

His voice had risen to a near shout. He stroked his arms, calming himself. "But the universe works for the best of all. If you had been used for Samhein, you wouldn't be Goddess of Beltane. That would be a shame."

"And I beg to differ with you, detective. None of those women were victims. They were recipients of a blessing, a very rare blessing, indeed."

"You raped them, and you call that a blessing?" Nancy struggled for control. "None of them wanted to have sex with you, Mr. Grimes. You

359

forced yourself on each of them."

Grimes stepped forward and held Nancy's chin between clenched fingers, his eyes awash with fury. She flinched, preparing for the punch. It never came. He backed off.

"Don't get me angry, Ms. Appleby. I don't want to bruise the Goddess of the Bel. And for your information, none of this has ever been about sex. It is about gift giving and receiving."

She wasn't about to debate that finer point at the moment. "But how did you get videos of so many women? Apparently, you wanted to see them nude before making your selection."

"You're right about that. I didn't want any Nordic imposters. One slipped in because of you, but I've forgiven you for that. I acted too hastily that night. You threw me off stride." He waggled a finger at her. "Once, but never twice.

"As far as how. Quite simple, really. I own a plumbing business. As a trustee and a contractor, I have free access to every shower and bedroom on campus. You'd be amazed at how many cameras I have scattered through the dorms and locker rooms. Not difficult at all if you have the intelligence, the equipment and the access." Grimes drew himself up to his full height. "I had all three, my goddess."

"In all I have collected videos of ninety-five co-eds. None, my dear, can hold a candle to you. Most of the co-eds are younger, and don't have your maturity. Nor do they possess the kind of skill you've mastered.

360

"My only regret is that we can't spend more time together. But then maybe we'll meet again in eternity. Enough of this," Grimes sputtered. "There is much to do before midnight.

"I want to show you what I've planned for us." Again, he stepped toward the couch; Nancy prepared to kick him in the groin. He pulled her gun from his waistband and held it on her.

"Don't try anything stupid, detective. I don't want to harm you, but I won't hesitate to put a bullet in your shoulder. I'm an expert marksman. A bullet wound might slow you down a bit, but it wouldn't spoil the gift giving ceremony."

Nancy stilled. "Okay, you've got the gun."

"Good. You are a wise woman, but to provide for our safety, why don't you slide on these leg irons." He handed them to her. "My brother can be quite helpful, especially when he doesn't know it."

"I've been working on this for some time, but I think you will find it worthy of you," Grimes said, with a trace of awe.

Nancy gawked at the ten foot high stack of timber and brush. A pole extended another ten feet above the pile's apex. She cringed at the maypole with colorful ribbons stirring in the slight breeze. In a pocket at the front of the pile she saw three gas cans, rags, and matches. He wasn't leaving much to chance.

A two foot high pallet of balsam boughs sat across the clearing from the woodpile. Grimes led her to the pallet.

"You might as well sit here and watch me complete the outside preparations. We'll make better use of these balsam boughs later." He gave her a lopsided grin. "I selected these with great care. All are fresh, and they're laid just right. No stray needle will poke or scratch your flesh. Nothing is too fine for you, my goddess." The man bowed and backed away from her.

The branches swayed with her shifting weight. Under other circumstances, they'd be quite comfortable. Grimes didn't seem very worried about her making an escape or attacking him. There were no options, with her wrists rawhide-bound and her legs shackled.

She'd bide her time. He'd have to remove the bindings, or at least loosen them, to rape her. *Keep your wits about you. Don't think too far ahead.* Would anyone realize she was gone?

Not likely. Matt might be surprised when she didn't show up for the lecture, but he'd likely write that off as her being pissed at him.

Bacardi. She was supposed to check in with him at six. Would he guess she'd been kidnapped? Or would he just think she was trying to go it alone one more time?

Malaki walked over and sniffed at the boughs. He nudged her leg. She leaned over and patted his head the best she could. "Sorry I got you into this, Mal."

Grimes dragged another log toward the pyre.

Nancy looked at Malaki. *Why not?* There wasn't

much she'd be able to do until that window of opportunity around midnight. Grimes wasn't about to spoil his goddess before Beltane.

"Mal, can you get Matt?" she whispered. The dog's ears perked at Matt's name. "Go get Matt." Malaki spun around and barked once.

Grimes looked up. "Get away from her, you stupid dog." He headed toward them on the run.

"Go, Mal," Nancy screamed, thankful that Grimes had not used his Mrs. Lindenhammer voice. "Get Matt. Run, Mal, run."

Malaki tore out of the clearing without looking back. Grimes chased after him, cursing, but soon stopped and bent over, grabbing his knees and gasping for breath.

"Think you're smart, detective?" Grimes returned to the bed of boughs. "That dog won't get far. I took his collar off when we arrived. Who'll want to deal with a loose Rottweiler without a collar? They're dangerous dogs, you know. Most folks will shoot before trusting a rabid, wild dog."

Nancy glowered at her captor and tried to blot out the image of Mal lying shot in a ditch.

Giving her an adoring smile, Grimes said, "Don't worry, my goddess, I'll provide you with all the comfort and security you require. We are quite hidden and safe here. Safe from the pressures of the world. Safe from prying eyes.

"Be patient, my lady. The bonfire is almost ready. Soon we will prepare you, for you must be properly pampered so your flower is eager and receptive of my Robyn."

She contemplated her funeral pyre and trembled slightly. Which would be worse, accepting his Robyn, or being consumed by fire? She squeezed her eyelids shut. *Don't think about it. Concentrate on getting away from him.*

"Don't fret, dear one. Such tension is to be expected the first time. Once I'm finished here, I'll make ready a potion for you that will help calm your virginal nerves. I'm quite experienced at initiating virgins, I can assure you. I'll make it as easy as I can for you. Don't worry, Robyn will fit."

Nancy stared wide-eyed at the man's back as he walked toward the pyre. He was flipping out. One moment, he was the rapist outwitting the detective, and the next he was a druidic priest, preparing his virgin goddess for consummation and sacrifice.

Malaki was no bloodhound, nor did he have the speed of a greyhound, but he was her best hope. The potion Grimes would prepare would likely include some kind of drug for numbing her senses and reactions, but probably not put her out. He wouldn't get his jollies screwing an unconscious or dead body. Should she be thankful for that? He wouldn't – he couldn't – do much until midnight.

- o -

Going over his lectures notes in his home office, Matt tried to shake off his funk. This was his last

364

lecture of the series. He needed to be at the top of his game.

But it was Beltane eve. Was she wired and ready to go? Was he ready to see her at the lecture? He'd do his best to ignore her.

She'd never called to explain or to apologize. He hadn't expected she would. Apparently, her little ruse hadn't produced results. He would have heard if the rapist had been caught.

Was he even still out there? Wouldn't that be a hoot, if she'd cost them their relationship for a guy who'd moved on?

Matt glanced at the clock on his desk. Six-thirty. Time to wrap up and get ready. He couldn't afford to rehash the past – he had a job to do.

He pushed his desk chair back and reached for his briefcase. Then he turned sharply, cocking his head. What was that?

Barking? Why not, there were lots of dogs in the neighborhood. But this barking seemed to come from his door step.

A fire alarm could not have clamored louder in his brain. *Malaki!* It *had* to be.

Matt dashed down the stairs two at a time. Malaki wouldn't be creating such a fuss if his mistress was making a social call. Matt flung open the front door. Malaki – wet, bedraggled, and full of caked mud – scratched at the screen. Matt let the dog in and knelt to hug him.

"What happened to you, Mal? You're a mess."

Mal gave him a pleading look, then he spun around and around. The dog pushed against the door and barked. He trotted back to Matt's side, nudged his knee, and retreated again to the door.

Forcing himself to stay calm, Matt snatched his cell phone from his belt. He punched in Nancy's home phone. No answer. He punched in her cell number. No answer. *Leave a message*. Right.

"I'll be right with you, Mal. Hold on."

Malaki continued barking and making a ruckus during the time it took for Matt to race upstairs and grab his gun. On the way back downstairs, he placed one more phone call.

"Is Chief Bacardi there? This is an emergency involving Detective Nancy Appleby."

He paused at the foot of the stairs.

"This is Bacardi. Who am I talking to?"

"Matt Bayfield, here. Nancy's dog showed up on my doorstep minutes ago. He is frantic, full of mud, and eager for me to follow him. And his collar is missing."

"Son of a bitch! Nancy didn't check in at six as we'd planned. The bastard must've struck early. Don't go traipsing off without me. I know the area. I'll pick you up in three minutes."

"Good, my address… "

"I know where you live, professor. Don't let that dog out of your sight."

Numb to the bone, Matt sat in the squad car moving at a snail's pace down an isolated dirt road. He marveled at the Rottie striding easily and deliberately in front of them. The dog jogged as if he knew they were running a marathon and not a sprint. He didn't waste energy.

"How much further do you think?" Matt asked, breaking the silence.

"Maybe another mile or two, if the women were correct with their estimates," Bacardi said. We've come a mile and a half. Given the stories we've heard, I doubt if he takes them more than five miles, likely closer than that."

"Damn, that could take a while yet." Matt shivered. He checked his watch in the dim light of the dashboard. "It's almost ten o'clock. Two hours. Wish Malaki had wings."

"He's our ticket. He'll get us there, if they haven't changed locations since he left. I'd put a chopper up, if I knew what we're looking for."

"Oh, there'll be something to see all right. He'll have a bonfire to celebrate Beltane."

"Could be a lot of campfires out there. Fishermen. Folks pushing the season. Others trying to keep the black flies down."

"I didn't say a campfire; I said a bonfire. This guy will build a huge one. He's probably had it ready for days. It will be a ritual fire. One large enough for human sacrifice."

"Human sacrifice!" Bacardi shot Matt a look of horror. "She never told me anything about that. Sweet Jesus."

Matt grimaced, fighting a gnawing stomach. "Nancy Crane Appleby is very astute at not telling the whole truth."

Bacardi glanced at the backup car following them with his chief deputy and Officer

Washington from campus police. Both had been at the station waiting to take their places on the planned stakeout. "I gather she's not likely to be harmed before midnight, before this Beltane thing actually starts."

"That's right. Everything in the universe would be out of kilter if he acts before Beltane begins."

"That's crazy. This guy's not going to do like some of those New Year's Eve celebrators by toasting on eastern time?"

Matt's blood chilled. "I doubt it. All the rapes occurred after the specific festival began or was even over. If he had wanted to, there would have been time to rape between the end of my lectures and midnight, but he never even grabbed a co-ed until after midnight."

"He did this time."

"Yeah." Neither he nor Chief Bacardi wanted to point out that this made the man even less predictable and a hundred times more dangerous.

"I'd call in for a chopper," Bacardi grunted, "but we're running out of time. They'd probably have to come up from Duluth."

- o -

"Hold on, girl," Nancy mumbled. "Fight it. Keep thinking." Since she'd swallowed the potion, everything was happening in slow motion: her movements, her thoughts. Where was Mal? Where was Matt?

She looked up to see Grimes peering at her.

They were back inside the cabin and he was dressed in a long black hooded robe with a rope knotted at its waist, making him look like a priest of some ancient order. The emblem hanging on a cord from around his neck was that of a ram. Nancy smiled to herself. He didn't look like he'd be much of a ram, not really. Where had that thought come from? What had he put in that drink?

"Your eyes are dilated quite nicely, my goddess. This is going to be such a delicious night." Grimes removed a hunting knife from the folds of his robe. "It's safe now for you to be unbound. You won't be going anywhere I don't want you to go. And you certainly won't be doing anything I don't tell you to do. You're going to be an obedient supplicant now, aren't you?" He placed the knife flat between her breasts.

"Yes," she murmured.

"Good. We need to get you dressed for the night. Sweat clothes will not do." Grimes sliced the rawhide binding her wrists and used a key to unlatch the ankle shackles.

Nancy tried flexing her fingers to increase circulation.

"Let's get these clothes off you."

She withdrew further onto the couch.

"Now," he ordered. "I've seen every thing you have to offer, detective. I've admired your body over and over again. Your luscious curves are etched into my memory. How does it feel to have achieved a form of immortality, my goddess?" He

369

snickered.

Thoughts tumbled in her mind trying to find coherence. She wasn't a goddess. Detective. She was a cop, not goddess. She had to hold onto that. She was the detective. He was the bad guy. Beltane. He wouldn't defile her before midnight. The hands on the clock blurred. Was that ten thirty or eleven thirty?

"Lift up your arms," Grimes said, pulling up her sweat shirt. She complied.

"Good. Now the bottoms," he said, tugging on her sweat pants. They slid off too easily.

"Very nice. Next, the bra. No," he commanded, "let me," The front clasp gave way and her breasts sprang free.

"Good God, even better in the flesh." He grazed a nipple. Before Nancy could shrink away, he yanked his hand back as if he'd touched a hot stove.

"Now the panties." He hooked his fingers over the slight material and ripped. They gave way.

He breathed rapidly, in short breaths. If only her muscles would respond, she could take him easily. She strained to move a hand. It lifted six inches and fell back to the couch.

Grimes licked his lips. His eyes bulged. "You are beyond beauty, my goddess.

"It's time to absolve you of your sins and prepare you for the seed and for the fire. Don't go anywhere," he cackled.

Several minutes passed before he returned holding a tray with two containers and various brushes from a makeup kit. After taking the cap off one of the jars, he dipped his fingers in it. Then he began to methodically apply white grease paint to Nancy's face.

"The goddess of the Bel must be a virgin," he explained. "When you are completely white, you will be absolved of all your sexual misdeeds and will be a virgin once again."

He used two fingers to spread streaks of white across her breasts and then massaged the grease paint into them until they glistened a white sheen. He moved to her belly. By the time he was finished, every square inch of her skin was pasty white.

She should feel mortified, but neither the color of her skin nor modesty was her biggest concern at the moment. Grimes was enmeshed in his priestly role. Even though he'd touched her everywhere, there had been nothing sexual about it for him. He was performing a priestly task.

He opened the second jar. "Now that you have been cleansed, now that you are a virgin, we can prepare you to receive." He chose a brush and dipped it into a jar. "The color purple I bestow upon you. The universal color of divinity." His eyes glazed. "You will become the receptacle of eternal life. You will accept my seed willingly. You will appease the fire of Beltane. No witches will dare haunt this place."

His mumbo jumbo did little to assuage her fears. She was dealing with a certifiable nutcase. But he had flashes of brilliance and considered himself invincible, and that might yet be his undoing.

With great care, he painted her lips purple. Then he did the same to her areola and nipples. He stared at the curls at the apex of her thighs. He hesitated, smacking his lips.

She watched him struggle with his own urges; his arousal was quite evident. He pinched the bridge of his nose and uttered an unintelligible incantation. He proceeded quickly to coat her nether lips with purple paint.

Nancy giggled to herself. If the guy ever had the chance to take her, he shouldn't miss the spot. Did the liquid he'd poured down her throat contain laughing gas?

Taking a step back, Grimes appraised his artistry. He appeared quite pleased. "Well done. I declare you fit and ready. You are not the only expert at disguise, my goddess. Years of performing and working behind the scenes in community theater have given me the opportunity to hone my makeup and acting skills. There is no role I could not play."

"We will have you don this white gown." He helped her raise her arms and slip the gown over her body. Its fabric hugged her skin. It was so transparent she might look more naked with the gown on than off. Certainly, more tantalizing.

"You make a most presentable receptacle for my gift. And the fire of Beltane will find you a delicious treat, no doubt.

"Shall we proceed to the fire? Time is going by.

We don't want to be late. Don't try to get up, you won't be able to walk. I'll carry you to the Beltane altar. We'll take a blanket along so you won't get chilled while you await the fire.

- o -

"Sweet Jesus," Bacardi muttered, watching the Rottweiler turn off the road and head into the woods.

"What?" Matt asked, bursting with adrenaline. "Do you know where he's headed?"

Bacardi pulled the car to the side of the road. "Around the bend is a driveway leading to David Grimes' lake cabin. He's the brother of the campus police chief. The dog is cutting through David's property. About quarter a mile through there is a lake. We'd better follow the dog. If we're seen coming up the driveway, it could all be over. There's a flashlight under your seat."

Matt nearly broke the door handle getting out. He heard Bacardi shouting to the others to fan out and shoot only if absolutely necessary.

By that time, Matt was twenty yards ahead following Malaki, who ran ahead along a deer trail and then came back to be certain Matt was still following. Matt held the Colt Python in his fist. They couldn't be too late. The last he'd checked his watch, which was only a few minutes earlier, it was only quarter of eleven. He swatted at a low hanging branch. Good God! They couldn't be too late.

Grimes laid Nancy gently on the pallet of balsam boughs and covered her torso with a white blanket. He had the hood of his robe tied snugly at his throat, giving him an otherworldly appearance. He left her without uttering a word.

It hadn't dawned on her till now that this was the Beltane altar. How fitting. She tried to bounce, testing the boughs, but she could hardly move enough to get a response.

She turned her head slightly to watch Grimes emptying the gas cans on the pile of logs and brush. While they'd been inside a full moon had risen, making it easy to see what was happening. Pitch black might have been better.

Several lit torches lined the front side of the pile. Grimes picked up one, backed away, and tossed it toward the stacked wood. There was a sudden whoosh, followed by flames stretching toward the sky. The flames settled some after the momentary rush, but the pile had caught. Nancy could already begin to feel its heat.

Grimes returned to where she lay. He knelt before her and placed a hand on her breast. Strange words came from his mouth. She couldn't understand what he was saying, though he was clearly praying.

Nancy closed her eyes to offer her own silent prayer.

His hand lifted from her breast, and he

returned to the fire. Again, Grimes shouted unintelligible words, only this time he also danced. Nancy watched him dance three times around the fire, and then he reversed direction and danced three more circles around the bonfire.

- o -

Matt stumbled to his knees. The sky had turned bright reddish orange. He staggered on, swearing he could already feel the heat. The gun in his hand felt like an anchor. *Dear God, don't let us be too late. Hang on, Nancy, we're coming. I love you.*

- o -

Nancy squeezed her eyes shut, resigned to her fate. Grimes had outfoxed her. She couldn't defend herself. She tried not to think. She tried blocking images of Mal and Matt.

She'd show no emotion for Grimes; he'd get no pleasure from her. That would frustrate him and prompt him to end things sooner than he'd planned. At this point, that was her best hope.

A crashing noise from the woods penetrated her haze. A blur of black sped by the pallet, racing pell-mell directly at Grimes. *Mal!*

Grimes broke from his trance in time to see the dog charging. He grabbed a burning torch and swung it over his head. "I'll kill you, you bastard," he cried. "You betrayed me."

Malaki never faltered. He leapt at the black

robed man and bowled him backwards into the fire.

Screams mingled with the crackling fire, shattering the night. Her body shook. Those weren't her screams. A stench of burned flesh filled her nostrils.

Her eyes blurred with tears. "Mal," she called out. "Mal, are you there?"

Sounds of branches breaking came from the woods where Mal had entered the clearing. "Good God!" She heard Matt exclaim. "Is she alive?"

She tried hard to lift a hand.

- o -

"She's alive," Bacardi said. "That's more than you can say for Grimes. You better put that gun out of sight and get that dog back from the fire before he decides to dive in after him."

Matt raced toward the dog, his heart pumping wildly. "You did it, Mal. Nancy's safe." Malaki continued barking and lunging at the fire. Matt knelt beside him, dug his fingers into the Rottie's thick coat, and pulled. "It's okay, boy. He'll never bother you or anyone else again."

The dog's sides heaved steadily and then began to slow. At last he slumped against Matt. Ignoring the tears streaming down his cheeks, Matt hugged the dog tight. "Come on, Mal. We better check out your mistress."

Officer Washington and Chief Bacardi stepped aside to allow Matt and Malaki to greet Nancy.

"Hi," she managed to say. "My heroes."

"You're the hero – you survived," Matt said, clutching her hand between his, ignoring her purple lips and white skin. Malaki laid his large head across his mistress' lap.

"Are you okay?" Matt asked. Was that a dumb question, or what?

"I've never been better. He only drugged me. It'll wear off. Don't know how long that'll take."

"That's okay, we've got all the time in the world."

Her eyes softened. "I'm so sorry, Matt. Do you still love me?"

Would she have asked that question with a clear mind? It didn't matter. Nothing before this moment mattered. "Yes, I still love you," he said, smiling. "How about you?"

A wisp of a grin made it to her lips. "Oh, most definitely. I love you so much I even have some body parts highlighted just for you." Nancy's eyelids drifted closed.

Matt flushed. Now what was she hiding?

- o -

Later that morning, Nancy sat at Matt's dining table with Matt, Chief Bacardi, and her aunt. She still had a mammoth hangover and hadn't slept for over twenty-four hours, but she'd showered and scrubbed all the paint from her skin. She felt like a new woman; she *was* a new woman.

She glanced down at her lap. Malaki wasn't

straying far. His head rested on her thigh. She squeezed Matt's hand. It was good to be alive. Definitely good.

She and Matt were running on adrenaline, almost giddy at times. They'd crash soon.

Most of the coffee Matt had made was gone and so were the pastries he'd run out and picked up while she showered. He had come for her. He'd gotten her away from the Grimes place as soon as he could and brought her here to his home. They'd talked and cried for hours. She squeezed more tears back.

"I can't tell you how elated I am with your decision, Nancy. You will be a real asset to the town of Trillium, and to Blackthorn."

"Thank you, Aunt Joan." She looked quickly at Matt. "We haven't had much time to work out the details, but I think the pieces are falling in place. I'm surprised Dennis Grimes resigned so quickly."

"I'm not," Chief Bacardi said. "Dennis wasn't involved, and I don't believe he ever suspected his brother, but he did help find the night camcorder for him. The shackles came through Dennis, knowingly or not. And he dragged his feet on this entire investigation before you ever got here."

"He would've been gone one way or another by the end of the day." Joan Williams tapped the table. "You're already officially on Trillium Police Department, Nancy. I don't think there's any question that you'll have the trustees' support as our next campus Chief of Police."

"So, Professor Bayfield," President Williams'

eyes sparkled, "are you finding this small northwoods town and college a little more appealing today?"

"Most definitely, President Williams. Most definitely. I doubt if Avalon was any more inviting."

Joan Williams cleared her throat. "How long will it be before you can call me Joan or Aunt Joan?"

Nancy laughed and stoked Matt's hand. "That might take a while," she said. "It took him a long time to call me Nancy."

"So have you told your mother yet?"

"No, I'll call later today. I want to savor this morning without having to provide too many explanations."

"Tell her I greatly approve and that she'd better get the entire family up here in June. Our little chapel isn't large, but it should accommodate everyone quite nicely. Well, we've been here long enough, Ed. Time to get back to work."

Nancy closed the door behind her aunt and Bacardi. She turned to face Matt. "Well, how are you feeling, professor?" She tried unsuccessfully to hold back a yawn.

"Absolutely the best." He brushed her lips with a finger. "But you're going to be sound asleep on your feet any moment."

"Will not."

"Come on, Nancy, let's put you to bed. More planning can wait. You can call your mother after you're rested."

Nancy yawned again and held Matt's hand as he guided her up the stairs. "What was that word Aunt Joan used?" she asked, when they entered the bedroom. "Accommodate. Yep, bet I still have enough strength to accommodate my man."

Matt tipped his head back and laughed. Keeping one hand around her waist, he yanked back the covers with the other. "You'll be asleep before you hit the mattress. But trust me, I'll be right here when you wake up. We'll do more than a little accommodating before the day is done."

He laid her on the bed and removed her slippers. "That sounds so good, Matt." She yawned and her head settled on the pillow. "Don't leave me."

"I won't. I never will."

The End

About the Author

Adriana Kraft is the pen name for a husband/wife team writing *Erotic Romance for Two, Three or More*. The award-winning pair has published over thirty erotic romance novels and novellas to outstanding reviews. Long and Short Reviews: *"scorching hot…refreshing...something to read when you want straight up hotness."* Romance Junkies: *"filled with warmth, blazing hot sex, well-developed characters…not for the faint of heart."* Romantic pairings include straight m/f, lesbian, bisexual, ménage and polyamory, in both contemporary and paranormal settings.

We hope you enjoyed *The Unmasking,* and we love hearing from readers! You can find all our links at our website:

http://adrianakraft.com

The Reunion

A dark and brooding bad boy, his petite Latina lover, and his unattainable former highschool crush ~ a sizzling, combustible threesome.

Definitely recommended at Rainbow Reviews: *This book sizzled as two incredibly sexy women and one gorgeous guy form a super hot triad, eventually. These three are by far and away the best smoldering trio I have read about. Oh, bring on more of this, but read this one first!* JJ

Top Pick at Night Owl Reviews: *A polyamory novel with real edgy characters with inclusive sexuality. I will just say this is not a read for the faint of heart. … All the characters are well developed and so colorful. Once you start reading you will be hard put to stop until you are at the end. … Very well written!* ArlenaDean

Top Pick at The Romance Reviews: *Stories written by Adriana Kraft are done with a twist on the usual plots that you find within the genre. In this m/f/f ménage, the twist is the women fall for each other and the man is left to wonder where he stands… All of the characters are well-written; the sex scenes are scorching hot. This is another great read from Adriana Kraft.* Laurie P.

The Best Man

Bad Boy meets Bad Girl. Is that all there is?

Five Stars at Shelfari: *I loved Kitty and Jared. Both are strong willed characters who will not run from their attraction… Watching them both fight their feelings made their capitulation so much sweeter.* ~ Shelia G.

Five Stars, Top Pick at The Romance Reviews: *What's supposed to be a brief, hot affair becomes so much more as they both slowly find their emotions engaged and they start to fall in love. The run towards and pull back and chase between them is an amazing journey to watch… I loved that while not really old, the characters were more mature than most are in romance books. The author proves that there is no age limit on finding love.* ~ Laurie P.

A Tempting Taste   *Swinging Games Series: Book Three*

A little voyeurism, some role-playing, a taste of m/m, ménage for three and four – the swinging world is heating up for Jennifer and Brett Andrews!

Four Stars at Night Owl Reviews: *Adriana Kraft has an eye for detail and likes to play that up, it works to her advantage. She writes fluidly, the story flowed well and the sensuality was very steamy.* ~ MonicaBBB

Ripening Passion   *Passion Series, Book Two*

Passionate about sex but relationship-phobic, Claire Johnson is about to meet her match. Can Max Wilson hang on for the ride with the icy temptress?

Four Blue Ribbons at Romance Junkies: *RIPENING PASSION is a sensual and spicy romance that will knock your socks off! Adriana Kraft excels at keeping the momentum going, and she knows how to inject sensuality into any character's story. Erotica fans won't want to miss this one! Hot! Hot! Hot!* ~ Wendy

www.ingramcontent.com/pod-product-compliance
Lightning Source LLC
Chambersburg PA
CBHW060145260626
47160CB00001B/129